Georgie's Secret
Book Three
Welcome to Chance

ELSA KURT

ELSA KURT

authorelsakurt@gmail.com
www.elsakurt.com

Ordering Information:
Quantity sales. Special discounts are available on quantity purchases by corporations, associations, and others. For details, contact the publisher at the address above.
Orders by U.S. trade bookstores and wholesalers. Please contact authorelsakurt@gmail.com or visit www.elsakurt.com.

Printed in the United States of America

This is a work of fiction. Names, characters, businesses, places, events, locales, and incidents are either the products of the author's imagination or used in a fictitious manner. Any resemblance to actual persons, living or dead, or actual events is purely coincidental.

ELSA KURT

Georgie's SECRET

CONTENTS

Georgie's SECRET

ELSA KURT

DEDICATION

To my husband, always.

To my very own Brightsiders (less the drama)
the beautiful, ever in love, Bobby and Annie. xoxo

ACKNOWLEDGMENTS

Chance is the home of my heart and becomes more so with each book. I'm deeply indebted to all who've had faith in this project, who've invested their time in following the saga of this fictional town, and who keep at me to 'hurry up with the next one.' My husband, parents, daughters, and friends have relentlessly cheered me on and applauded my successes and tooted my horn for me when I couldn't or wouldn't. This would be impossible without you. Thank you, a thousand times over. To my publishing company, editor, and marketing team, my faith in you has been well-founded. Thank you for taking a chance on Chance (wink, wink) and me.

A couple of years ago my husband and I met a couple who personified everything we love about... love. Fifty years of marriage and they're more in love than ever. They're not afraid to show or share it, either. Bob and Annie are marriage goals times infinity and the model for the epic love my Charles and Georgie Brightsider share. Thank you both for coming into our lives. Paul and I adore you! xoxo

ELSA KURT

1 New BEGINNINGS

The church bells of St. Paul's rang in measured tolls. Each one resounded across Chance—carried on the breeze through open windows, grassy green fields, and newly budded trees—beckoning them to come. On this day all faiths—believers and non-believers, children and adults, friends and enemies—would gather for not one, but two of their own. No matter what happened in their respective lives, they'd come together.

This would be a day of remembrances and rejoicing, tears and laughter. Old acquaintances who'd become distant would reconnect and new ones made. As winter turned to spring, it was only befitting that it was a time of goodbyes and new beginnings.

It was a reminder—this subdued day—of something easily forgotten in the frigid winter months, everyone hibernating in their own little worlds. Unity. Communal spirit. They constituted more than just people who lived in the same town; they were a family. Dysfunctional at times, yes. But family, nonetheless...

2 Georgie

August 14, 1965

"Daddy, I *am* going. Mother said I could."

"Your mother has no idea what you girls have planned."

Georgie tried another tactic. "Gloria's parents said it was fine by them."

"Gloria's parents are nincompoops, sweetheart."

Georgie stomped her foot. "Daddy, stop being facetious. This is a big deal to me. You, of all people, should understand. I mean, what kind of musician doesn't appreciate the magnitude of this event?"

"One who appreciates talent, I suspect."

There was no reasoning with the man. Georgie made a sound somewhere between a scream and a growl, then stomped her foot once more before stalking out of the room in search of her mother.

"Mother, Daddy is *still* saying no. Won't you talk to him for me, please?"

Mavis Perri glanced up at her daughter over her reading glasses, setting her knitting down with a sigh. From the other room, where her husband was, came the sound of a needle touching vinyl. Of *course*, Gene would put on Louis Prima now, just when she settled in for a quiet sit.

"Young lady stop that scowling. You'll get lines on your face and the boys won't like you."

"I don't care if the boys like me," pouted Georgie. She stopped scowling, though.

"What did I tell you to do?"

"Don't sass Daddy. Talk sweet and compliment Daddy, then ask him," recited Georgie, directing an insolent gaze toward the ceiling.

"Mhmm. I told you, if he knows that—that Beatles band razzes your berries, he's sure to say no."

"But Mother, it's the *Beatles*. Shea *Stadium*." She drew out the word, breaking down the syllables for emphasis. "It is the event of my *lifetime*."

"Oh, honestly, Georgina Rose. Those fellas need haircuts and music lessons. Why can't you listen to real music? Like Frank or Dean, or Perry. I'd even prefer Elvis, for heaven's sake."

"Mother, please. This is important to me."

Mavis sighed. "Fine, then. I will talk to your father. You girls *are* going to have a chaperone, right?"

"Yes, Mother," said Georgie, her fingers crossed behind her back. "Gloria's older brother, Samuel and his friend James."

"That sounds like a double date, missy."

"Eww, Mother. They're *old*. Sam is twenty-eight. He's *ancient*."

At forty-nine, Mavis had a thing or two to say about that, but considering her daughter was twenty and about to go on a car ride with boys, she thought better of correcting her.

Instead, Mavis said, "Go on with you, now. And do not make me regret this, missy."

"Yes, Mother," said Georgie before dashing out of the living room and upstairs to her bedroom.

Georgie closed her door and pulled out her Philips portable along with her *Beatles For Sale* album. With reverence, she slid the shiny black disc from the sleeve, carefully set it onto the player, and flopped onto her bed, album jacket clutched to her chest. Toe-tapping and head bobbing, she lifted the album jacket to study the picture. Paul McCartney's dreamy, sleepy eyes gazed back at her. Knowing it was silly, Georgie pressed her two fingers to her puckered lips, then to Paul's.

"I will see you tomorrow, Mr. McCartney," whispered Georgie.

3 The Ides OF MARCH

Feather Anne puzzled over the foreign words. It was English, but not any English she knew. Across the table, William sat on his laptop, tapping the keys with rapid, sure fingers. She rested her chin in her hand and stared at him. His glasses sat low on his straight nose, a two-day beard shadowed his jaw and part of his cheeks with more salt than pepper. His tousled hair gave him a boyish appearance.

Without glancing up, William said, "Is there something I can help you with, Feather Anne?"

"Well, since you asked—yes. It's this stupid assignment. Mr. Kapinski—my English teacher— wants us to explain, like, why people say Beware the Ides of March. I mean, who even *says* that? *I've* never heard it before."

"Hmm, Julius Caesar? Heavy reading for sixth grade. Would you like to use the computer?"

"Yes, but we're not supposed to. He wants us to figure it out from this." Feather Anne waved the staple sheets of white paper in the air, then slapped them back down on the table.

"And what have you figured out so far?" William smiled patiently.

"That the Ides of March is on the fifteenth, which was thirteen days ago, so it doesn't matter anymore. Oh, and I also figured out that they talked really weird back then."

"That they did. I'm rusty on my Shakespeare, and my Roman history, at that. However, I seem to recall a soothsayer giving Caesar a warning, and Caesar not heeding the omen. Then, he gets murdered. Sound about right?"

"I guess," said Feather Anne skeptically. "But I can't use the word soothsayer. I don't even know what the heck that is."

William grinned again. "Like a fortuneteller. Don't you dare tell your sister I'm giving you the answers."

Feather Anne sat up straight and spoke in a solemn, officious voice. "Your secret is safe with me." She deflated. "I still don't get it, though."

"Bring it over here, and we'll find the answer together."

Fifteen minutes later, Feather Anne had her answers and William had his peace and quiet back. However, all this talk of ominous predictions and threats of trouble ahead had turned his mind to worrisome thoughts. Mae was due on June fifteenth—the ides of *June*, so to speak—so perhaps this was a sign of foreboding?

With an impatient shake of his head, William cast away the absurd notion. He was not a superstitious man by any means, but merely a man worrying about his wife and unborn children. Perfectly normal. To take heed of a warning from a play written in the fifteen hundreds, ridiculous. Glancing at his watch, he stood and stretched.

"All right, kiddo. Time to pack it up. Gina and Mae will be back shortly, and they'll expect us to be ready to go."

Feather Anne chewed her lower lip, then said, "I've never been to one of these things before. What's it going to be like?"

"Well," said William thoughtfully, "it'll be somber for a while. Then, as people relax a bit, they'll lighten up some—tell stories, share memories—and before you know it, it'll be done."

"Do I really have to wear this dress?" Feather Anne looked down at her navy-blue dress and low heels in contempt.

"Yes, I'm afraid so. And you look lovely, dear. Except, maybe you should go brush your hair."

"Yuck. Fine," said Feather Anne with an exaggerated eye roll.

William chuckled and shook his head at the retreating figure. He swung his suit jacket off the back of the chair and put it on just as Mae and Gina came through the door.

"I knew you wouldn't be ready," scolded Mae playfully.

"I beg your pardon, madam. I am indeed ready. Just had to put my jacket on," replied William, sweeping his wife into his arms and leaning towards her round belly to stage whisper, "Your mother is a slave driver, kids."

Mae laughed and slapped at his arm. "Oh, you. If I was a slave driver, I'd have made you come with us to the café and load everything into the car."

William looked to Gina, suddenly serious. "I hope she wasn't carrying those heavy trays or—"

"Relax, Papa Bear. Bruce and I did the heavy lifting. This one bossed us around. You know, like a—"

"All right, all right you two. Hilarious. Where's Feather Anne? I hope she—"

"Chill, Mae. I'm right hear. And I'm wearing the stupid dress. *And* I brushed my hair. So, there."

Mae waved a hand dismissively at all of them and ordered them to the car. "Come on then, we don't want to be late."

William grabbed hold of her hand, causing her to pause in the doorway. Her eyebrows rose in question. He studied her face, concern etched in his.

Mae gave a small laugh. "What? What is it?"

"Nothing, I suppose. I just wanted to be sure you're all right."

She kissed him and pressed a tender hand to his cheek. "I'm all right, William. Please don't worry so much."

He observed her a moment longer, then kissed the tip of her nose. "Very well, then. Off we go."

4 Charles

March 17th, 1967

Charles Brightsider, violin case in one hand, saxophone case in the other, approached the house—a raised ranch style home that almost identically matched the rows of houses surrounding it—feeling more nervous than was right for the occasion. At the point where the sidewalk met the asphalt driveway, he paused and took a deep breath.

The garage door stood closed, but Charles heard the muffled sounds of swing music seeping through the wood and the cracks. A curtain in the window above the garage fluttered. A young woman peeked out at him, a slight smile on her lips. Charles lifted his hand to wave, but she'd already let the curtain sweep shut.

Charles set down the trumpet case, pulled his handkerchief from his back pocket, and mopped his brow. The front door opened, and a woman called out a greeting.

"You must be Charles. Come on in through the house and I'll walk you down to the boys. They've already started playing, as I'm sure you and the whole neighborhood can hear."

"Thank you, ma'am," said Charles as he climbed the stairs on his long legs. "I, uh, hope I'm not late?"

"Don't you worry, you're right on time," smiled the woman. "I'm Mavis Perri, Gene's wife. My daughter, Georgina, is around here somewhere, too. I'm sure she'll be coming down to see the new fella play any time now. Follow me."

Charles thanked her again and followed obediently. He had to duck a bit as they went down the stairs, which gave Mavis a chuckle.

"Luckily for you, the garage has a high ceiling. Although, in the winter they move it all into the basement here, so you may have a little trouble around the beams."

"Yes, ma'am. Hopefully, I'll be around to have that trouble."

"Oh, I'm sure you'll do just fine, dear."

She opened the door separating the basement from the garage. Music and cigarette smoke poured through the entryway, hitting Charles square in his face. They stood there, waiting for the song to end. The moment the last notes died off, Mavis called out to her husband.

"Gene, your new—what is it you play, dear," asked Mavis.

"Ah, well, a bit of everything, ma'am. Mr. Perri asked me to bring both my sax and my violin. But I can—"

"Come on it, son. Meet the boys. Thank you, my bride. I'll take the boy from here."

"Go easy on him, Gene," admonished Mavis.

"Aww, c'mon, now. We'll treat him mighty fine, don't you worry your pretty head. Get in here, boy 'fore she starts mother hennin' you."

Mavis waved a hand at her husband and the rest of the band as they guffawed and left them to it. Now she only had to wonder at how long it would take her daughter to spy the handsome young man.

At the top of the stairs, Georgie hissed, "Mother, what did you think? Is he a drip?"

Well, that didn't take long. To her daughter, she said, "Oh, Georgina Rose, were you spying on that boy already?"

"I wasn't spying, Mother. I just happened to be looking out my window when he came up the walk. He looked tall. Is he very tall?"

"Let me by, now. And yes, he's tall. Handsome fella, too. I don't think he's 'a drip' either." Georgie started creeping down the stairs. "Oh, no you don't. Stay up here with me and help start supper. You can go down later, when they're near done."

"But Mother—"

"No 'but Mother,' get in that kitchen. The boys will want a nice meal after they're done. I'll bet your Daddy asks Charles to stay for supper, too. So, if you want a nice boy to like you, then you need to show him you can cook just as good as the next girl."

Resigned, Georgie put on an apron and began peeling the big bowl of potatoes her Mother thrust into her arms. It was a full hour before Georgie could finally sneak downstairs and slip into the garage.

Charles's back was to her. She leaned an elbow on Vinnie's piano and studied the broad shoulders and long legs of their soon to be new band member. He turned halfway, and Georgie rested her chin on her palm as she took in his profile. Long—not too long—straight nose. Square jaw. Nice cheekbones. He even had nice ears.

"There's my girl," bellowed Gene. "Say hello, Georgie."

"Hello, Georgie," said Georgie with a smirk.

"That's my girl, a real wisecracker, she is. Sweetheart, this is Charles—what'd you say your last name was, son?"

"I—it's Brightsider, sir. Charles Brightsider. It's a pleasure to meet you, Miss Perri."

Charles gave a polite little bow in her direction and Georgie had to bite back a giggle. My, was he ever formal.

"Pleased to meet you as well, Mr. Brightsider. Am I too late to hear you play?"

"I—we, I think we might be all done—" stammered Charles. He hadn't taken his eyes off Georgie, nor she off him.

"Oh, heck, we can give her one song, can't we fellas? Whatcha wanna hear, sweetheart?"

Georgie thought for a moment. Her eyes traveled back and forth between Charles' violin case and his saxophone. She tapped her chin with one finger and looked skyward.

Batting her eyes, she said, "Oh, I don't know. How about Seven Steps to Heaven?"

Georgie knew well what a challenging song it was to play. Charles looked questioningly at Gene, who shrugged and nodded at Vinnie who took his place. Charles took out his trumpet again and waited for his cue from Georgie's daddy.

When they'd finished playing, Gene asked his daughter, "Well, sweetheart, what do you think?"

"Oh, I like the way he plays, Daddy. I think you should definitely put him in the band. Assuming you're interested, Mr. Brightsider?"

"Why, yes, Miss Perri. I very much am. Interested, that is." Catching himself, he turned to Gene. "Sir, I—yes, I'd be very much interested in joining your band, sir. I didn't mean—"

"Relax, son. Stay for supper, why don't you. Mavis makes a mean pot roast and Georgie here makes a mean martini. Oh, and we rehearse on Tuesdays and Thursdays. Hope that works for you. We can discuss the rest over supper."

"Thank you, sir. I'd be much obliged."

"One more thing, son."

"Yes, sir?"

"You've got to stop calling me sir all the time. It's Gene from here on out. All right?"

"Yes, s—Gene. That's all right by me," grinned Charles.

Charles stole another glance at the pixie-haired, bright-eyed Georgie. She smiled so prettily at him that his heart stuttered. He knew, right then. He would marry that girl, if she'd have him.

5 Under WRAPS

Brianna reached a shaky hand for the towel on the rack above her head. Her stomach roiled again, and she gripped the sides of the porcelain bowl and retched violently, this time only heaving up strangled air.

Into the crook of her arm she hissed, "God damn it." With a mighty effort, Brianna forced herself to stand, panting as she did. She staggered on rubbery legs to the bathroom sink, splashed water on her face and rinsed out her mouth. Meeting her own eyes in the mirror, she swore again.

"You fucking *idiot*." She turned off the faucet, dried her face and hands, and smoothed her hair.

From downstairs, Mrs. Teccio called in her heavy Italian accent, "Missy Brianna, you come a down for break-a-fast?"

Brianna answered back in her regular speaking voice, "Yes, I'm coming for fuck's sake."

"I no can a hear you, Missy Brianna? You come?"

Brianna bit back the urge to scream and called her affirmative—less the cursing—louder. At the full-length mirror, she assessed her appearance. Puffy eyes, check. Pale, pasty face, check. Waistband of black pencil skirt digging uncomfortably into her middle, double check. She turned sideways, flattening her blouse to show a tiny bump where a firm, flat belly had been up until recently, and swore again.

From the bedroom doorway, Mrs. Teccio said softly, motherly, "Missy Brianna, why you no tell you husband? Eh? He should know."

Brianna jumped and gave an exasperated sigh. "I've already told you. If Ricky comes back, it should be because he *wants* to, not because he *has* to."

"But a *baby*, this is reason to come home," said Mrs. Teccio stubbornly.

The nanny come housekeeper never understood Brianna's ways. To her, she had wild moods and a cold personality. It probably shocked her that, somehow, her husband loved her. Even after her terrible mistake. Not that she came out and said an of that to Brianna.

The older woman clacked her tongue and said, "A man like a that, you don't wait for him to decide. You decide for him and let him *think* he decide."

"Believe me, Mrs. Teccio, I want my husband back. And not because we're going to have another baby. But I have to know he's back because he *wants* to be. I—I've already done enough damage. I can't bear it if he always looked at me with—" the tremor in her voice betrayed her resolute expression.

Mrs. Teccio understood better than to push to hard and simply said, "I make a you some toast. Mr. Ricky will be here soon. You put on the makeup, look a pretty, yes?"

"Yes, of course." As she turned to leave the room, Brianna called out softly. "Mrs. Teccio?"

"Yes, Missy Brianna?"

"Thank you."

Mrs. Teccio smiled warmly and nodded once. *Missy Brianna* made very few emotional gestures. When she did, it was best not to make a fuss about it. Everyone knew *that*.

Once Mrs. Teccio had padded down the stairs on her sensible shoes, Brianna sniffed once, straightened her back and looked herself dead in the eyes.

Disdainfully, she said, "Get a hold of yourself."

If only she might recall her former iciness with some authenticity, maybe she wouldn't be so easily reduced to tears at the drop of a hat. Or perhaps she'd have cared less that her husband still refused to come home. Or that she was three months pregnant and alone.

She would not ask Ricky to come home again. Not after the last time, when she had sobbed and begged, practically groveling at his feet. Who was she trying to kid? She *did* grovel at his feet. He'd looked almost ready to crack, to give in, but he started to turn away. It undid her. She fell to her knees onto the hard, cold kitchen floor.

"Whatever you want, I'll do it, Ricky. Anything. Anything, just please—"

He'd spun and looked down at her with an expression she couldn't name right then, lifted her roughly, shaking her once—not hard, but enough to shock her—and his eyes bore into hers.

"Don't do that," he'd said, his teeth clenched. "Don't ever do that," and released her as suddenly as he'd grabbed her.

Before she uttered another word, he slammed out the door and his truck screeched out of the driveway. That was one month ago.

She'd taken a home pregnancy test that morning, shocked but *not* shocked by the results. Brianna thought back to when they'd last made love—New Year's Eve—and the math had worked out simply enough to be certain.

Another time, another *Brianna* would've used this genuinely unexpected pregnancy to get her husband back, not caring the manipulativeness of it if it meant getting her way. However, the Brianna of today—the broken, scared, lost Brianna trying desperately to keep it together—she hadn't the shrewdness for such games. Not after that expression on his face when he'd stared down at her on the floor.

It was pity. That first wave of emotion that swept across his face. Pity. For a split second, she'd mistaken it for love, and it gave her hope. Something in his eyes changed, hardened, and he lifted her so quickly off the floor that she may well have been a rag doll. She was okay with that—the anger. Anger she recognized well. It had been her constant companion growing up a Bourdreau. Especially the low, seething kind that got camouflaged and hidden in public. But the pity? The pity brought back all the shame and humiliation. The pain, the secrecy.

Ricky knew all of it. Or at least enough of it to be sickened by Gordon and Martha Bourdreau and fiercely protective of Brianna. He kept their secrets, though. Against his will and for her sake, he kept them. She'd rejected his pity all those years ago and asked him his silence. Ricky had honored her wishes since they were fourteen years old and up until that night, had kept whatever pity he'd felt for her under wraps. If forced to choose, she rather have his hate than his pity.

Thirty minutes later, Ricky stood in suit and tie at the front door. Like a guest. Brianna invited him in, but he stared at her a long moment.

"What?" Her hand flew up to smooth her hair.

"Nothing. I don't know. You seem—different, or something. Never mind. You, uh, ready to go?"

"Just fixing Cassidy's hair. You know how she is. Come help me?"

Ricky half-turned, as if to walk back to the car to wait, then changed his mind and gave in. "Yeah, sure. I'll distract her with the duck song while you do her hair."

"Great," said Brianna, trying not to smile.

"Mr. Ricky, how good to have you home," said Mrs. Teccio effusively.

Brianna widened her eyes at her, and Mrs. Teccio put her hands out and shrugged before returning her attention to Ricky. He was as warm and friendly to Mrs. Teccio as if she were his own grandmother, making Brianna roll her eyes.

From down the hall came the high-pitched squeal of three-year-old glee. "Daddy! Daddy! Dad-deeeee," exclaimed Cassidy, throwing herself into Ricky's arms.

"There's my baby girl. I missed your face," said Ricky, holding her tightly and kissing her little neck.

Brianna's eyes welled, and she had to blink hard to make the disobedient tears retreat. Ricky's eyes met hers. They were red rimmed as well. They both looked away quickly. Would this ever get easier?

6 Shabby CHIC

"Rosie! Rosie Posie! Come on, babe. We've got to roll."

"One more minute. Geez, Miles. What's your hurry?"

Rosabelle pushed the backing of her earring through the sterling silver post and dabbed perfume at her throat. She was the one who should be nervous, not him. It was after all, her painting that would be front and center for the ceremony, there for everyone to judge her work.

Oh, my God. I am nervous.

She placed her palm to her diaphragm and ordered herself to breathe slower, remember her meditations. She considered doing yoga poses she'd learned at Brittany Sheffield's studio, but Miles called from downstairs again.

"Rosie, come *on*."

She heaved a resigned sigh and stood. It was too quick a move and a stab of pain shot through her pelvis. Most days she was fine, if she remembered to get up slowly. It was only when she moved too fast, or sat or stood for too long, that she had any difficulty. Miles had been disappointed when she asked to change their wedding date to June but agreed that they'd have much more fun if they could dance and walk around without her needing to take breaks every five minutes.

"There she is," breathed Miles.

"Oh, relax. The church is five minutes from here. We've already dropped off the portrait and my parents are on their way here."

Miles face blanched. "What do you mean *here*? I told *my* parents to meet us here," said Miles, mounting panic blooming across his face.

"Miles, I told you last night, my parents are meeting us here, *your* parents are meeting us there."

Rosabelle pinched the bridge of her nose, closed her eyes, and muttered, "I love my fiancé, I love my fiancé, I love—"

"Are you mad?"

She opened her eyes and gave him a tight smile. "No. Nope. Not mad at all. Just—let's get through this, then we can relax." She softened her tone, "It's fine, really. I'm just on edge. What if no one likes it? Or *any* of my work, for that matter. All that time and effort. Listen to me, worrying about myself. I know today isn't only about me, I just—"

"Hey, I get it, Rosie. Everything will be fine. Your work is spectacular. If someone doesn't love it, it's because they're blind."

The doorbell rang, and in walked Ruth and Steven, followed closely by Chet and Jeannie.

"Hello, hello. You kids ready to go?"

"I didn't realize you'd be joining us, Ruth," said Jeannie, shooting raised, perfectly sculpted blonde eyebrows at Miles.

"We didn't realize *you'd* be joining *us*, Jeannie," replied Ruth, giving Rosabelle an identical, if not as manicured, look.

Mile jumped in, "Slight miscommunication. No worries. Plenty of room in the Navigator."

"Honestly," declared Ruth, "that thing is like a house. A whole family could live in there comfortably. Imagine the carbon footprint —"

"Nothing better than a solid, American made vehicle," said Chet, clapping Steven on the back.

"Nor an energy efficient, fuel saving hybrid," volleyed Steven.

"*Both* are excellent," said Miles. "We just wanted something extra safe for Rosie, is all."

Rosie missed her adorable Mini Cooper—the pre-accident version—but had to agree with Miles, she felt much safer behind the wheel of the Lincoln. She had been slightly surprised by how nervous she'd felt driving again after the accident and long recovery.

The big car with its multitude of air bags and safety features had eased her trepidation, but she'd yet to go through the intersection where the wreck happened. Instead, she took the long way around, parking at the far end of the street. Avoiding it forever would be close to impossible, but postponing it—well, it suited her nerves for the time being.

"It looks as if the whole town will be there. They've set up seating outside," said Jeannie, her eyes traveling the small house's interior as she spoke.

She kept her expression neutral; only a keen and knowledgeable observer of Jeannie Hannaford's behaviors could see the flicker of disdain that flashed across her face. Miles noticed.

"Rosabelle, dear. You must tell me who your decorator is. Your style is so… what do they call it? Shabby chick?"

Rosabelle offered a cool, polite smile, as aware as Miles of the underlying condescension in his mother's deceptively innocuous compliment. Her eleven-hundred square foot house was not a place Jeannie Hannaford saw her son living for any length of time. She couldn't comprehend why they'd moved into the tiny dollhouse, rather than Miles' twenty-four hundred square foot townhouse, with its modern furnishing and minimalist design so similar to their own. By comparison, Rosabelle's place—with its floral patterns, lacy trimmings, and soft, worn seating—was something of a shock.

"Why, thank you, Jeannie. Yes, shabby *chic* is a lovely way to describe it. I decorated it myself, actually. I'd be happy to help you with *your* house. You know, soften up some of those hard lines and cold, empty spaces."

Jeannie blinked several times, and Miles turned a laugh into a cough. "All right, then. We should hit the road. Don't want to be late, do we?"

The six soon-to-be family members piled into the Lincoln with the expected amount of polite arguing as to whom should sit where. Somehow, Chet had finagled the first row of passenger seats behind Miles and Rosabelle for himself and Jeannie, remanding Steven and Ruth to the far back seats. Rosabelle expected to hear about that later, she was certain.

7 Georgie

October 10th, 1965

"Georgina, you're not making any sense. Why on earth do you want to go to upstate New York to be a-a nanny when there are perfectly fine babysitting jobs here?"

"I already told Mother, Daddy. I just need a change, is all."

"Aren't you happy here, ladybug?" The hurt in Gene Perri's voice was as clear as his bafflement by his daughter's sudden changes.

The usually vivacious, sassy girl had been behaving like a sullen, moody teenager. Mavis had reached her wits' end and Gene was close behind. Georgie knew this and provoked it. It was her only chance to gain their permission to move almost five hundred miles away from the only life she'd ever known.

"No, Daddy, I'm not. I need *more*. You of all people should understand that." She turned her head into her pillow.

There was silence from her bedroom doorway for a minute. Gene sighed heavily. That's when she knew she'd won.

"All right, sweetheart. Upstate it is."

Georgie held her own sigh of relief until he'd walked downstairs. Then she cried herself to sleep.

8 *The* PORTRAIT

Gloria Van Bergen strode toward the front of the empty church, her back straight as ever. Soon, every polished oak pew would be filled with Saint Paul's congregation and guests to the church. For now, though, she had the ornate, solemn space to herself.

She paused and gazed up at the cross high above the alter, then made her way to where an easel with a cloth-draped painting stood in wait for viewing. Two tall, symmetrical flower arrangements flanked the easel, both with long plastic card holders gripping small rectangular cards with words she couldn't read without her reading glasses.

With a tentative hand, Gloria reached for the corner of the cloth. A peek wouldn't hurt. Rosabelle Waterman had been so secretive about her work, and Gloria had respected this, but now it was so close to the ceremony. No one would be the —

"Pardon me," called a voice from midway down the aisle.

"Oh," said Gloria, snatching her hand back, her cheeks heating.

"Sorry to startle you. You must be Gloria, right?"

"Quite all right. And, yes. Gloria Van Bergen."

Gloria reached out her hand to the familiar-looking man.

"Pleased to meet you. I'm—"

"Craig Davidson," exclaimed Gloria, at once comprehending why he seemed so familiar. It was like her dearest friend Georgie's eyes were staring back at her. "It's lovely to meet you, dear. I'm afraid you've caught me red-handed."

Craig looked puzzled a moment. Gloria nodded to the draped easel, and he chuckled. "I'm curious myself. What do you say we peek together? We'll be one another's accomplice, so neither can rat out the other."

"Oh, you *are* Georgie's son, for certain," giggled Gloria.

"Is that so? I imagined her being a proper rule-abiding young woman," said Craig with a grin.

"Ha. Georgina Perri was a rapscallion, believe me. Led us both into more trouble than we could get out of."

"Hmm. Says the woman leading me into trouble. In the Lord's house, no less," said Craig, his eyes twinkling with mischief.

"Oh, hush now. You grab that corner. I've got this one. Ready?"

"Ahem."

The sound came from beside the alter. Pastor Thomas stepped down from the dais, crossed his arms over his chest, and gave his best look of forbearance. However, he had a thin, rubbery face and build that called to Craig's mind Dick Van Dyke, making it easier to imagine him breaking out in song than a reprimand.

"Oh, hello Pastor Thomas. Don't you have a ceremony to prepare for?"

Gloria attempted a caustic tone, but it was less than effective thanks to the renewed flush to her cheeks and the incriminating fabric still in her hand. She glanced down at it and released it as if scalded.

He glanced down at the swaying material, then back at Gloria and Craig. "I can assure you, Mrs. Van Bergen, I am entirely ready. Are you?"

"I am. Pastor Thomas, this is Craig Davidson."

Pastor Thomas's sternness dropped as smoothly as a cloud drifts from the sun and he smiled in priestly benevolence at Georgie Brightsiders' son. Georgina had confessed to Pastor Thomas many, many years ago about her illegitimate child, relieving a small amount of weight from her burden. That was his hope for her, at least. He'd told her then that God's forgiveness was hers for the asking and encouraged her to forgive herself as well. He never knew if she had done so but seeing her son in Chance gave him cause to rejoice for her.

"So pleased you could join us today," said Pastor Thomas.

"Thank you. My wife and two of my sons are here too, outside. We arrived earlier than expected, and—"

"No explanation needed, my son. Well, I must finish up preparing for the ceremony. I'd love to chat more with you after." He moved to take Gloria's hand in his. Leaning in closer to her, he smiled and said, "Go on and take a peek. I won't tell."

Gloria smirked, placed her free hand over their clasped ones, and nodded once.

After Pastor Thomas had left them, Craig said, "I'll leave you to it, then."

Gloria cocked her head. "You're not going to peep with me?"

"I think I'll wait until the ceremony. Unless you need—"

"Not at all, dear. Go on. I'll see you shortly."

She waited until the heavy church door clapped behind him, its echo bouncing off the high ceiling and walls. She lifted the cloth up and over the back of the easel in one smooth sweep, then stepped back to view it in full. Gloria tilted her head this way and that, then stood for a long moment with her cheek resting in her hand. She swallowed hard against the lump in her throat. Her hand reached out to touch the oil color image of her husband.

"The girl has done well by you, Andrew."

Indeed, Rosabelle Waterman had captured not only Colonel van Bergen's likeness but also his spirit. She had also understood Gloria's need for preserving the Colonel's dignity, of which his first stroke had robbed him. Rather than depicting him bound in his wheelchair, half his face drooped, Rosabelle gave him back his stature and restored his strong, proud jaw.

The Colonel had so wanted to take part in what they suspected would be his last Memorial Day parade. It was not to be, though. His passing came quietly ten days before. Gloria had returned from a luncheon with Georgie and a few of the Ladies Auxiliary Club to find him slumped in his chair. She knew right away but spoke his name anyhow.

"Andrew?"

Her vocal cords had betrayed her, it was a whisper. Gloria patted down the wisps of thin white hair on the top of his head and nodded. She gazed out the bay window onto the street, then around the room.

Perhaps some might find it strange—were she to tell them—that she did not call for help right away but sat beside him in her rocking chair. She didn't cry. Tears would come later, she knew. Gloria wanted to pretend, if only for a few more minutes, that she and her husband were sitting in companionable silence. That it was just a regular Tuesday and soon, Drew and Melanie would come by with the grandchildren for a visit with Colonel and Gran.

"Mrs. Van Bergen?"

It was Pastor Thomas again, this time dressed for service.

"I suppose it's time then?"

"Yes. Your son- and daughter-in-law have just pulled into the parking lot. Others are arriving, too."

With care, Gloria draped the cloth back over the portrait, nodded to Pastor Thomas, and took her seat in the first row of pews. The time had come for a final goodbye.

9 *End* OF AN ERA

"Georgie, sweetheart?"

"Yes, Charles, what is it?"

"It's still hard to believe, isn't it?"

Georgie slipped her hand through the crook of Charles's arm and nodded. Their pace was slower than it had been this time last year, but they were still walking, arm in arm, as they'd always done before. The doctors had commended them both on their healthy lifestyle, leaving out the implications of what the alternative may have led to. She was one hundred percent recovered from her stroke, and he had his medication dosage adjusted for his heart.

Charles told anyone who'd listen that they'd *lowered* his dosage, not raised it. Georgie had warned him not to be smug, it was unbecoming.

"The Colonel had been failing for some time, Charles."

"Yes, yes. Of course. I just mean," he paused and looked at the ground, "it's the beginning of the end of an era. Our era."

"Oh, now," began Georgie, intending on shushing such talk. Only it had the resounding ring of truth to it, and Georgie fell silent.

"We're nearly there, my bride. My, there's a lot of people," said Charles.

"Yes, it is a lovely turnout for the Colonel, don't you think?"

Georgie stopped walking, halting Charles. He looked at her, a question in his eyes.

"Oh, Charles. When I think of Gloria on her own now—and forgive me for being selfish—I think, *what would I do without you?* It's unfathomable."

Rather than attempting to pacify her with platitudes, Charles nodded his understanding and tucked her arm in tighter to his side.

After a moment he said, "I suppose we do as we are doing now, Georgie. *Living.* Let's not worry about what we can't control, hmm?"

"Look at you, being the sensible one all of a sudden," tutted Georgie.

Charles chuckled. "There's my Georgie."

They followed the sidewalk to where it abutted a cobblestone path leading to the side entrance of the church. They preferred this route over the one that led to the front entrance, as it wound around a rose garden. Georgie and Gloria had been maintaining the garden for St. Paul's for over ten years, and she liked to check the rose bushes before each Sunday's Mass.

They paused before a small, newly planted bush. Tight orange buds, cupped in deep green sepals, pointed skyward. The small bronze plaque set in the mulch below it read,

In Memory of
Colonel Andrew Van Bergen
1932-2018
The 'About Face' Rose
Grandiflora

Georgie had helped Gloria plant it just three days ago, and she gave a brisk bob of her head in approval before they carried on.

"Georgie, Charles," called a voice from behind them.

"Craig, Marianne. Thomas and Nate. So good to see you," said Georgie, a smile spreading across her face. To Charles, she said, "They came, how wonderful."

They greeted one another warmly and went inside together, with Craig telling them of his too early arrival and Marianne's interrupting that she'd told him they'd left too soon. Charles and Georgie's eyes twinkled, and they exchanged amused, knowing glances. It was like listening to their own conversations.

Their voices hushed as they entered the nave and made their way to the row behind Gloria van Bergen. Her son- and daughter-in-law sat to her left, and Gloria's brother, Samuel and his wife, Teresa beside them.

Georgie turned to Charles, an expression of dismay on her face. Charles—assuming it was her sorrow for her friend that made her look so distraught—put both hands on her shoulders and gave a gentle squeeze before taking her hand as she sat.

10 Charles

April 23, 1967

Charles, all six-foot-four of him, stood grinning in the center of his small rented room. He gazed around the square, sparsely furnished space, barely registering the mustard, brown and rust colored floral wallpaper or the spindly legged furniture and matching twin bed. The nose-twitching smell of mothballs didn't even faze him. In fact, if the whole room vanished, or burst into flames, he'd not have noticed. His mind was on the events of just a half hour earlier.

In it, he still danced across the gritty wood floor of the town gazebo with the most beautiful girl between his arms. Her dark hair beneath his cheek tickled his nose while her soft voice continued to hum and vibrate against his chest long after they'd stepped apart. After, her perfume lingered on his clothes.

"Georgina Perri, I love you," he'd said.

She'd looked up at him with that impish grin of hers and said, "Well, Charles. I think you should kiss me now."

So, he did. Sure, he'd kissed girls before. Plenty of them—not that he'd brag—but kissing Georgie Perri made him feel like it was the Fourth of July, Christmas, and his birthday rolled in one.

When they broke apart, Georgie breathed, "Goodnight, Charles," and sauntered down the gazebo stairs.

"W-wait," said Charles, "does that mean you— do you, you know—"

"Silly man, I've loved you from the moment we met. I've just been waiting for you to catch up. Oh, and yes. I'll go on a date with you."

Georgie blew him a kiss and continued her swaying walk across the grass to her father's waiting Oldsmobile. Charles waited until they'd turned the corner before picking up his case and heading across the lawn in the opposite direction to the Rudiwitz's grand, Victorian style home on the corner.

Tomorrow, he'd have to apologize to Raymond and Edith Rudiwitz—and their daughter, Eloise, he supposed—for declining their invitation to join them for dessert. He'd seen Eloise's hopeful gaze turn crestfallen but pretended not to notice. He wanted nothing to interrupt his replaying of the evening.

Two hours before the woman of his dreams said she loved him back, Gene Perri's All-Star Band had kicked off the Chance Music in the Park Sunday series to a large crowd. Picnic blankets and lawn chairs spread over much of the fresh green grass, all but for a space in front of the gazebo for dancing.

They'd played the standards for the older folks in the crowd, but at the behest of Georgie, Gene reluctantly added some more modern hits like, *Can't Take My Eyes Off of You, Please Love Me Forever,* and a surprise song, sung by Georgie— *These Boots Were Made For Walking.* Gene, though not a fan of the song, beamed at his daughter.

As for Charles? Well, someone could've knocked him over with a feather. He grinned like a love-struck schoolboy at Georgie and she smiled back at him. When her song ended, he was supposed to lead them into the next one, but he'd been too busy watching the love of his life walk off the makeshift stage to remember.

Gene gave a sharp blast on his trombone, causing Charles to jump. The band had a big laugh at his expense, but he didn't mind. Charles Brightsider was in love and nothing else mattered. His future father-in-law took notice—everyone had, it was impossible not to notice the giant man-boy mooning over Gene Perri's sassy, smart-mouthed daughter—and seemed to approve. Or at least not be mad.

Gene confirmed his hope when, during the packing up of equipment, he said, "She is quite something, my Georgie, isn't she?"

"Yes, sir. She is," said Charles.

He scanned the thinning crowd. When his eyes fell on her, standing with her mother and gazing back at him, he dropped his case. Gene laughed.

"Son, you've got it bad, I'd say. I'm gonna tell you—man to man here—my little girl is one in a billion. Not a million, son. A *billion*. Maybe even a trillion. But I suppose I may be biased."

Gene looked over at his wife and daughter and a troubled look passed over his face. The man had more to say. Charles waited. Gene went back to winding a long electrical cord, speaking as he did.

"Georgie hasn't been herself for quite a while. She, uh, lost her spark. Her mother and I have been worried sick about her, to be honest."

He set down the coil and gave Charles a long, thoughtful appraisal.

"Then you come along with all this—" Gene waved a hand at Charles, "with talent to boot, and just like that, my little girl is back again."

Gene squared up to Charles, and even though he had to crane his neck to look Charles eye to eye, there was no question of the man's superior position.

"So, here's what I will say to you, young man. My little girl has taken a shine to you. I'm fairly confident the feeling is mutual. Am I correct, son?"

"Yes, sir. Very much so, Gene."

"All right then. You have my very cautious approval and permission to see my daughter socially. Take her out on a date, have her home by ten."

Charles grin split his face in half. "Yes, sir. I will. If she's willing, of course."

"Well, son, you have about fifteen minutes to ask her. That's about how long it'll take me to bring this stuff to the car and load it up."

Gene grabbed the handle of his case and walked out to where Georgie and Mavis stood. He said something to his daughter and jerked his head in Charles's direction. Georgie's gaze found him, and she nodded with a soft smile.

He hadn't planned what he'd say to her, and even if he had, he'd have forgotten it the moment she turned those blue eyes his way. What finally came out of his mouth sounded like gibberish and he cringed, certain she'd laugh at him and walk away.

"Charles Brightsider, are you asking me on a date? Before we've even had a dance together?"

Charles blinked at her. "Y-you want to dance?"

"I thought you'd never ask."

She sighed and stepped forward, one hand raised, the other extended and waiting for him to take her in his arms. He obliged with a surge of elation at the prospect of holding her close.

"We don't have any music, though," murmured Charles into her hair.

"Do you sing, Charles?"

He gave a self-deprecating shrug. "I'd say I hum better than I sing, Georgie."

"Then we'll hum."

She rested her head against his chest and began humming *Can't Take My Eyes Off of You*. It would forever be their song. When it ended, he'd only intended to ask her out on that date again, but that's when his heart spoke for him. An hour and a half later, he still replayed their words in his mind.

"Georgina Perri, I love you."

"Well, Charles. I think you should probably kiss me now."

"Goodnight, Charles."

"W-wait, does that mean you—do you, you know—"

"Silly man, I've loved you from the moment we met. I've just been waiting for you to catch up. Oh, and yes. I'll go on a date with you."

11 *Silent* SHOWDOWN

Gina followed behind her daughters and William. The eyes of those already seated scalded her with laser intensity. *You're oversensitive*, Mae had said. *No one cares, Gina*, insisted Feather Anne. But she knew better. Anywhere else, they may have been right. Not here, though.

Any moment now, *he'd* take his place on the side of the dais. The bastard. Gordon Bourdreau, with his slick black hair, hooded eyes and hook nose. She shuddered.

"Do you have a chill, Gina? Take my jacket," said William, now beside her in the pew.

"No, I'm fine, thanks." She offered a wan smile.

His presence, along with Mae and Feather Anne's. made it better. Made her safer. The need sickened her, though. Gina Byrd hadn't ever needed anyone to protect her. She took care of herself.

Even as the defiant thoughts flitted, another side of her mind—the quiet, little girl voice that sometimes spoke up in the night—said, *you did so need protection. All those years ago, you needed it.* But it wasn't there. Not then, when she was just a little kid. Not later. Never.

Guilt flooded color into her cheeks. She'd been no better than her own mother. Gina Byrd wasn't worthy of protection because she fulfilled Connie Byrd's prophecy.

You're no good, Gina.
You're worthless.
You will always be a loser.

Maybe she didn't deserve the abuse as a child, but she did when she became an adult. She gave Mae to Keith with the ease of handing over a sack of groceries. She barely took care of Feather Anne, and then she left her. She was an alcoholic, white trash, loser.

"We are all children of God, and he loves us despite our faults. He forgives…"

Pastor Thomas had begun his sermon several minutes earlier—Gina heard it as if from a distant radio—but at this, her head jerked up. It was like the words were meant for her. A tremulous smile pulled at the corners of her mouth. Then, she saw *him.*

Smug. Pseudo-pious. Evil. Those were the words that sprang to mind. The word she didn't know, but understood on an emotional level, was Machiavellian. Gordon Bourdreau had convinced an entire town he was a God-loving family man. What had Mae called him? *A pillar of the community.* She shuddered again.

William whispered, "Please, take my jacket."

Gina let him drape the garment over her still too thin shoulders, but her eyes remained glued to the wolf in deacon's clothing beside the dais. She watched as his deceitfully sleepy eyes lazily scanned the congregation and waited until they landed on her.

Would he allow a flicker of recognition change his countenance? Would fear drain the color from his cheeks? Or would he give her that awful smirk before dismissing her without a word or second glance?

Her body tensed as if spring loaded. Feather Anne, perhaps sensing a shift in her mother's energy, looped her arm through Gina's, looked up at her, then followed her gaze. She dropped her hand over Gina's and held it.

The child didn't know the cause of Gina's agitation aside from an inexplicable profound dislike for the Bourdreau family. One that seemed to even extend to the youngest, Brandon. Gina denied her obvious and almost palpable hostility when the boy came over to study or 'hang out' as the kids called it, but she made herself a fixture, like a sentinel each time.

Feather Anne accused her of hovering and being nosey. Mae teased her. They didn't know what Gina knew, though. Someday, she'd tell all. Gordon Bourdreau deserved to have his dirty secrets cast into the light, but she wouldn't for as long as he thought he might be—

It felt like an ice pick pierced her heart. Gordon's heavy-eyed gaze landed on her and stayed. There was mockery in his eyes, a taunting. He expected, in all his arrogance, for her to avert her eyes.

Not this time, you bastard.

She returned his stare, raising her chin and setting her jaw. A flicker of—of something flashed in his eyes. Fear? Yes, it was fear. He masked it quickly, replacing the nonchalant veneer and adding his own lift of chin and narrowing of eyes. He tried to convey a dare with that look, one that said, *go ahead. Try it, and see what happens to you,* but the beads of sweat that dotted his forehead spoke otherwise.

It dawned on Gina. *He's afraid of me.* The sudden shock of it exhilarated her. A memory surfaced.

"You listen to me, you filthy whore. I know your secrets as well as you know mine. Tell someone what we did—that's right, *we*—and I'll tell them every despicable detail of your pathetic life."

"I don't care, Gordon. They already think I'm trash. You can't hurt me. I-I'm going to tell the world you raped me." Gina's voice shook with rage and defiance.

"Rape? Don't be absurd. You were more than willing. You came on to me, remember?"

Gina's resolve wavered. "No—I—that's not what happened. I didn't—"

Gordon's tone softened and became sickly sweet. "You had too much to drink. As did I, I admit. When you came into my home, I had no idea what you had in mind. In fact, I feel as though *I* may have been taken advantage of."

"No, I came to you for help. I wanted to—"

The next thing he said came out so casual, Gina doubted she'd heard him correctly. "Besides, who'd believe you? I'm a God damn saint in this town. And you? You're a *sinner*. A lying, no good, loser who sold her child."

It was like a slap in the face. She'd told him in confidence—a confidence he'd coerced her into with promises and lies—and he had no qualms of telling. Gordon knew she'd rather die than betray Keith Huxley *or* Mae. He'd been the only man in her life that had treated her with kindness and respect. Their arrangement wasn't seedy like Gordon portrayed it.

When Gina told Keith she was pregnant with his child, his first question wasn't, *are you sure it's mine*, but *are you all right*? He offered financial help, his home to stay in, and asked to raise the child together. It was Gina who wanted him to raise the child, Gina who severed all contact, and Gina who walked away.

Never once had Keith treated her poorly. She owed him her silence, even though he never asked for it. In her own way, Gina may have been a little in love with Keith, even though she'd always known he was gay. He'd been a sweet kid who grew up to be a classy, charming man. And handsome, too.

When he asked her to be his first—and likely only—female lover, she was more than willing. That was the only time in her life alcohol hadn't decided for her, although it may have fueled *his* choice. She never asked.

He was reverent and gentle that night, more awed than repulsed by the female form. When it was over, he helped her up and shyly asked if it was all right for her. She told him the truth. It was perfect. *He* was perfect.

She would protect his and their daughter's reputation from the likes of her at any cost. It was a promise she made to herself, and to Keith. Although he protested, Gina could see the guilty relief on his face when she told him the plan. It hurt her, but she didn't blame him for it. Who'd want Gina Byrd sullying their good name?

Gordon gleaned that information off her when she was most vulnerable, and he used it to keep her silent. But now, all these years later, Gina's secrets—at least the ones Gordon held over her— were out. She held the upper hand now, and they both knew it.

Gordon suspected and feared that Feather Anne might be his child. Gina knew he wasn't, but for the first time ever, *she* had the upper hand. She considered it payback for his cruelty when they were kids, and for his treatment of her when she'd asked for his help.

If only Feather Anne hadn't befriended the boy. Brandon.

When Gordon finally dropped his gaze, Gina looked over at the second row on the opposite side of the aisle. There sat Martha Bourdreau in a Puritanical, floral print dress, eyes straight ahead. Beside her, the boy. He craned his neck to see Feather Anne, but when he caught Gina's eye, he spun away.

It was the resemblance to *him*. That's what sent a tremor of fear down her spine. The hair was lighter, the eyes, too. But it was there in the head's tilt, the laugh. It was definitely there. Wasn't it? Maybe her panicked mind imagined it. Maybe he was a good kid who'd grow up to be a good man.

Gina could only hope the children's friendship drifted apart. They were only eleven and twelve. Surely, they'd make new friends, and this phase would end.

But if it didn't? If they grew closer, if their feelings became more than platonic… no. They were still too young to even worry about it. She *wouldn't* worry about it. Not yet.

"Earth to Gina? Come on, let's get out of here."

The service had ended, and everyone was standing and chatting. She'd blanked out the whole hour long memorial. Gina stood and muttered an apology. She shot a surreptitious glance to where Gordon had sat, but the chair was empty. She'd survived—and maybe even won—their first showdown.

12 What THE HEART WANTS

"It's so weird to see them together, right?"

"Who?"

Elise swatted Bruce's arm and hissed in his ear, "Brianna and Ricky. Did you hear anything I've said in the last ten minutes?"

"No, because I was trying to listen to the sermon from Pastor Thomas. Anyhow, why's it weird? They're married, so—"

"Ugh, never mind. You're useless when it comes to this stuff. I'm going to find Brittany."

"But the service isn't—"

It was too late. Elise, pulling her phone from her purse, slunk out of their pew and sashayed up the aisle. The door opened and closed with a loud creak and a click that echoed. Bruce winced in embarrassment.

Damn it, Elise.

The second those five reunited they started their antics all over again. It was like no time had passed, no betrayals had occurred, and they held no grudges. Only, that was a lie. They still sniped at and about each other. Bruce couldn't understand it, and he never would.

He considered the friendships between Mae—sitting two pews ahead—Rosabelle, Marisol, and now Charlotte, who flitted between the two groups. No drama. No fights. No claws. Why couldn't Elise join in on *that*?

Despite his better intentions, Bruce took a second look at the Bakers. Ricky lost weight since their separation. Brianna... well, he'd never say it aloud, but Brianna might have *gained* some weight. Not a lot, but just enough to soften some of the sharpness to her features. They sat with Cassidy between them, eyes ahead, and postures board straight. Occasionally, Brianna snuck furtive glances at Ricky, but he never returned her gaze.

Bruce felt sad for his longtime friend. The poor bastard was still madly in love with his wife, but he was trying like hell to fight it. Man to man, Bruce told him he had to do *something*.

"Just, I don't know, do whatever you think is right."

"Ah, well there's some sage advice. What exactly *is* right in this situation, Moose? She *cheated* on me, man. I want to hate her. Seriously, it would be so much easier if I did."

They were in Elise's—now Elise and Bruce's—garage. Bruce handed him another beer.

"But you don't, bro. You love her. The heart wants what the heart wants."

Bruce almost asked, *What about the guy? Do you know who it is?* But Ricky bust out laughing.

"*The heart wants what the heart wants*? The fuck, man. You turnin' gay on me? Kidding, I'm kidding." He flicked the tab on his beer can, took a long sip, and said, "Yeah. That about sums it up."

Bruce tossed his wrench into the toolbox and wiped his brow. "So, what are you gonna *do*, my friend?"

"Well. I think I will let her win me back." A slow grin spread across his grease streaked face.

Bruce repeated back Ricky's words. He shrugged. "So, you're gonna make her grovel and beg. I get it. Cheers."

Ricky half raised his beer can, then halted. A look of dismay clouded his face. He looked like he might get be sick.

"You okay, bud? You're looking green."

Ricky recovered his composure and shrugged off Bruce's concern. "All good. Let's get this engine in and take this baby out for a spin."

That was two weeks ago, and the Bakers looked neither further nor closer to reconciling. Bruce, despite Elise's nudges, wasn't one to pry, so he said nothing the last couple times they got together to work on the Camaro.

Ethan slid down the pew, Gianna on his lap, and whispered, "Where'd Elise go? I think Gigi needs a change."

Bruce mimed two beaks chatting and Ethan sighed. Then he tried to hand off Gianna to Bruce, who nudged her back to her father. The men went on with this until Elise's mother reached between them and plucked Gianna from their hands. She may have called them both idiots, Bruce couldn't be sure.

Minutes later, the service for Colonel van Bergen ended and Pastor Thomas invited everyone to the luncheon in the community hall next door. When Bruce took his turn to file out from the pew, he weaved through the slow-moving crowd to walk beside Mae.

"Hey, Huxley. That's quite the—"

"If you say waddle, I'll punch you, even if we are in a church," said Mae.

"Easy, killer. I was going to say… I was about to say…"

He'd been about to say duck waddle and now he had nothing.

"Oh, shut it, Grady. You and Elise going to the luncheon? Wait, where is Elise?"

Bruce spread his arms wide—whacking Feather Anne in the forehead—and said he didn't know.

"Watch it, you big ape," said Feather Anne.

"Sorry, sport. Geez, you Huxley girls are vicious. How do you survive, William?"

William turned back and tipped his hand to his lips as if holding a drink. The men laughed. The women did not. Bruce looked to Gina for support, but her focus was on something far down the aisle.

"What's up with Gina," asked Bruce.

"Dunno. She's been acting weird since we got here." Mae shrugged and glanced back at her mother.

Pedro Villeneuve caught Bruce's eye and waved him over. Bruce held up a finger. "Wonder what Pedro wants."

Mae followed his gaze as they continued to shuffle along the aisle. "Oh, I know. They're going to add an in-law apartment to their house. I think he wants to offer you the job."

"Me? I'm a roofing guy, not a contractor."

"Yeah, but he knows you built the addition on your house by yourself. Said he'd rather hire you than some—what was the word—ladrón? Anyhow, he wants you."

"Huh. Well, it has been slow lately." Bruce scratched his chin. The extra money would be nice. Especially with the wedding plans Elise had.

As if reading his mind, Mae asked, "Elise still have her heart set on the country club?"

"Yep," said Bruce.

Before they could say more, Elise materialized at his side. It was like she had some kind of radar whenever he got anywhere near Mae.

"Sorry, got held up," said Elise as she hooked her arm through Bruce's. "Hi, Mae. How you feeling?"

"Like I'm carrying the world's largest watermelon," said Mae.

"Ah, you'll get back to your old self in no time. After Brittany had her twins, she fit right back into her old jeans. But she was always super athletic, so…"

"Whereas I'm—"

"Hey, look," cut in Bruce, "there's an opening up ahead, maybe we can squeak through and get outside."

"You two go on, there'll be no squeaking through anywhere for me," said Mae as she waved them on.

Elise needed no encouragement and yanked Bruce forward. He called back, "See you guys next door," before they disappeared in the throng.

Outside, Bruce stepped out of Elise's grip. It was too hot for that. Elise took it wrong, naturally.

"What? Does my public display of affection bother you, Moose?"

They was a challenge in her tone, but a child-like hurt in her eyes.

"Lissie. It's ninety degrees. I'm hot, that's all. Don't look for a fight. Please?"

They were saved by her parents, who had Gianna toddling between them on her chubby legs.

"There you kids are," said Joanna Martino. "Your dad and I aren't staying for the luncheon, so give our love."

"Where are you going?" Asked Elise. "Let me guess. The casino?"

Anthony Martino pumped his arm like he was pulling a slot machine handle. "Cha-ching. You guessed it, baby doll."

Elise rolled her eyes. "Well, have fun and don't gamble away my inheritance, please."

"Inheritance? What inheritance?" Anthony laughed and patted his daughter's cheek. "Don't you worry, sweetheart. Your old man is gonna live to one-hundred."

As the three Martino's jabbed and teased one another, Bruce stood back, well aware he wasn't who'd they'd have chosen for their daughter. He didn't make enough money for their liking, his job was too blue collar, his lifestyle pedestrian.

At last, they walked away, and Elise returned her attention to Bruce. Her smile faded. "Oh, Moosie, relax. They'll come around. Eventually."

"Yeah, yeah. Come on, I'm starving."

13 Hope AND FEAR

The hall, usually decorated minimally, was resplendent. The lights had been turned down just enough to make the long, rectangular room look cozy. Bouquets of blooming orange roses adorned every ivory tablecloth draped table, candles flickering in their centers. Fairy lights lined the wainscoting, and a band set up on stage played soft music.

Brianna's eagle-eyed gaze took in the scene, assessing and seeking fault or flaw. There was none. She observed the reactions of each person as they walked through the doors, fanning themselves and prattling about the heat or the service, or a combination of both.

As their eyes adjusted, a look of surprised awe overcame them. Brianna smirked. Most of these people have never seen a party of this elegance.

She'd set each of Rosabelle Waterman's paintings—gallery style—on easels around the room, each just below an angled spotlight.

"Brianna Baker, this is… I am just speechless. You are a gifted young woman, my dear," said Georgie Brightsider.

She took Brianna's hands in her soft, papery ones and kissed her cheek.

"Thank you, Mrs. B. I'm so glad you like it. Your painting is up front, to the right. I think it might be my favorite one, but don't tell the others, hmm?"

Brianna didn't have to like Rosabelle Waterman to admire the woman's obvious talent. Each painting depicted its subject—be it town scenes or portraits—with such attention to detail and vividness of color they made you want to climb inside.

From beside her, Ricky looked down at Brianna with an expression that could only be pronounced as incredulity. Perhaps even approbation. When the Brightsider's stepped away, Ricky placed a hand on her elbow.

"You did all this? How—I mean, with everything—you never said a word. I would've—I could've helped…"

Brianna's normally fierce pride melted and her chin—damn the thing—quivered at his kindness. Her composure left her every time he showed a softening toward her, despite her best efforts to control it.

"It was nothing," said Brianna breezily. *Tried* to say breezily. She looked away.

Ricky took her chin in his rough, warm hand and said, "It's spectacular, Bri."

Everyone disappeared for a moment. It was just Ricky, looking down at her like he used to. She swayed toward him, her gaze on his lips, his on hers.

"Holy shit, Bri—oh, sorry."

It was Brittany. *Idiot.* Ricky's hand dropped away, and he excused himself with an incoherent mumble. Brianna wanted to throttle her moronic, shit-for-timing friend but instead said, "It's fine. Did you check the bar like I asked?"

"Yes, they—"

"Good. Now, go see—" Brianna stopped.

A sharp pain shot across her lower abdomen and she paled.

"Go see what?" Asked Brittany, unaware.

"Just, go—"

Another stab. She clutched Brittany's arm and folded.

"Bri? What's wrong?"

"Go get Elise. Meet me—meet me in the ladies' room. And be discreet, damn it."

That was like asking an elephant to tip-toe, but she had no other choice. She sucked in her breath, straightened and walked toward the women's restroom, praying no one would stop her. Brianna was never that lucky, though.

"Brianna Jean."

She flinched. "Hello, Dad."

"Am I to understand this was your doing?"

He waved a disdainful hand at the room.

"Yes."

"Yes, what?"

"Yes, *Dad*. I-I'm a party planner now."

He laughed as if Brianna told a joke. "A party planner? Oh, that's rich, Brianna. What on earth makes you think you could—Tom, Margaret. Great to see you."

His tone changed on a dime. It always did when outsiders came around. Brianna stepped backward. It was her chance to escape. Gordon Bourdreau would have none of that, though. He grabbed her upper arm—hard, but not quite hard enough to hurt—and pulled her beside him. At the same time another pain pierced her stomach.

Gordon was smiling. "You two know my daughter, don't you? She—"

Ricky, appearing out of nowhere, stepped aggressively toward Gordon, blocking Tom and Margaret Luschek's view. He put Gordon's upper arm—the one holding Brianna captive—in a vise-like grip. Both men smiled menacingly.

Ricky bent close to Gordon's ear and hissed just barely over a whisper, "Fuck off, Gordon. Or I will make that scene you're so afraid of."

Gordon released Brianna's arm and stepped back, laughing a hearty—and fake—laugh.

"Hey, there son. Good to see you, too. I think I see my wife looking for me, so you all will have to excuse me."

He strode off without a backward glance. The Luschek's made polite, confused salutations and drifted away. Ricky looked at Brianna, his jaw clenching rhythmically.

"You okay? What's going on? Brit said you're not feeling well."

"I-I'm fine, really, I think I just—" Another lightning bolt. This, enough to double her over.

Ricky half-walked, half carried her to the ladies' room and sat her on the small sofa. When the door *whooshed* shut, she let the tears fall.

I'm losing the baby. I'm losing the baby. No. No. No.

"Bri, you're scaring me. What the hell is wrong?"

"I-I'm so sorry, Ricky. I didn't want you to find out. Not like this. Not when we're still—"

"You're pregnant."

It wasn't a question, but a statement. She dared not look up at him. To see the disgust and anger… it would be unbearable. She nodded her head and whispered, "Yes."

"We're going to have another kid? Holy shit. How far along are you?"

"Six months."

Ricky kneeled beside her, took her hands in his, and implored her to look at him. "Bri, babe. We need to get you to the hospital, okay?"

"Are you mad?"

He dropped his forehead on her lap, then gazed up at her, his eyes shining. "No, I'm not mad. Shocked, but not mad. Now can we get you out of here and to a doctor, please?"

She stood shakily, expecting another stab of pain. When none came, she offered a tremulous smile. The door burst open again and Brittany,

Elise, Charlotte, and Katie flooded in. They froze when they saw Ricky and turned their questioning eyes to Brianna.

"He knows," confirmed Brianna.

Elise and Katie let out their held breaths while Charlotte and Brittany gaped in confusion.

"Knows what?" Asked Charlotte.

"I'm pregnant," said Brianna.

Brittany punched the air. "I *knew* it." Then she frowned. "Wait. Why do *these* two know and not me?"

"Or-or me?" Asked Charlotte. Hurt shown in her eyes.

"Ladies, can you have this conversation another time, please? I need to get Bri to the doctor. She's having pains."

"Can you guys make sure the coast is clear? I don't want to make a scene."

The foursome went into to Black Ops mode. Brittany monitored the door and Elise brought the Baker's car up to the side entrance. Charlotte grabbed an hors d'oeuvres tray and drew in the attention of those nearest the restroom. Katie strode to the stage and took to the microphone.

"Ladies and gentlemen, if I could have your attention for just a moment…"

It was Brianna and Ricky's cue to exit the bathroom and beeline for the side door. Brittany and Charlotte flanked them like Secret Service agents until they were safely ensconced in their car.

"You doing all right? Any more pains?"

Brianna exhaled. "Not as bad as the first ones. I-I don't want to lose our baby, Ricky. Even if we never get back together. I—"

"Shh, now. We won't know anything until the doctor sees you. We'll... we'll figure out the rest... after."

She didn't know what that meant, but what she *did* know was that he hadn't let go of her hand since they got in the car. And that was enough for her. There grew a seedling of hope in her heart.

14 Georgie

June 22, 1968

Gloria adjusted Georgie's veil for the fifth time while Georgie herself smiled dreamily out the window.

"How in heaven's name are you so calm, Georgie? I'm a wreck and it's your wedding day, not mine," said Gloria.

Georgie laughed. "Because I'm marrying my best friend, that's why. What's to be nervous about?"

She dotted rouge over her cheeks and tilted her head this way and that in the mirror. When she met her friend's teary-eyed reflection, she jumped up and hugged her.

"What are you crying for? You and Andrew will be married the moment he gets back and then the four of us will have a gay old time."

Gloria dabbed the corners of her eyes and sniffed. "It's not that, you ninny. I'm just so happy for you. After we came back from New York, so much happened. You became so distant, then you went away for real. My brother and Susie broke up and he moved to Michigan. My two favorite people in the world, gone, just like that."

Gloria's chin quivered. "I-I thought I'd lost my best friend. Even after you came back from that nannying job upstate, you were different. But then dear, sweet Charles came along and you came back to us. Then, to make it even better, my mother told me this morning that Sam's coming back home."

Georgie tensed at Gloria's recollections, but her friend seemed not to notice. It wasn't until the last sentence, *Sam's coming back home*, that she saw the color drain from Georgie's face.

"Oh, Georgie, what is it? Are you ill? I knew you couldn't be this relaxed on your wedding day. My, goodness, you're shaking. I'll call for—"

"No," said Georgie with more vehemence than she'd intended. Softer, with a hand on her dearest friend's arm, she said, "Don't call attention, please, Gloria. Just sit with me a moment."

Georgie had held a secret from everyone for three long years, and she was tired of the burden. Even if she couldn't tell all of it, especially to Gloria, she could tell some. She took a breath and began.

"That weekend? The one we went to Shea Stadium? Something happened—I-I did something. I was so ashamed, Gloria. I *am* ashamed still."

"Georgina Perri, what on earth? You stop that right now. There's nothing you could say to me that could make me think less of you. You're my very best friend in the world. Whatever it is, you can tell me."

Georgie believed her friend meant what she said, but still could not burden her with the worst of the tale. It would devastate Gloria. Instead, she shared the one part of her shame that could only hurt herself.

"I-I got pregnant while we were in New York. Please, don't ask me any of the details. It's too mortifying. I was foolish and let's leave it at that."

Gloria stared uncomprehendingly at her for what felt like an eternity. "But... we were all together. All the time."

"Not *all* the time, Gloria. We'd had a lot to drink, remember? After the show. You and James went in search of pizza, and I—"

Gloria stiffened. "And you and Sam stayed back." Gloria looked out the window. Her voice became firm. "You went out and left Samuel behind." She turned back to Georgie and begged her with her eyes and tone. "That's what happened, right? You went out and left Sam at the hotel."

Georgie had led Gloria to the conclusion. To the man who'd taken her virginity and impregnated her. And she'd repelled from it. Her adored older brother could never have done something so vile and wrong.

Georgie said what she knew she had to say. She took Gloria's hand in both of hers. "Yes, Gloria. That's exactly what happened. Sam stayed behind, and I-I went out. I met a boy in the lobby and—well, you can figure out the rest, I'm sure. Now let's not speak of it ever again."

Obvious relief coursed through Gloria, making her go limp. She recovered her composure when a new, slow understanding ran across her face, like she was replaying the last couple years with a new lens.

"You didn't go away to be a nanny, did you? You went to—to have the baby?"

Georgie bowed her head and nodded.

"Oh, you poor dear." Gloria took Georgie's face between her hands then embraced her tightly. "You could've told me. You should've told me. I-I'd have helped you. Don't you know that?"

"I know, really, I do. But I just—it was just too shameful, Gloria. I hope you understand."

Ever sentence weighed heavy now with double meaning.

"I suppose I do. Georgie, I know you don't want me to ask, but—the boy—does he know about… about the baby?"

Georgie shook her head violently. "No, no. He doesn't. That's all I want to say about that. About any of it. I'm sorry I burdened you with this, Gloria. But really, I just want to move on and never think of it again. Say you'll do that for me?"

She could see the conflict in Gloria's eyes, but she agreed.

"Very well. We shall never discuss it again. Unless you change your mind, of course."

"I won't. Now, let's get back to this wedding, shall we?"

Georgie stood. Gloria grabbed her wrist. "One last question. Charles? Does he know?"

Quietly, barely above a whisper, Georgie said, "No."

Gloria patted her hand and also stood. A moment later the rest of the bridal party entered the suite and Georgina Perri got on with the joyous event of marrying the handsome, sweet, and wonderful Charles Brightsider.

15 *Siblings*

Feather Anne jabbed Brandon's arm with her elbow. "Where's your sister going? Isn't this her party?"

Brandon rubbed his arm and followed her gaze. Ricky had his arm around her waist as they slipped out the side door. Her friends were acting like bodyguards.

"Uh, yeah. Well, she's, like, and event planner or something now. Wonder why she's leaving? My dad'll be pissed, watch."

"Why would your dad be pissed?"

Brandon shrugged and changed the subject. "Who's your mom talking to?" He jerked his chin in Gina's direction.

Feather Anne followed his stare and saw her mother in conversation with a tall, sandy-blond haired man. He looked familiar, but she couldn't place him.

"No idea. Kinda familiar though, no?"

Brandon looked again. He laughed and said, "Holy shit. I know who that is. Fat Chris. Only, I guess you can't call him fat anymore."

"Brandon."

Gordon Bourdreau had come up behind them.

Brandon jumped. "H-hey, Dad."

He stared at Brandon a moment; his eyes dark. It made Feather Anne uneasy. But then he gave them a beatific smile and his tone changed to something that sounded like a dad on one of those old black and white sitcoms Mae loved to watch.

"Son, I think your mom could use a little help over by the dessert table."

"Help with wh—" Brandon stopped, then perhaps seeing something in his father that Feather Anne missed, said, "Uh, sure, Dad. Come on, Feather Anne."

Gordon put a hand up. "Just you, son. I'd like a chat with... Feather Anne."

She saw then what had paused Brandon. Though Gordon's smile never left his lips, it also never reached his eyes. Brandon looked back at her apologetically.

Gordon stared at her. "I hadn't realized you and my son are so chummy. How old are you, Feather Anne?"

"Eleven. I'll be twelve in October. Why?"

Gordon laughed as if she'd said something amusing. "Aren't you precocious? I was just curious about the young lady my son has been spending time with. Tell me, why is it you never come over our house? Martha and I would love for Brandon to have his friends over more often."

Because Gina says you're a piece of shit and I should stay away.

"Thanks, but Mae and Gina prefer I stick close to home."

"Hmm. I see." He glanced around the room. He was trying to look casual, but Feather Anne saw through it when his gaze paused on first Mae, then Gina. "Lovely chatting with you, Feather Anne. Enjoy the rest of the party, hmm?"

He turned as if to walk away, but then he came back, his hooded eyes locked on her. The smile remained. "My son is an honor student, you lady. Make sure you keep him out of whatever trouble you like to get into. Understood?"

Feather Anne, taken aback by the meanness in his voice and how it contrasted with his jovial demeanor, but also never one to back down, said "Actually, he's an honor student *because* of me. But, sure thing, Mr. Bourdreau.

Gordon stepped forward, towering over Feather Anne. There was blackness in his eyes. For a split second, she thought he might hit her.

Instead he hissed, "Nasty, insolent girl." From behind Feather Anne, Pastor Thomas called Gordon's name. His countenance smoothed, and he called, "Coming, Pastor Thomas."

Without a second glance, he strode away, leaving her feeling like the dirty, white trash kid she used to be. Like the one she'd deep down always be.

"Feather Anne? Everything all right?" It was Mae.

"Uh, yeah. All good." She lied.

"What did Gordon Bourdreau want?"

She hesitated. "Nothing. He just wanted to say I'm welcome to hang out at their place with Brandon."

Mae studied her a little too worriedly—just like she always did—and at last said, "Oh. Well, that was nice of him. But given the way Gina feels about—"

"I know, I know. Over her dead body."

They both looked over at Gina, still talking with not-fat-anymore Fat Chris.

"Is that—" started Mae.

"Yep," said Feather Anne.

"Wow."

"I know."

It seemed like the two were flirting. Gina had an almost girlish air—shy, giggly even. The sisters watched the pair for a minute longer. When they could take no more of the bizarre sight, they went on their separate ways. Mae, to find William, and Feather Anne to find Brandon.

16 Happily EVER AFTER PLANS

"You did it, kid. And you sold five paintings," exclaimed Miles as he lifted Rosabelle into a hug.

She squealed, "I can't believe it, Miles. It was… it was *amazing*."

She grabbed his arms. "And, I didn't even tell you the best part."

Miles laughed. "You mean, it gets better than making five grand in one day?"

Rosabelle fanned herself, barely able to contain the scream of excitement welling in her chest.

She spoke slowly. "The town library commissioned me to paint a mural for the main lobby. They were going to hire a guy from out of state with the grant money they received, but when Judith Morrison saw my latest work, she said the job was mine if I wanted it."

"Damn right, she chose you. My girl is the best. So, how much are they going to pay you?"

He couldn't help himself; Miles Hannaford was all about the money. Rosabelle knew this, knew it was part of his upbringing, but she couldn't help but be true to her nature, too.

"Oh, I don't care about that part so much. It's just an honor in itself."

"Oh, God. Please tell me you didn't say that to Judith Morrison." Miles steepled his hands under his nose as if in prayer.

"Well, no. I mean I didn't really get a chance to say it. She said they had a grant for ten-thousand and that they could probably get a little more from private donors."

Miles sat down hard on Rosabelle's sofa. *Their* sofa. "Ten-thousand? Did you just say ten-*thousand* dollars?"

"Ah, yes. They'll give me a retainer of four-thousand, and the rest upon completion."

He was looking at her strangely. Kind of like he might pick her up and run around the house with her held high like a trophy. Or like he might have an aneurism.

"Rosie, do you realize what this means?"

"Um, well…" She supposed it meant a few things. She had a job she loved. It could provide a real income. Affirmation that she was talented. What Miles meant likely had more to do with the financial aspect.

"Babe, the house on Great Heron. Across from the Villeneuve's." Rosabelle stared at him. "The one I just listed. Still nothing?"

He stood again, taking her face in his hands. "Rosie, babe. *We* can buy that house. You said yourself it was a dream house."

Rosabelle pulled back, her brow furrowed. "Oh, Miles, I didn't mean *I* wanted it. It-it's too much."

The notion of such an imposing, grand home made her slightly queasy. Yes, she'd said it was beautiful when Miles took her through. But she'd imagined someone like a Brianna Baker type in it, not a Rosabelle Waterman. Although the gardens in the backyard were breathtaking.

"Remember what you said about the gardens?" It was like he'd read her mind.

"Yes, they are beyond incredible. But the asking price… even if they took less, it's still more than we can afford. Isn't it?"

It embarrassed her to realize she had no actual idea of how much or little Miles made. She'd always assumed he did well for himself—expensive car and condo, high end clothes and salon haircuts—but they'd never discussed their incomes.

Before her art showing, Rosabelle made enough to maintain her tiny, low mortgage, twelve-hundred square foot house. The after-showing earnings had the potential to be great… or it could slow to a trickle. If they stayed where they were, they'd never have to worry. If they moved into that mini-mansion, they'd be forever forced to strive and possibly struggle.

"Rosie, let me worry about the details, okay? Just say you're in. That's all you have to do. Say you're in, and I will give you a dream life."

She wanted to say—even started to say—she already had her dream life. But the excitement and need in his eyes changed her course. "I… of course, I'm in, Miles. If you think we can swing it, then I'm all in."

Miles hugged her into a quick spin before setting her back down and pulling out his cell phone. He already had it to his ear, one hand covering the mouthpiece to say, "Calls to make, babe. I love you."

"I love—"

"Nora, listen. I need you to freeze that listing on Great Heron. Yeah, I have a buyer, all right. Great. I'm coming into the office."

He tapped his keypad rapidly. "Hey, Pop. Got some great news. I'm going buy the house on Great Heron." He caught Rosabelle's raised eyebrow. "We, I mean, we are going to buy the house."

Miles strode down the hall and out the back door, into the little backyard as he spoke. Rosabelle sighed and looked around her sweet little home. Ludo gazed up at her with his strange, bright cat eyes.

"Oh, Ludo. What have I just gotten us into?"

Miles's call to his father almost immediately after getting Rosabelle's assent send a rock-hard knot into the pit of her stomach. Buying the house on Great Heron would please the Hannaford's immensely… and the Waterman's, not at all. True, a newfound affection for Miles had budded, but it still bore traces of doubt and mistrust for their future son-in-law. And she mustn't forget the continuous bickering between both sets of parents.

What would it be like when they had children, for God's sake? Visions of Ruth and Jeannie having a snarling tug-o-war with her precious—albeit currently nonexistent—baby made her shudder. More images, like movie clips, popped in her head. Chet Hannaford clapping her father on the back hard enough to make him wince and clench his jaw beside a grill—both wearing Number One Dad aprons—while Rosabelle ran drinks back and forth between the mothers. Meanwhile, Miles's phone would be glued to his ear as he talked *first-time buyers* and *listings* and *sellers' market* all while holding up a *one more minute, babe* finger at her.

To the distressing scene, she added a large breed dog chasing Ludo around the expansive yard and a group of grown-up mean girls—Brianna Baker and clan—cloistered in a corner, pointing and laughing at her. She'd probably have kept on piling image after overwhelming image had Miles not returned to the living room with exuberant glee.

"I've got the code to the lockbox. What do you say we take a ride over to the house and take another look around, hmm?"

"Oh, I—Miles, I'm exhausted from today's excitement. Tomorrow, maybe?" His face fell and Rosabelle felt a twinge of guilt. "I'll tell you what. Give me an hour to rest, then we can go, okay?"

Like a child whose parent suddenly agreed to give them ice cream after repeated *no*'s, Miles brightened. "Perfect. Rest up, Rosie Posie. I'm going to go for a run while you relax."

He dashed up the stairs two at a time. Five minutes later he galloped back down and out the door, his headphones already jacked in his ears. He blew her a kiss and she waggled her fingers back.

Rosabelle stretched out on the sofa and pulled her book from the coffee table. *The Writer's Romance*. When she'd stopped into the new bookstore in town—aptly named That Book Store— the owner had recommended it. The back cover promised it to be a sweet, romantic comedy, and she was sold on it.

With Miles out of the house for a bit, maybe she'd read in peace and quiet. Her cell phone rang.

"Miles?"

"Rosie, babe. I know you're resting, but, hang on." Rustling on the line, then the sound of a car horn. "Sorry, switched over to Bluetooth."

"Aren't you jogging right now?"

"Yeah, yeah. Listen, I was thinking. Is your heart set on getting married at the cafe?"

"Ah, well, I thought so, but I'd be willing to consider—"

"Great. Hear me out, okay? I'm thinking once we buy the new house, we should get married right there. I mean, I know it's no English garden, but it's close, right? Unless you really *did* have your heart set on Mae's Cafe."

A small smile tugged at Rosabelle's mouth. Every time she thought *he never listens*, he came out with something so thoughtful and sweet, it made her eyes sting. He really *had* been listening when she'd said her dream wedding would be in an English garden.

"I think it has potential, Miles."

"Good. Okay, that's all I've got. Go back to resting."

She pressed the phone to her chest. Was a garden enough reason to buy a house? She envisioned the sprawling green, manicured lawn, the curved stone ledges that bordered each section of themed garden. Succulents and verdant greens in the shade, followed by a bonsai and bamboo oasis, complete with a koi pond. Further along an arch of wisteria vines draped the path that wound around a moss and vine enshrouded gazebo. On the other side of that, a rose garden filled with dozens of varieties, many of which she'd never seen.

There would be no rest now. One wedding delay had followed another. Could *this* one stick? Rosabelle's mind flooded with wedding ideas. If they married early August, everything would be still in bloom. But August was right around the corner. They *could* manage it. Or, had she gone mad? The answer was yes, a temporary insanity had overcome her, but she didn't care. She sat up, set the book back on the table and called Miles back.

"Go, Rosie," panted Miles.

"I've made a decision, Miles."

His breathing was loud in the phone. "About the house?"

"No, about getting married."

"You want to push back the wedding again?" His voice went up an octave. "Babe, if it's about the house—"

"Hush, silly. I don't want to push back the wedding again, Miles. I just want to get married in our new backyard."

"Soon, right?"

"Right."

"Like *how* soon?"

"Like August soon."

Silence. Then, "That's technically pushed back, you know."

Rosabelle laughed. "By a week or so, Miles. But do you think we could be in the house in time?"

"Rosie, if I tell you something, promise not to get mad?"

She sank back against the cushions. "What did you do, Miles?"

"I put a deposit on the house last week. I-I knew you'd kill it at the showing, and well—"

"Oh, Miles. What am I going to do with you?"

She could almost see him smiling. "Live happily ever after, Rosie Posie. That's what."

She tapped the phone to her forehead, then sighed. "I'm going to hold you to that, you know."

She hit end and stared out the living room window. Giddy, almost hysterical excitement welled in her chest. She wanted to laugh and cry, run around and take a nap. It was sensory overload. She needed to paint. It was the only thing that settled her jangling nerves.

17 *Perfect* SYNCRONICITY

"It was different back then," said William. He shrugged and handed Mae a cup of tea. "Women didn't have the options—hell, they didn't have the *rights*—you do now. Sounds as if Georgie made the best of a bad situation."

"I know. Really, I understand. It's just..." she rested her free hand over her round belly, "I can't fathom giving up these two little ones. It must have been so awful. And being forced to pretend it never happened?"

William kissed her temple and wrapped his arm around her. There wasn't any more he could add. It *was* heartbreaking. Her expression was so troubled, he felt compelled to remind Mae of the good parts of the Brightsider's story.

"Craig grew up happy, healthy and well-cared for. Now, they get to build a relationship. All's well that—"

"You're kidding, right? *All's well that ends well?* They lost over forty years. And the *grandchildren.* Don't get me started on that. It—I'm sorry. I didn't mean to yell at you, William. It's the hormones."

"Uh-oh, William. Is Mae biting your head off, too?" Feather Anne peeped her head around the kitchen doorframe.

"I'm not biting anyone's head off, thank you. I'm emotional." Mae sniffed.

William and Feather Anne exchanged *here we go again* glances before returning to their respective tasks. For Feather Anne, it meant test studying with Brandon. For William, it meant placating his irrational, emotional, and immensely pregnant wife.

"So, what shall we watch?" William braced himself. If he had to watch My Man Godfrey one more time…

"My Man Godfrey sound good?" Mae smiled sweetly.

"Perfect," said William.

Feather Anne groaned from the kitchen.

"Be quiet in there," growled Mae. "William, would you mind getting the watermelon from the fridge?"

"The—you want the whole—"

"*Yes*, William. I *do*. Is there a problem with that?" Asked Mae.

"Ah, nope. Not at all, sweetheart. One whole watermelon coming up."

In the kitchen he silenced Feather Anne and Brandon's laughter by putting his finger to his lips. He mouthed, *Don't you dare*. They pursed their lips and tried to focus on their open books. Or pretend to.

William shot several surreptitious glances their way as he cut the melon. There seemed to be more elbow nudging and muffled laughs than studying in his opinion. He'd talk to Mae about it. Although, he might wait until she was less… sensitive.

"How's the studying coming along you two?"

"Fine," said Feather Anne.

"Very well, sir," said Brandon.

Feather Anne mimicked him.

"That's called respect for your elders. Don't tease him, young lady."

"More like fear of being beaten by the Deacon, I bet."

"Oh, Feather Anne," admonished William.

They bantered back and forth, but when he looked to Brandon, he saw the boys face had gone ashen. He met William's gaze then quickly looked down at his open book. William questioned Feather Anne with only his eyes and she shrugged.

He looked again at the boy. He and his older sister, Brianna, had always reminded William of a pair of Parian dolls he'd seen once in Germany. They shared the same porcelain complexion, pale blonde hair, and cornflower blue eyes.

At only twelve, Brandon's height and build showed a promise for a spot on the Chance Chargers when he got to high school. Despite his size, the boy had a gentle nature and was exceptionally well-mannered. Especially compared to Feather Anne.

William opened his mouth but thought better of it. What would he say anyhow? *Brandon, is everything okay at home? Are you in danger?* Yes, those were questions that might need to be asked… or he simply read too much into a gesture. Mae would know what to do.

He cleared his throat and said, "All right, back to work, you two. Mae and I are right around the corner if you need us, and Gina is… where *is* Gina?"

"Didn't you hear?" Feather Anne smirked. "Gina's out on a date with Fat Chris." She frowned and said, "Only, I think he's just Chris now."

"I see," said William. "So—"

"William," hollered Mae, "how long does it take to cut a watermelon?"

"Coming, my love."

He left the pre-teens laughing in his wake and hurried to his hungry, cranky, and round-bellied wife. She'd already begun the movie without him and was speaking Gail Patrick's lines along with her.

"How'd you like to make five dollars," they said in stereo.

William, having seen the movie enough times, said in perfect synchronicity with William Powell's Godfrey, "Well, I don't mean to seem inquisitive, but what would I have to do for it?"

Mae rewarded him with a smile that more than made up for her often combative and erratic mood swings of late. It would be a mistake to bring up his concerns over the kids' study habits, or those about Brandon. Instead, he sat beside his wife and pondered ways to get more information on the Bourdreau's without raising questions.

18 Playdate

"He drives me nuts sometimes," said Elise. She threw a dandelion for emphasis. It hit Charlotte on the nose.

"Ouch," said Charlotte.

"It was a dandelion, for fuck's sake, Charlotte. It didn't hurt." Brianna sneered and rolled her eyes.

"I-I know, it was just a reaction. Like a knee-jerk. It's like when you—"

"Yeah, we know what knee-jerk means, Char," said Brittany. She looked to Brianna for 'burn' approval, but Brianna had already moved on.

"So, tell me again how impressed everyone was with the luncheon."

Elise stifled a yawn. How many times could they discuss how *wonderful*, how *amazing*, how *beautiful* Brianna's first event was? And why had she thought they'd all turned over a new leaf after the last fight?

Clearly, they were right back to their fucked up version of normal. Brianna holding court like Queen Elizabeth—although she'd prefer being likened to Posh Spice— and the rest of them at her feet. Literally, too. It was their weekly park play date, and they sat under the same massive oak tree they'd always sat under. The one with *Ricky + Brianna 4ever* carved in its rough bark, along with a dozen other teenager's handiwork. Only, instead of sitting on blankets like Elise, Charlotte, Brittany, and Katie, Brianna sat on an expensive cushioned collapsible chair from L.L. Bean.

As Brianna preened on her throne, Elise squinted at the tree trunk behind her. *Ah, there it is.* In a cryptic and discreet location on the trunk there the letters ELM were notched. Elise never confessed it had been her work. *Elise Loves Moose.* Most people figured some drunken idiot had mislabeled the maple tree to be ironic or something.

"I thought you were ordered to bed rest, Brianna," said Charlotte. She caught Elise's grateful expression and gave a quick wink.

"Something in your eye, Char?" Asked Brittany. She eyed her with suspicion and a dare.

"Ah, yep. Eyelash," answered Charlotte pointedly. She stared back at Brittany—eyebrows raised—until she turned away in exaggerated disinterest.

Okay, so *some* things had changed. Passive Charlotte had lost her anxious, eager to please manner and replaced it with a calm confidence. She was still ditzy, though.

"It's not exactly bed rest," justified Brianna as she inspected her nails with sudden interest. "It's more like… light duty."

Elise took that to mean she'd have everyone jumping to do whatever she had no interest in and doing only that which served her. She couldn't help but goad her.

"Ah, so you got Ricky right back where you want him, hmm?"

"It's not like that, Elise. He's a very busy, hard working man. I'm not going to take advantage of him. Not… never again."

Damn it. Just like that, Brianna pulled on her sympathies again. She wasn't pretending, either. Losing Ricky—even if it had only been for a short while—had broken open something in her. A willingness to be vulnerable? Elise thought so, and both Katie and Charlotte had agreed. She didn't bother asking Brittany.

Katie, resembling a Weeble Wobble, half-rolled toward Brianna to pat her knee. People kept asking her if she had triplets in that giant belly, but she good-naturedly repeated over and over, "*Nope, fifth pregnancy. That's all it is, folks.*"

She was as big as Mae, and *she* expected twins. If anyone thought Mae would've been the Zen-like, yogi preggo, they were wrong. She was surly, grumpy, and outright prickly. Guess Miss Perfect wasn't so perfect after all.

"What are you grinning so devilishly about?" Asked Brianna.

Elise wiped the smile away. Charlotte and Katie wouldn't approve her mean-spirited thoughts, and Brittany and Brianna would relish in them. Both excellent reasons to keep her spiteful glee to herself. And naturally, she felt bad almost immediately. Mae tried like hell to be Elise's friend. On the surface, they were good. But every time Bruce came back from the café, or from Mae's house, it twanged a raw nerve.

Without missing a beat, she said, "I was picturing Rosabelle's face when she saw Miles talking to Julianne Morgan at the luncheon."

Brianna leaned ever so slightly forward. "Really? Hmm. Julianne *is* very pretty. Way prettier than Rosaline. She probably should worry."

None of the women corrected her. Ever since Miles and Rosabelle went public, Brianna had deliberately called her by every variation of her name she could come up with. It wasn't that she had any feelings left for Miles—aside from moderate revulsion that she'd slipped and fell for his smarmy charm for a hot minute—but her hyper-competitive nature wouldn't let her do otherwise.

Charlotte, not thinking, said, "Well, prettier than the old Rosabelle. New Rosabelle is gorgeous. It's like when they suddenly replace an actor in your favorite show with a better look—"

"Let's talk new news, hmm? Elise?" Katie clapped her hands.

Elise flipped her long, black hair over her shoulder and sat up straighter. "Well, as you know, I've been a little... stuck on what to do now that I'm a single mother."

She paused for pity. The women obliged by offering her pitying nods. Satisfied, she continued. "You're going to love this. I bought that cute little building on Parsonage. You know, the one with the yellow door and cobblestone walkway?"

"I think it's flagstone," interrupted Brittany.

"Whatever, Britski. Anyhow. I've decided to make it a girl's boutique spa." The others stared blankly at her. "You know, like, where they can have fancy birthday parties and get manicures and pedicures, and then shop. It's a *great* idea, thank you."

Elise thrust her jaw at them, waiting for their criticism or mockery while trying to feign indifference.

"Elise Martino," said Brianna, "that is… fucking *brilliant*."

Even though she hated herself for it—and would never admit it— but if she had feathers, she'd have fanned them out like a peacock. Elise could tell Brittany wanted to throw cold water on her and douse her pride and excitement, and it only made her more giddy.

"Oh, my God," said Katie, "that's *you*? Every time I drive by, I try to figure out what the heck is going in there. It looks like a little paradise island."

"Right? Bruce is over there now painting. Each room is going to have a different theme. You know, like, a pop star room, and a princess themed room, and—"

"Ooh, could you do a unicorn themed room? I love unicorns," said Charlotte.

"It's for kids, dum dum," said Brittany.

"Did you just call her *dum dum*?" Katie laughed.

Brittany sniffed. "It's the twins' favorite word of the week. Whatever."

"I guess it's better than last week's word. What was it again? Oh, I remember. Dickface, right?"

"That was Bart's fault, not mine," said Brittany defensively.

Elise sighed. "Anyhow, back to my spa, please? We plan on having the grand opening end of July, so mark your calendars. It needs to be spectacular, so Brianna, will you be my event planner?"

Brianna forgot herself for a second and nearly squealed with excitement. "Really? Me? That would be—" she caught herself. "I'm sure I can fit you in my schedule. We'll do lunch tomorrow and discuss details, yes?"

Elise grinned. "That would be lovely, thank you."

They spent the rest of the playdate discussing themes, décor, and brainstorming a name for Elise's new business. In the end, she declared her own idea—Enchanted Oasis—the winner. She emailed her sign maker immediately.

What Elise left out from the story was Bruce's initial resistance to her idea. She wanted them to think he was the perfect, ultra-supportive fiancé. Which, ultimately, he was. It had just taken some convincing. And apologizing.

Two weeks earlier Elise had taken him out to dine at one of his favorite places to eat, Harry's

Place in Colchester. They grabbed the only open picnic table and sat. Bruce had already dug into his first burger when Elise began her rehearsed speech.

"Bruce? We need to talk. I, uh, I kind of did a thing."

He glanced up, burger poised, and waited.

Elise wiped her hands on her shorts. "It's not a *bad* thing. It's just, you know, a thing."

He set down his burger with a small groan and scraped the napkin across his mouth. "Spill it, Martino. No, wait. Let me guess. You bought those ridiculous, over-priced shoes? No? Okay. Hmm. Please don't tell me you booked that Clemens Castle place for the wedding. Oh, I know. You—"

"I bought a building," blurted Elise.

He repeated her words back to her, slowly. "I don't understand."

Elise, in a rapid-fire delivery, explained that she'd had the idea brewing for a couple months, but was afraid he'd think it was silly or stupid. Then her dad had been talking to Miles about the property on Parsonage.

"But don't freak, he wasn't the one handling the listing. It's Nora's and she's been trying to unload it for almost a year, but the seller's asking price was too high and they'd refused to drop it."

It turned out the seller was an old friend of her dad's and, "Well, he said, *make an offer*, and so, my dad made an offer and the guy said, *okay, it's a deal*, and now it's mine."

Her lips pulled back into what was meant to be a smile but fell short. Bruce's face remained stony.

He pushed his burger away and pinched the bridge of his nose.

"Elise, what the fuck, babe? Where's the money coming from for this?"

"Daddy," said Elise. *Naturally, it was from him. Duh.*

"Your father bought you a building so you can have a... what did you say? A *kid's* spa? That doesn't—it's not—I don't even know what to say here."

"I don't expect you to understand. You're a guy. Girls love being pampered, Moosie. It's going to be amazing, you'll see. There's nothing like it anywhere near us, so—"

"Elise. We're a couple, aren't we? We're engaged to be *married*. You didn't think you should maybe, oh, I don't know, *discuss* this with your partner in life?"

She opened and closed her mouth. Elise had no good answer to that question. Why *hadn't* she discussed it with him? If she were completely honest, the thought never really crossed her mind. Saying that to him, though, would've made matters worse. So, she lied.

"I wanted to surprise you, babe. Plus, you've been so busy with working on the Villeneuve's addition. And I know how you are. You'd work yourself to the bone trying to do everything for everyone. I just wanted to spare you extra work." She added, "Not that there's much to do. Just painting and decorating, really. And I've already ordered a shit ton of stuff online, so..."

She stopped there. Any more would be overkill. It did the trick. The hard lines around his gorgeous blue eyes and stubble rough jaw softened. He picked up his burger again. He wasn't done admonishing her yet, but he started warming to the idea.

"You can't do shit like that, Lissie. We're supposed to be a team, okay?"

"Yes, Bruce. I'm sorry for buying a building without asking you first."

He rewarded her with a small, snorty laugh. She smiled back at him. After he'd eaten his second burger, he crossed his big forearms on the table any told her to tell him everything. Elise treated it as if her were a bank loan officer and laid out her business plan, which—if she'd say so herself—was pretty fricking impressive.

At the end, he said, "Damn, Martino. I thought you were an Arts major. How'd you know all this stuff?"

She shrugged. "Simple. I minored in business. Daddy made me. He said the odds of making a living off an arts degree weren't as good as a business degree. So, we compromised."

For a moment, he looked like he'd been about to say something, but changed his mind. In the end, he decided on congratulating her and offering his services as her handyman, even if it was grudgingly. She had him start that afternoon.

In two short weeks, the little building that once was someone's house had transformed into something that resembled an island oasis. The Hannaford's landscapers had followed her specifications and surrounded the building with sand and beach roses. Fairy lights wound around the two artificial palm trees flanking either side of the arched entrance, and shrubs trimmed into fanciful shapes lined the stone walkway.

The clapboard house went from a faded, powder blue to flamingo pink. The white shutters became aquamarine, and the yellow door remained the same. Sure, plenty of people in town would be calling it an eyesore, but every little girl would lose her ever-loving mind and beg her parents to go inside. That tacky little building was about to be Elise's financial security.

19 Charles

June 22, 1968

The organist played the first notes of Mendelssohn's Wedding March, cueing the guests to stand. Charles, as if in slow motion, turned to watch his bride. Her gaze swept across the church pews, a mild smile on her lips. When her eyes met his, the smile widened.

His heart nearly burst with a surge of love for the stunning creature making her way toward him on the arm of her father. Charles, with great effort, tore his gaze from her face to appreciate her figure. He'd claim later that he'd been admiring her champagne-blush dress—as unique a choice as was the woman wearing it—and she'd chide him that she knew very well what he'd been admiring.

When she was at last by his side before the pastor, he whispered, "Now I understand why the tailor gave me such an usually colored bowtie."

"You look dashing, my love."

"You look radiant, darling."

The pastor cleared his throat and Charles and Georgie's startled expressions made the congregation erupt in a twitter of subdued laughter. Once again, and at their own wedding, they'd forgotten there were other people in the room.

Sheepishly, Charles said, "We-we're ready now, Pastor." More laughs followed.

Less than an hour later, they were taking their first spin around the dance floor as husband and wife. The toasts and dinner were a blur. His chicken cordon bleu could have been prime rib, and he'd have not known the difference. His mind had taken the leap from wishing the night would never end, to hoping it would go faster. He wanted to take his breathtaking wife back to their hotel room and do the things he'd been imagining since that first kiss a year ago.

At long last they dove breathless and laughing into the back seat of the waiting limousine, falling against each other. Georgie's head rested on his chest; her arm strewn across his lap. It was enough to awaken his lust. Their laughter hushed and their breathing changed. Her arm nudged against the hard swell in his trousers.

Charles tipped her chin and claimed her mouth with his. She returned his kiss with delicious, wine tinged passion. It took all his self-control to not take her there in the back of the limousine. The driver cleared his throat.

"All right you two lovebirds, we're here. Congrat—"

Charles and Georgie sprang from the car and up the hotel steps before he finished. At their suite, Georgie almost walked in ahead of Charles.

"Wait," exclaimed Charles. He swept her into his arms. "This is the way we're supposed to do it."

Georgie giggled and swatted his arm. "Just don't whack my head against the frame, Hercules."

Pale pink roses and peonies filled the room. A cart with champagne and strawberries stood in one corner and their suitcases open on top of the dressers.

Georgie excused herself to the bathroom, lifting a small bag off her case as she passed. Charles removed his jacket, undid his bowtie and kicked off his shoes. He tried to think of what to do next.

"Champagne, dear," called Georgie.

"Champagne, right," muttered Charles as he hopped to it.

He also closed the curtains, dimmed the lights and turned on the cabinet stereo. Should he turn down the bed? He stood over it, his chin in his hand, deliberating.

"It's not going to turn itself down, dear," said Georgie from the bathroom doorway.

"R-right, no, it's—oh. Hello, you."

A dopey grin spread across his face and the stirring in his loins returned with a vengeance. Good God, she was stunning. Georgie had on a short but demure nightgown with a sheer, loosely tied dressing gown over it. As she walked toward him, one sleeve fell off her shoulder.

She rested her hands on his hips and stood on tiptoes to kiss him. A groan escaped his lips. Charles wrapped his arms around her waist and lifted her, holding her to him.

"Mrs. Brightsider," he growled in her ear, "I am going to make love to you now."

"Is that so," she teased back.

He pulled back and waggled his eyebrows at her. With a smirk, he tossed her onto the bed.

"Ooh, you bad man, you," gasped Georgie, laughing.

Before she could say another word, Charles pounced on her, stifling her giggles with kisses until they became groans of pleasure. They shed their clothes in a tangled flurry and when he at long last had her bared beneath him, he marveled at the wonders of his new wife.

To his great and welcome surprise, Georgie was a willing, if not initially shy, partner. Once he'd gently and slowly entered her, he stayed still inside her, caressing her skin in light strokes, kissing her throat, breasts, and mouth until her body relaxed beneath him.

His thrusts started small, rhythmic. Georgie's hands, which had gripped his forearms, now stroked his arms, then they moved to his hips. Her body began to respond, and her legs spread wider to let him in deeper. Charles let her control their pace; he wanted her to want him as badly as he wanted her.

Her climax came with a gasp and a moan, and it sent him over the edge. After, he held her close and rained kisses on her brow and temple.

"I love you, Georgie."

"And I love you, Charles." After a moment, she giggled. "So, is *this* what married life will be like?"

"I certainly hope so," said Charles with a content sigh.

"Me, too."

When Georgie rose to use the bathroom, Charles thought he'd spare her embarrassment by removing the bloodstained sheet. Only there wasn't any. Georgie came out to see him puzzling over the bed.

"What are you doing, Charles?" Dawning overcame her confusion and her face crumpled. She ran back into the bathroom and slammed the door.

"Georgie, sweetheart, come out. Please? I'm not—it's just—well, I don't… I mean, I guess I thought, oh, hell. Please come out so we can talk?"

Muffled sobs were her reply. Charles sighed and pressed his forehead against the door. "Georgina Brightsider, you are the one and only love of my life. That does not mean I didn't have a life before you. Nor did I expect *you* to not have a life before me."

He placed his fingertips on the door right about where he hoped hers were. "The only things that matter to me are our present and our future."

A sniffle, then, "Promise we won't have to talk about it."

Charles grinned. "I promise."

"Not ever?"

"Not ever, darling. I'm going to pour us some champagne, now."

Charles left her to gather herself together. He poured their drinks, loaded a tray with strawberries and chocolates and brought them to the bed. When the bathroom door opened, he turned to see his wife, the tip of her nose pink and her eyes red-rimmed, staring at him with a look of... well, he didn't know what the look meant.

"Charles," she said, "you're naked."

He looked down in surprise. It was true, he was naked. In all the fuss and worry, he'd not thought to dress.

"So, I am." He gave her a wicked smile. "And you're overdressed, my dear."

Georgie narrowed her eyes at him, the corners of her mouth twitching. She'd hastily snatched only her sheer dressing gown when she'd run to the bathroom and it disguised none of her curves. Charles felt his arousal grow. Georgie could see it and it emboldened her.

She untied the satin strings that held the garment closed, slid it off her shoulders and let it fall to the carpet. Despite the blush that crept up her cheeks, she held his gaze and moved toward him as gracefully as a dancer. Georgie coiled her arms around Charles's neck, and he lifted her against him.

They made love for a second time that night, then again in the morning before they left for their honeymoon. Charles held to his promise to not ask any questions of her past, nor did she volunteer any answers. It would be a lie for him to say he wasn't curious, but he respected and cared too much for her feelings to press her. If she ever wanted to talk, he would listen and not judge. When he told her this, Georgie's eyes welled again, and she kissed his cheek, whispering, "Thank you, my love."

20 Mayberry

Mae stood behind the counter, one hand resting on her round belly, the other twirling a lock of hair.

"They make a cute couple," said Claudia with a shrug.

She followed the young waitress's head tilt to see Gina and Fat Chris—*just Chris*—on the café's patio. They sat across from each other at one of the wrought-iron tables, their bodies curved toward one another over the tabletop and arms resting inches apart. They were like shy teenagers. Mae couldn't decide if she found it adorable, or gross.

"Eww," said Feather Anne. Her opinion was clear.

"Get used to it. I believe they're an item now," said William as he passed by them to his table in the corner, laptop satchel hanging from his shoulder.

The sisters rolled their eyes in unison. Mae said, "Well, you can have the honor of waiting on them. I'm too—"

"Fat?" Feather Anne batted her dark lashes at her big sister.

Claudia took the moment to make her escape. "I'll take care of them. You two try not to kill each other."

Mae scowled. "Don't you have a summer reading packet to begin?"

"It's literally the first day of summer vacation, Mae. Geez. Lay off, will ya?"

"No, I won't lay off. Mrs. Patterson said you need to read these books for next year. I know you, you'll put it off until the last week of summer and then cry and complain that it's too much work."

"Whatever," said Feather Anne. She stomped off to the kitchen, swiping a peach champagne muffin from the case and sticking her tongue out at Mae as she went.

"Got your hands full, huh, baby Mae?" Miles sauntered to the counter, swinging his keyring on one finger. He took an exaggerated double take at her belly. "Damn, you look ready to pop. When are you supposed to squeeze those little footballs out, anyhow?"

Through gritted teeth Mae said, "Eight weeks, four days, and counting. And if you piss me off, Miles, I swear to God I will beat you blind with this egg white sandwich."

The waiting customers around the counter chuckled behind their hands. Mae's cantankerousness had become as much an attraction to the café as had her formerly sweet nature. Some regulars had begun making various bets as to what pastry item she might throw at someone on any given day, which orders she'd mix up, and how many times she'd knock a glass off a table with her belly.

Everyone from William to Rhonda the mail carrier had suggested she take a maternity leave and let Gina and the Petrova twins take care of things in the café. Bruce even had the audacity to hint that she should close for a couple months. Mae let them know just what they could do with their suggestions. After that, they stayed clear *and* quiet.

Miles started, "Aw, baby M—"

Rosabelle hurried in, grabbed his arm, and said, "Miles is going outside and out of your way. *Right*, Miles?" She gave him a push and turned back to Mae. "There, all better. I'll take these so you can get the next customer, okay?"

Mae's face smoothed again as she inhaled, exhaled, and then smiled. Serenely, she said, "Thanks, Rosabelle. That would be awesome."

From his corner, William raised a questioning eye at Mae. She pulled a face reminiscent of Feather Anne's frequent displays of silent, passive aggressive resistance to authority. Not that William ever tried exerting authority over Mae. *Influence*, maybe.

After the last of the lunch customers left, Gina found Mae in the kitchen, rubbing her back. It'd been aching and spasming all day. When she saw that Gina had Fat Chris—*just Chris, damn it*—in tow, Mae made more an effort to stand straighter and force a smile.

"Uh, Mae? You have a minute? If not, that's okay. We can talk later—"

"It's fine, Gina. I wish everyone would stop walking on eggshells around me. You all act like I'm Attila the Hun. *Am* I Attila the Hun?"

She crossed her arms on top of her stomach and glared.

"No, not at all," cajoled Gina.

From behind her, Chris piped in, "Y-you look great, Mae."

She narrowed her eyes at them then huffed. "So, what's up? Let me guess. You want a day off?"

"Ah, no. I mentioned to Chris that you were thinking about hiring a part-time cook. And, well, speak for yourself," she said to Chris.

He stepped forward, removing his baseball cap and wringing it in his hands. "Uh, yeah. I, um, well, I'm actually a pretty good cook."

Oh, God. He probably thinks making boxed macaroni and cheese qualifies as being a good cook.

She kept her expression placid and friendly. "Oh, that's very nice of you to offer, but—"

"I-I went to Bristol Tech. Their culinary arts program? And, yeah, I got my degree. I just, you know, never followed through after."

Mae struggled and failed to keep the surprise from her face. Chris O'Brien—formerly and possibly forever known as Fat Chris—part-time roofer, the guy whose van plowed into Rosabelle Waterman's Mini Cooper last winter and almost killed her, was also a culinary school graduate. Would wonders ever cease?

"I—we'd have to start with a trial run, of course. Does that work for you, Chris?"

He bobbed his head enthusiastically. "That'd be great, Mae. I won't let you down."

"I'm sure you won't. Wednesday breakfast crowd is usually light. Come in then?"

He agreed with more eager enthusiasm and Gina mouthed thank you as they left. Truth was, Mae was starting to get desperate for help. With her due date looming and her ever-mounting responsibilities, she felt like a frayed rug. It pained her to need to lean on others for help, but there was no way around it, she was exhausted.

"Kid, you look like you swallowed a watermelon."

Mae looked up to see her Aunt Katrina in the doorway.

"Tree! What are you doing here? I thought you and James weren't coming back until the end of the month?"

She and William's publisher had hit it off over the holidays and jumped into a whirlwind romance that involved flying to Europe on a whim and eloping while in Paris. No one had been surprised. She was tan and glowing with happiness, and Mae's heart swelled at the sight of her wild, vivacious aunt beaming at her.

"And miss the birth of those two? Not a chance, kid."

Katrina tottered across the kitchen in her high heels and placed her hands on either side of Mae's stomach. She put her face an inch away from her navel.

"Hello, my little chickadees. It's your Auntie Tree-Tree."

"Tree, I'm not due for another eight weeks."

Katrina straightened and waved a dismissive hand. "Bah. You'll go early, mark my words."

"Oh, is that so? How do *you* know?"

She spread her arms wide, palms up, and she tipped her head back to gaze at the ceiling. "Because the universe has told me so." She dropped her arms and head, picked up a pickle, and said, "Plus, twins usually come before their due date. Your father and I did."

"You could've led with that," said Mae.

"Eh, not as dramatic. So, what's the latest in Mayberry?"

Mae pondered. "You know, it's been relatively quiet. I think things have finally settled."

Katrina dropped her pickle on the counter and shook her fists at Mae. "What, are you crazy? Saying something like that is a jinx. Go knock on wood. Here throw this over your left shoulder. Or is it right? Shit. Do both."

Mae's aunt frantically threw handfuls of salt over her own shoulders, then knocked on the butcher block. Mae scoffed, but obliged. Just in case.

Joel Asheby popped his head into the kitchen. He was in uniform. "Uh, Mae? We've got a situation. Is Feather Anne around? I'm going to need to speak to her."

Katrina gave her a theatric, *what did I tell you* look. Mae ignored her.

"Ah, she was here a few minutes ago. Why, what'd she do?"

Feather Anne was no stranger to getting in trouble, but never with the law. Not until now, at least. Mae went through the mental list of possibilities. Maybe she took one of her pranks too far and now a teacher wanted to press charges. Or, she punched yet another kid, and *their* parents wanted to press charges. Or—

"It's nothing she's done. We're looking for Brandon Bourdreau. Gordon came by the station this morning. Says Brandon hasn't been home since yesterday afternoon."

"Oh, thank God," said Mae. "I mean, not thank God about Brandon. I just thought—"

"No worries, Mae. I knew what you meant. He doesn't seem *overly* concerned. Just wants his kid to check in with him."

"And he thinks Brandon's at my house? I think I'd know something like that," said Mae.

"Gordon didn't say that exactly. He, uh, seems to think she'll know where to find him, though." Joel hedged. "I kind of get the idea he doesn't much like those two hanging out."

"Well, he can join the club. Gina hates it."

Joel hesitated again. "Gordon implied the reason Brandon's not coming home is because Feather Anne is a bad influence on him."

"That's crazy," sputtered Mae. "And let me get this straight. The guy's kid is basically missing, and he's not even concerned?"

"Well, missing might be—"

"You said he hasn't heard from Brandon since *yesterday afternoon*, and he doesn't want an Amber alert put out immediately? I know I would."

Joel gave an exasperated sigh. "Yeah, tell me about it. I don't like it, but he thinks the kid's just throwing a temper tantrum and trying to piss off his old man or something. The mother seems calm, too."

"Aren't those the people Gina hates?" Asked Katrina.

"Gina? What does she have against the Bourdreau's?" Joel pulled out his notepad and a pencil.

Mae widened her eyes at her aunt, who mouthed back, *What*, in exaggerated innocence.

"It's nothing, Joel, really. She just doesn't care for them, that's all."

"She say why?" It was Joel's turn to sound innocent and nonchalant, but Mae saw the tension in his hand.

Mae's back pain suddenly wrapped around to her front. Her abdomen tightened. She knew what Braxton Hicks contractions felt like, but this felt different.

No, it's too soon. She'd just stood too long and needed to sit.

"I think it was something… something to do with… something—"

"Mae? Everything okay? You look a little funny."

"Yeah, I'm…" Breathtaking pain blotted out the next words. She gasped and reached out for the counter to brace herself.

"Jesus, Mae. How long have you been having contractions?" Joel went into medical emergency mode.

"Contractions? No, I'm—it's too soon." She hadn't been having contractions. Just some mild cramps on and off all day. And the back pain. Not contractions. Even as she thought the words, the understanding hit her.

"Where's William? Someone get William, please?" Mae's voice sounded calm, but inside she panicked. It was too soon. *Not dangerously soon, though.*

"Katrina, stay with her and time the contractions. I'll get William, Mae. You just relax as best you can."

"Sure, no prob—ow, fuck," gasped Mae.

"There's our delicate flower," chuckled Katrina as she looked at her watch. "five and a half minutes in between."

William burst into the kitchen as if there was a fire. "Mae, sweetheart. Are you all right? What do you need? Should we get to the hospital? I think we should. Should we?"

"Whoa, slow down, there, Papa Bear. Everything is fine. We're timing her contractions. No need to rush over to the hospital just yet," said Katrina.

"I'm okay, William. I think—oh." Mae looked at the floor. "My water just broke."

Another contraction followed, doubling Mae over. William brushed her hair back and murmured in her ear. Her brow smoothed, and she nodded at him.

"Okay, guys. I think maybe we will get her on over to the hospital now," said Joel. "William, I'll lead you there in the cruiser."

The next contraction came. "Two and a half minutes since the last one," said Katrina. There was a slight tremor in her voice.

As they walked Mae out, she called back orders and instructions.

"Feather Anne, call Bruce. Paulina, check the mini quiches in the oven in ten minutes. Claudia, see if Gina—damn, hang on."

Everyone stopped and waited with tense faces as a contraction gripped her. When it passed, she continued.

"See if Gina can get my suitcase and bring it to the hospital. Is Rosabelle still here?"

"Right here, honey," called Rosabelle from the patio railing.

"Great, okay. Can you get Feather Anne home?"

"Of course, no problem, Mae."

She made her small swarm stop again. "What am I forgetting? Oh, I know—"

"Mae, sweetheart, try not to worry. Everything will be taken care of," said William.

She let him lower her into the car while Katrina jumped into the backseat. More than half the café's patrons and the staff crowded at the entrance, waving and calling out their well wishes. A contraction cut short her return wave. When it subsided, a new wave of worries overcame her.

"William, we haven't decided on names yet. We can't call them Baby A and Baby B after their born."

"No, I'd imagine not," said William.

"Are you two really going to keep it a secret until they're born? Come on, what's it going to be? Identical? Fraternal? Two girls? Two boys? One of each?" Their silence on the matter exasperated Katrina.

"We want it to be a surprise, Tree," said Mae in between shallow breaths.

"Hang tight, Katrina. Won't be long now," said William. He grinned at her through the rearview mirror.

Eight hours later, they were still waiting. Nurses and the doctor had come and gone numerous times. The intervals of Mae's contractions had become irregular, and they were monitoring the babies heart rates.

"Why haven't they—I don't know—induced you or something?" Katrina's concern made her prickly.

William said, "Because her water's already broken. She's *in* labor… it's just slow going."

"Well, she's exhausted. Shouldn't they do a C-section by now?"

"Guys? I'm right here. You can talk to me, you know," said Mae. Her voice sounded reedy and weak.

Mae's face looked waxen in the fluorescent light, all but for her flushed cheeks. Her eyes had a feverish, glossy shine. William strode to her side and pressed a hand to her forehead. He glanced up at Katrina, his brow creased.

"She feels—" he caught himself, "you feel hot, love. I'm going to call for the nurse again."

"I'll get one. You stay with her." Katrina quick-stepped out into the corridor.

Her clacking heels echoed down the quiet ward. It was so quiet that they could hear her admonish someone at the nurse's station at the opposite end of the floor.

Mae chuckled weakly. "They're going to hate us by the time this is done, aren't they?"

21 Georgie

September 1974

"Isn't it just wonderful to have the fellas home?" Georgie sighed her contentment.

Gloria chuckled. "Mostly. Andrew thinks the boys and I are his regiment and keeps trying to order us about. He'll need setting straight."

"Oh, dear. Well, if anyone could do it, it's you. He does realize you *run* the Ladies Auxiliary, doesn't he?"

They laughed. Staff Sergeant Andrew van Bergen, home from the war now two years, was a career military man, and that made the van Bergen's a career military family. Georgie had watched her best friend evolve from a flighty and whimsy girl to a self-possessed and assertive mother of three exceptionally well-behaved boys.

"Charles's idea of unpacking his instruments and suitcase is to set everything in the foyer and hope I'll put it all away. He's been back from a tour a week now and it's still right where he left it."

"Oh, dear. Sounds like war to me." Gloria laughed.

"It sure is. And I'm going to win, mark my words."

"Get a look at those two out there. Trying to keep up with the young ones."

Despite having little in common besides their wives, Charles and Andrew forged a friendship of their own over the years and were heading up a rousing game of baseball on the town green. Georgie, Gloria, and some other wives and mothers prepared sandwiches and cups of lemonade for when they finished.

"Hey Gloria. Georgie," called out Eloise Rudiwitz, a yellow Tupperware container pressed to her stomach.

Georgie rolled her eyes at Gloria, and Gloria swatted her arm.

"What," hissed Georgie, "she tried making the moves on my man, Gloria Jean. I despise her."

"Oh, stop that. It was years ago, and you've got the man. Take pity on the woman, for heaven's sake. She married *Calvin Merkle*, after all."

"Hm," sniffed Georgie.

She glanced over Eloise's shoulder at Calvin. He'd been a year ahead of them in school, and Georgie would've barely remembered him had it not been for his shockingly large, hooked nose. She found it as hard not to stare at it now as she did back then.

"Stop staring," whispered Gloria. She called back to Eloise, "Hello, Eloise. So glad you could come out for the fundraiser. Are those your famous deviled eggs?"

Georgie made a small retching noise that Eloise may or may not have heard. She found it hard to tell by the woman's expression—it always had that pickle-bit look to it.

"I wouldn't miss it for the world, Gloria." She glanced at Georgie or rather, somewhere vaguely over Georgie's shoulder. "Georgina. Looking... trim as ever."

It wasn't intended as a compliment. Of all the young, married couples in their social circle, Georgie and Charles were the only ones without children.

"And you're looking quite—"

"Let's put your dish over on that table over there," cut in Gloria.

Eloise blinked several times at Georgie, then at Gloria. The dare in Georgie's eyes was more than she wanted to contend with, so she huffed and clomped away.

Before Gloria said a word or reprimand, Georgie said, "She started it."

"She's just jealous of you, Georgie. She always has been. Do try to be more charitable. She's been on her own in that old Victorian so long now, it's no wonder she said yes to the first man who asked for her hand."

"Well, at least now that she's got a husband it doesn't look so unseemly to have transients in and out of the place."

"Travelers, Georgie. It sounds much nicer than *transients*."

Georgie, still stinging from the *trim* comment, sniffed and declined a response. She tried to not let the whispers and innuendos bother her. Or the times someone nosily asked, "So, when can we expect a little Charles or Georgina running around?" Although, eight years in, the questions *had* become more infrequent. They were replaced more often with well-intended, "Not everyone is meant for parenthood," and, "Well, at least you two have your freedom."

There was no known medical reason why Georgie couldn't get pregnant. There'd been several almost-maybes, but each resulted in disappointment. Charles maintained a pragmatic mentality and assumed the burden of fault. Deep down, though, Georgie believed it was God's way of punishing her for her deceptions. She told Gloria this once, after one of their many letdowns.

"You mean to tell me you think God is mad at you for giving up your baby? Georgie, honey, what *else* could you have done in the situation?"

"I could've told my parents. Or the boy—" she tried to stop the words, but she was too late.

"Ah, yes. the mysterious boy," said Gloria. She opened her mouth to say something more but changed her mind.

Georgina turned away. "Let's not discuss it anymore."

Georgie's SECRET

Gloria honored her friend's wishes. Some things couldn't be spoken of.

"Well," said Gloria in a too gay voice, "all's well that ends well."

"Yes, exactly," agreed Georgie.

The truth was, she and Charles had a wonderful marriage. Fun and passionate, comfortable but exciting. She had more than happiness; she had contentment. Their life together was enough. It had to be.

22 *Invisible* SCARS

Brianna sipped her tea and grimaced. "Ugh, what *is* in this, Mrs. Teccio? It tastes like… I don't even know what it tastes like."

Mrs. Teccio smiled her most beatific smile and wiped her hands on a worn dishcloth hanging from the pocket of her apron. "It is old family secret recipe. Is to keep baby, you know."

To express her meaning, she slapped her hands together and laced her fingers tightly.

"Stick?" said Brianna.

"Yes, how you say? Stick together."

Brianna rubbed her temple. Adopting her most tolerant voice, she said, "Thank you, Mrs. Teccio. The doctor said everything is fine. I just can't do any heavy lifting or stand for too long a time. No special tea needed."

She handed back the cup, ignoring the disapproving tutting from her nanny and housekeeper. The two women had an unspoken agreement. Mrs. Teccio did not speak excessively of how much she enjoyed taking care of Brianna and her family, and Brianna would never say how much she loved being taken care of by the motherly woman.

It was something she'd never experienced growing up a Bourdreau. Martha, as both a mother and wife, was both brittle and nervous. She never did or said anything without Gordon's explicit approval and spent much of her spare time vacuuming, cooking, or doing laundry.

Her idea of love and affection involved phrases like, "Did you eat?" Or "Wear a coat tonight, it'll be chilly." Even those were said distractedly and sounded like a recording to Brianna's ears. She'd look up from drying a dish or ironing one of Gordon's shirts with a look of confusion. As if her daughter came from another planet and was wholly unconnected to her. Sometimes Brianna answered, other times not. It never mattered either way.

The Bourdreau women did have some things in common, though. They had the same gut clenching tension during silent dinners dominated by Gordon's heavy breathing. They had a shared twitching rabbit sense for when his ever-simmering temper began to boil. Both were experts in walking on eggshells. And each could take a kick to the ribs or a punch in the gut like a champ. So that was something. Oh, and they both knew how to keep secrets and appearances.

"Missy Brianna, you go dark place again, no?" Mrs. Teccio sat beside her and together they watched Ricky and Cassidy in the yard. "Every time you go there ina you head, you stop and say, '*No*,' and you look here, at your life, your beautiful life, okay?"

In a surprise move, Brianna tipped her head onto Mrs. Teccio's soft, round shoulder. "Okay, Mrs. Teccio."

They said no more. The woman didn't know exactly what happened in Brianna's childhood, but she somehow seemed to understand her. Perhaps better than she understood herself.

The therapist she'd been seeing helped. Most times, after leaving Dr. Hannah's office, a sense of peace and hope filled her. Their session that morning had not. Dr. Hannah had asked her about the dynamics of her relationship with Ricky. Brianna recognized it as an attempt to see if she had continued the cycle of abusiveness.

"Just so you know, my husband is the dearest, sweetest man. He may look like a bull in a China shop, but he's a lamb. If anything, I'm the—" She stopped, stricken.

Dr. Hannah waited, a benign half-smile resting on her coral painted lips. "You're the what, Brianna? What were you going to say?"

Brianna looked out the window of the cozy home office. Her jaw clenched. She ran a damp palm along the length of her linen pants. The words remained locked in her throat. The realization was too large.

Dr. Hannah spared her. "You were going to say, *if anything, I'm the abusive one*, weren't you?"

Brianna nodded. *She was her father*. Bile rose in her throat and she reached for the glass of water on the table between them. The buttery-smooth voiced doctor waited for her to compose herself. Then she said the words that felt comparable to a balm on scorched skin.

"You are not your father, Brianna. You have free will, the ability to choose how your relationships will be. Do you believe this to be true?"

"Yes." The word came out strangled.

"Good. That's *very* good, Brianna. The scars he inflicted on you—they weren't just physical wounds. They were emotional ones and those last way longer than anything else. The things you've done, choices you've made, your behavior—it is perfectly normal given what you've experienced."

"H-how do I—where do I even begin to make up for the way I've treated my husband? And my daughter." She looked up, a horrified expression on her face. "I've never laid so much as a finger on Cassidy, I swear on my life. I-I've just been so… cold. Disconnected, I guess. I love her with my whole heart, but—"

"You're afraid. It's understandable. We're almost out of time for today. Let's take a moment and talk about the good things you've done in your life, Brianna. We'll have plenty of time to discuss the other things, but I think it's vital to recognize the positive, too. Tell me something good."

Brianna frowned, trying to think of one damn good thing she'd done. Then she gave a small laugh. "Well," she said, "I somehow managed to find the greatest guy on the planet. Of course, I almost ruin—"

"Ah-ah. Only the positive right now. What else?"

"I brought a beautiful, smart little girl into the world." She smiled even though tears threatened.

"Good. Go on."

"I started a business, even with the craziness going on in my life. I-I'm actually very good at what I do, too." She sat up straighter.

Dr. Hannah said, "I have no doubt about it. You've accomplished so much for someone with such odds stacked against them. Whenever you start to get down on yourself, I want you to remember that, okay?"

"I'll try," said Brianna. "I mean, I *will*. I'll remember."

"That's what I want to hear. See you next Thursday?"

Brianna had driven home after with a tangle of mixed emotions. She tried to hold their last words at the forefront of her mind, but the cold-water splash of realization struck her repeatedly. *She was the abusive one*.

Fifty-one percent of child abuse victims ended up in abusive relationships. It was a statistic she'd read once. Brianna had prided herself—vainly and naively—on not being one of the casualties. *She'd* married a man who consistently treated her like gold. Better than gold. *She'd* not fallen into the cycle of abuse.

Wrong, she had. Her assumption had been the statistic referred to victims remaining victims, not victims becoming abusers. It seemed so obvious now. Even if she'd not escalated to physical abuse, she'd emotionally abused her husband for years. And he took it. Ricky was a victim, and she... she was a monster. She didn't deserve him, or their daughter, or their unborn child, or—

"Babe? Yo, Bri. You okay? You're a million miles away," said Ricky. He had Cassidy on his shoulders and her little hands gripped his hair tightly.

"I—yes, I'm fine. Cassidy, honey, don't pull Daddy's hair, you'll hurt him." She scolded gently.

"Ah, it's fine, doesn't hurt much," said Ricky.

Brianna set her cup down and placed her hand over his on the porch railing. "No, Ricky, it's not fine. It's not fine to let someone hurt you." Her voice shook.

Ricky exchanged glances with Mrs. Teccio. He said, "Hey, Mrs. T., mind taking Cass in for a snack?"

"A'course I take little Missy. Come, come," said Mrs. Teccio to Cassidy. She reached out to take the willing girl from her father's shoulders and brought her inside. Not before giving them both warm, mothering smiles, though.

When they'd gone, Ricky joined her on the shaded porch, wiping his brow. He slid a chair over beside her and gazed steadily at her profile, waiting.

"It's nothing," she said. It came out automatically, a habit. One that needed to be broken. "I-I'm just a little... shaken, I guess. My session with Dr. Hannah this morning."

"It didn't go well?"

"No, it's not that. I mean, it went very well, but..." she hesitated.

"Babe, you can tell me anything. You know that. What happened?"

"Do you ever feel like... like I'm abusive to you?" She looked down at her lap. Already knowing the answer, she couldn't bear to see the truth in his face if he tried to lie.

He laughed once through his nose, then he must've realized she was serious. "Aw, babe. Bri, *no*. Of course not. Sure, you've got some... sharp edges, but I know you don't mean it when you get like that."

"Sharp edges, huh? That's a mild way of saying it."

She tried to laugh, but tears got in the way. Without warning, she began sobbing, her words choked out between gasps and shudders.

"I-I've been awful to you. I'm a terrible wife, a terrible person. H-how have you put up with me? *Why* have you put up with me? I-I don't deserve you, Ricky. I don't, and I know it, but I can't imagine my life without you, and—"

Ricky, in one swift, bear-armed move, scooped Brianna up and pulled her onto his lap. She buried her head into his shoulder and let herself be held as the unpretty tears soaked his collar. When she'd exhausted herself, he spoke, his cheek resting on her head.

"You remember that time when we were about seventeen and we got into that fight outside of Dairy Queen?" She nodded. It had been a big one. "I thought Jimmy Vincent and you were flirting at the game. Lost my shit. Yelling at you, getting in your face. I was such a dick."

He shook his head against hers and held her tighter.

"I knew already about your dad, what it was like for you at home. And still, I acted like that. You were shutting down, backing away, and I kept going, like an asshole. And I remember I raised my hand—I think I was gonna, like, push my hair back or something—and you—" his voice shook. "You, uh, got this look of terror—not fear, fucking *terror*—in your eyes and threw your arms up to protect your face, a-and you dropped to the ground and curled up in a ball. A-all you said, over and over, was... was, *don't hit me, don't hit me.*" He sniffed. "That broke my fucking heart, Bri. *Killed* me."

Ricky nudged her up so he could look her in the eye. He wiped her tear-streaked cheeks and stroked her hair back. "I never realized, until then, just how bad it had been for you, babe. I made a promise to myself that I'd never, ever give you a reason to have that look in your eyes when you looked me. No matter what."

Brianna rested her forehead against his and wiped his tears away, too. "You've been the greatest boyfriend, husband, and father any girl could dream of, Ricky. I'm so sorry I haven't been who you deserve."

"Don't apologize, Bri. We're all just, I don't know, works in progress."

Brianna grinned. "Works in progress, huh? Where'd you hear that?"

Ricky chided her. "You're not the only one who's gone for some counseling."

She pulled back, surprised. "Really? When? I had no idea."

He looked away, as if embarrassed. "Not long after that night. I, uh, wanted to learn how to help you. Then again when we separated."

Brianna was incredulous. "You went to a-a therapist when we were kids? For me? Do you ever stop being amazing?"

"Nope," said Ricky. Then he kissed her, and she kissed him back with a passion she'd forgotten she had for him.

It left them both breathless. Their first real kiss since they'd been back together. The old, familiar lust for him pulsed at her core. She ran her fingers through his dark hair and kissed him again. Ricky groaned against her lips and danced his fingertips across her back, sending chills of delight up her spine.

Then the back door bounced open and Cassidy stomped out, popsicle in fist and smeary red grin on her sticky face. Mrs. Teccio hurried out behind her. When she saw them, sitting together—Brianna still on her husband's lap—a delighted 'oh' burst out and she clapped for Cassidy to come back.

"Let's go back inside, Cassidy." She called.

Brianna sighed, resting her temple on Ricky's forehead, and said, "It's fine. Mrs. Teccio. Come here, you little sticky monster."

Cassidy ran to her parents and raised her arms to be lifted. Both used their free hand to lift her onto their lap. She offered them a taste of her cherry red pop, which they accepted with mock gratitude.

The depth of love Brianna had for them, their life, ran deeper than she ever could've imagined possible. Just as deep and fierce was her determination to be the best wife and mother she could be.

She would *not* repeat the cycle or be the victim of her past. Nor would she allow her precious family to be victims of it either. Gordon Bourdreau had for too long been the puppet master, and then the looming black cloud of Brianna's life. No more, though.

The shame of her childhood, her home life—that wasn't hers to bear, it was *his*. Gordon was the villain, not Brianna. Not her mother—who's complicatedness was ruled by fear and intimidation—and certainly not her young brother's, who she scarcely knew.

Brandon. How easily she'd disregarded and often forgot about him. He was a toddler when she'd married Ricky and got out of that hell hole. And anyhow—she'd justified to herself time and again—the violence had always arced around the boy and onto Brianna or Martha. *They* were the subjects and recipients of Gordon's wrath, not the handsome, quiet little boy who watched them all with round eyes and silence. She would make more an effort to connect with him.

Brianna's cell phone rang. Ricky glanced at the caller ID and grimaced. She knew without looking who would be on the other end of the line. She answered.

"Brianna, I'm glad you answered. It's about your brother. He's missing."

23 *Seventy-Two* HOURS

William smiled down at Mae. "They won't hate *us*, darling. Just your aunt."

He kissed her scalding temple and tried to keep the worry from his face. Katrina returned a few minutes later with a terse looking nurse whose expression softened upon seeing Mae.

"Hang on, honey. I'm going to grab a cart."

She left, but not before exchanging scathing glares with Katrina, who stood arms crossed over an ample chest in the room's corner. In a flash, she returned, wheeling a small metal stand with a blood pressure cuff, thermometer, and electronic pad.

"All right, sweetie. Let's take your temp, hmm?" She rolled a wand over Mae's temple and forehead, looked at the reading, and darted a glance at William. In a calm, maternal voice, she said, "Okay, then. So, you're running just a bit of a temperature and your heart rate is a little faster than we like. I'm going to page Dr. Morgan and see if we can get these babies born quicker, okay?"

"Okay," said Mae.

She sounded like a small child. William's heart clenched, and he followed the nurse out of the room.

"Nurse? What's going on? Should we be worried?"

The petite, olive skinned woman gave him a placating smile. "Now, Mr. Grant. Everything is perfectly *fine*. However, her fever *is* rather high, and that justifies the elevated heart rate, so we like to err on the side of caution."

"But is she—"

"Mr. Grant? Try to relax. Your wife is in excellent hands. Go on back to her room, and I'll get the doctor for you."

After an eternity, Dr. Morgan stepped into the room. Katrina and William stood, Mae lay wanly, eyes closed. The last contraction had spent her.

"Let's see what we have going on here, shall we?"

He awarded them a pearl-white smile, then looked at Mae's chart. The smile faded and a frown line creased his forehead. When he looked back up at William, the smile returned, but it didn't reach his eyes.

"Let's go out in the hall a moment, yes?" Dr. Morgan tilted his head toward the door.

William led them out with a request to Katrina to stay by Mae's side.

The doctor made no preamble. "So, your wife's fever is high—103.2—and since she didn't come in with it, I'd say it's intrapartum. There's little concern for the babies, however, it poses some potential post-delivery complications."

William swallowed. "Such as?"

"As inconsequential as Caesarean delivery— which I expect we'll be doing—to retained placentas and… post-partum hemorrhaging."

"H-hemorrhaging? Jesus." William pressed his palm to his forehead and rubbed. "Doctor, I can't… you have to—"

"Mr. Grant, Mae is in good hands. We're going to do everything we can to make this all go smoothly. I'm going to get everything moving now, okay? The anesthesiologist will be in shortly."

He left William standing slack-jawed and sickened with distress for his wife and unborn children. The fears he'd tried to convince himself as unfounded, now rang clear and true. Even in this age of modern technology, at a state-of-the-art hospital, he could lose his beloved in labor.

He forced the tremor in his jaw to cease and raked back his hair. Mae could not see the apprehension in his eyes. He joined Katrina bedside.

"How is she?"

"What'd he say," countered Katrina.

He shifted his gaze from Mae to her aunt. His eyes told her everything, and she nodded grimly.

"What's going on? Are the babies okay?" Mae lifted her head like a wobbly colt then dropped it down again. "William, don't let anything bad happen to them. I—"

"Shh, shh. Sweetheart. Everything is fine. The babies are fine. You have a fever, is all. They, uh, they want to do a caesarean."

A tear rolled from the corner of her eye. "I'm so tired. Just so—"

A contraction silenced her.

"Why the hell haven't they given her an epidural yet," hissed Katrina.

"No," said Mae with surprising force. "I don't want one. I want to have the babies naturally."

"I'm afraid that's not an option, Mae," said Dr. Morgan striding into the room. "A and B are being too pokey for our liking and you have a fever, so we're going to help move things along now."

She looked to William. He nodded. "Dr. Morgan knows best."

Her head dropped back again, defeated, exhausted, and resigned. She reached for William's hand and gave a faint, tremulous smile. "Well, then, let's go meet our babies."

The next twenty minutes were an orchestrated flurry of activity. A pair of efficient but kind nurses gowned and maneuvered William with precision to the head of Mae's operating bed. He stroked her hair and offered placations. Her gray eyes met his.

"I love you, William. If anything happens to me... I—"

"Hush, now. None of that. You and our babies will be perfectly fine. I insist on it."

"As do I, Mae," boomed Dr. Morgan. "That epidural should take effect now, so it's go time. You two ready to meet... what are their names?"

"We haven't decided yet. We're waiting to meet them first," said William.

"All right, then. A and B it is, for now." He clapped his gloved hands and gave his nurses more instruction.

Ten minutes later, the first angry, insulted cry rang out.

"Welcome to the world, Baby A," said Dr. Morgan.

The nurse gave them a glimpse of the little red, furious bald baby.

"Hello, son," said William through laughter and tears.

"Hello, sweet boy," sighed Mae.

Three and a half minutes later, another gusty wail punctured the air.

"And hello to Baby B," announced Dr. Morgan.

Again, the nurse held up the newborn, this one smaller and raven haired.

"There's our girl," chuckled William.

He looked down at Mae. Her eyes fluttered, then rolled back. A monitor made a series of rapid tones, then a long beep. Suddenly, the atmosphere changed from buoyant to businesslike.

"Mr. Grant, come out here with me." A nurse took his arm and pulled him away, toward the doors.

"No, I'm staying with my wife." He pulled his arm free.

The nurse used both hands now. Her peaceful, everything-is-fine tone sharpened. "You want them to help her? Then you need to get out of the way. *Now*."

The change in tone was a slap in the face and William let her lead him out to a private waiting area. Not long after, the same nurse walked Katrina into the room.

"Thought you could use the company while you wait," said the nurse.

William, anguished, said, "What's happening in there?"

"Her blood pressure dropped. That's all I know right now. Dr. Morgan will come see you as soon as she's stabilized."

"Jesus Christ," said Katrina. "How serious it this?"

The nurse glanced uncertainly from one to the other and hedged. "I-it depends on the cause of the drop. It could be nothing, or…" she trailed off. "I'm sorry, but all you can do right now is hurry up and wait."

"The twins? How are they?"

At this, the nurse smiled. "Healthy, strong, and beautiful. You can see them any time now."

"I-I can't. Not until I know…"

"Of course," said the nurse warmly. "I'll be back as soon as I can."

Thirty-three minutes later—William knew this with the exactness of a man who'd counted every single one as they ticked past—Dr. Morgan entered the private waiting room. Gina and Feather Anne in the meantime had joined them, and they stood.

William blurted, "How is she?"

Dr. Morgan squeezed his surgical cap in his hands as he looked to each of them. When his eyes found William's again, he said, "Mae had an *amniotic fluid embolism*. It caused her blood pressure to drop drastically, among other complications. It's quite rare—one in a hundred-thousand—and almost impossible to prevent."

"What are you saying, Doc? Is she all right?" Katrina's voice, one notch below hysteria, cut through the room.

Dr. Morgan put his hand forward in a placating gesture. "She's stable, but I'm not going to lie. This is serious and we'll need to watch for developments like blood clots, seizures, ventricular distress…"

"Are you saying—are you saying she could die?"

This time he put both hands out. "Mae is in excellent hands, William. We are watching her closely and the next seventy-two hours will tell the tale, I believe."

He hedged and looked down briefly. "There's something more. Your daughter, Baby B as we've affectionately moniker'd her, experienced some oxygen deprivation while waiting her turn to come out. She's on oxygen and her vitals are being monitored."

"Oxygen deprivation? That's serious, isn't it?" Asked Gina.

"It can be," said Dr. Morgan. "It's possible we won't know the effect on her for a while, I'm afraid."

Katrina asked, "What kinds of effects are we talking about?"

William had gone mute in his numbing fear and worry for his wife and child. He let them ask the questions frozen in his throat and dreaded their answers.

"Abnormalities in cognitive development, for one. There is also a chance—slight in her case—of cerebral palsy. However, the length of time she lacked oxygen was short and we feel sufficiently confident her risk is low."

"Jesus," said Katrina.

She and Gina flanked William, and each looped an arm through his in support.

"Once we get Mae settled in her room, I'll have a nurse come for you. You'll each be able to visit for a short time."

"I'll be staying with her," said William.

If the doctor intended on arguing with him, the steely glint in William's eyes dissuaded him. "Very well. I'll let the nurses know."

He left the shell-shocked foursome with his apologies. No one spoke. It was Feather Anne, silent until then, who spoke first. "I'd like to go see my niece and nephew, please."

Gina, likely still unsure in her role, jumped at the chance to be of use. "That's a great idea, Feather Anne. Lets you and I go see the babies. William, if there's anything I can do, just say the word."

William collected himself. "Thank you, Gina. Knowing family is with the babies is a comfort. I-I can't right now, I—"

"No explanation needed, William," said Katrina in a firmer voice than her pale complexion suggested her capable of. "We're *all* going to get through this fine. I'll come spend some time with Mae, then make some calls, let Mae's friends know what's going on."

24 Desperate TIMES

"Where've you been? It's been *hours*." Brandon took the sandwich from Feather Anne's hand with greedy rapture. He spoke around a mouthful of food. "I'm starving."

"No one's been home, dummy. You could've gotten something from the kitchen yourself."

Brandon shrugged. "I considered it, but I kept thinking someone might walk in right when I—hey, what's wrong? You look upset. Are you mad at me? I can go somewhere else, Feather Anne. I don't want you to get in trouble on my account."

"It's fine. I'm already grounded for life for telling Mr. Solange his toupee was on backwards."

"So, what is it then?" He set his sandwich down.

"My sister. She had the babies."

"That's cool. Wait, they're early, right? Are they okay?"

"Yeah, I think so. I mean, Baby A is fine, they say. Baby B might have something wrong with her. But Mae—" She stopped as her chin quivered.

Brandon put an awkward arm around her shoulders. "Hey, hey. It's all right. Whatever it is, it will be fine."

She dropped her head on his bony shoulder. "But what if it's not? What if she…"

"Don't think like that, Feather Anne. You gotta be positive, and like, pray on it."

She sniffed and picked her head up to look at him. "You still believe in all that stuff? Even after your father—"

"Just because he's a hypocrite, doesn't mean the God stuff is bullshit. I mean, you gotta believe in something, right?"

Feather Anne had never given God much thought. She wasn't raised religious like Brandon, but she supposed it couldn't hurt to try. The front door opened and slammed close.

Gina called, "Feather Anne? Time to head back to the hospital."

"Shit," said Feather Anne. "Get in the closet, quick."

Gina knocked once then opened the door. She cocked her head at Feather Anne. "Everything okay in here?"

"Yeah. Totally. W-why?"

"I don't know. You look… guilty or something."

145

"Guilty? What? No, don't be weird, Gina." She sprang from the edge of the bed and brushed past her mother. "Come on, I want to see the babies."

Gina let Feather Anne pass, but took a sweeping glance around her room, her eyes landing on the ham and cheese roll on the bed.

"I thought you hated ham?" Gina's eyebrow shot up.

"I do. I mean, I did. I-I like it now. Big deal."

"Well why don't you finish it instead of leaving it there?"

A dozen retorts raced through her brain, but none of them would get Gina and her suspicious squint out of her room faster than just taking a bite of the vile sandwich.

"Fine. I'll take it with me. Let's go."

"Sure. Take a bite first, though. You must've been pretty hungry to make a sandwich the minute you walked in the house, right?"

Gina had walked into the room and stood in front of the closet; arms folded over her chest. Feather Anne felt a wave of panic well in her chest.

"Fine, Jesus." She took a tiny bite and tried to not gag. "There. Happy? Can we go now?"

"Sure." Gina took two steps, then stopped. "Just one thing first." She pivoted to the closet door and yanked it open. "You two really need to learn how to be more discreet."

"Shit," said Feather Anne.

"Hi, Mrs. I mean, Miss Byrd," said Brandon from the floor of the closet.

"You realize you have half the town looking for you, young man? And you, harboring a runaway? Aren't you in enough trouble already from you last antics?"

"Sorry," said Brandon as he righted himself. "It's my fault Feather Anne got involved in my mess, ma'am."

"Oh, Feather Anne is a natural mess finder, don't worry."

"Takes one to know one," muttered Feather Anne.

"I'll ignore that. So, what the hell is your plan here, kids? Wait, don't. I—we don't have time for this right now. You," she pointed at Brandon "you can stay until we get back. Then… Ah, we'll figure something out. You," pointing at Feather Anne, "get in the car. You can explain what the hell you two are up to on the way."

Feather Anne pulled a face but did as told. She mouthed sorry to Brandon and stomped from her room to the car. They didn't speak until they'd turned onto the highway.

"So? Talk," said Gina. She set her mouth in a firm, *I mean business*, line.

"Gina, we can't send him back to that, that asshole. We *can't*."

"Language, Feather Anne. I'm going to need more than that. What happened? What'd that asshole do?"

Feather Anne tried not to smirk. Gina had never been the best mom—not by a long shot—but theirs was a bond like no other. Their trailer home history made them something apart from everyone else in Chance, and from Mae. The scrappy, *us against*

147

them mentality still ran strong—even if it hid below the surface now that they were civilized—and would cause Gina to protect Brandon instinctively before she knew the facts. Her hatred of Gordon Bourdreau didn't hurt, either.

"Well, nothing to Brandon, exactly. To his mom. Brandon says Gordon beats her up. It's bad, Gina. Last week, he said he tried to stop him, but Gordon just threw him off like he was a doll. That's why he left. He said if he stayed there another minute, he might kill Gordon."

"Wait. Last *week*? Has he been hiding out at Mae's for a week?"

Feather Anne didn't answer.

Under her breath, Gina swore. "Fucking hell." She looked at Feather Anne anew. "You know I hate Gordon Bourdreau, but this, Feather Anne, this is serious shit. If he finds out his kid's been with us all this time, he'd probably accuse us of kidnapping."

Feather Anne scoffed. "He would not. He didn't even try looking for him until two days ago. Even then, he didn't want the police to do anything. He asked Joel Asheby as a *favor*, not as a cop."

Gina bit her nail and her one-handed grip on the steering wheel was white knuckled. Feather Anne squinted at her mother. Her already pale face had gone even whiter.

"You're afraid of him." It wasn't a question, but a fact Feather Anne understood to be true, but not why.

"No, I'm not. I used to be, but not anymore." Her tone was defensive and not entirely believable.

Feather Anne shifted in her seat to face her mother's profile. "Gina, what happened between you and the Bourdreau's? You can tell me."

Gina shot a furtive glance at her daughter, then another. She seemed to force her grip to ease and shoulders to drop. Her brow smoothed, and she took a full breath.

"I-it was a long time ago. Before you were born. Things were, uh, pretty bad. I had no money, no place to live, no family. The guy I was seeing took off with all my stuff and the last of my money. Desperate times, as they say."

She stopped talking for so long that Feather Anne thought maybe she'd decided not to say anymore. Before she could nudge her mother, she spoke again. This time, it was a far-off monotone, a voice barely recognizable as her mother's.

"Hector and I were pals back then. He said, *go to the church. They'll help you.* So, I did. Eleven at night, I showed up at Pastor Thomas's rectory. I was such a mess I didn't even know it was Christmas Eve."

The recollection forced a hollow laugh from her throat. By then, they'd pulled into the hospital parking garage, but Gina just put the car in park and let the engine run as she spoke in that dry, steady voice.

"Pastor Thomas was in the church for the candlelight service. That's what Gordon said when he opened the door—*after* he looked me up and down for a minute. I told him I had nowhere left to go, and I needed help."

She wiped her hands on her pants repeatedly. "He asked if I had anyone else with me. I told him, *no one. It's just me.* He dug around in his pocket and said, *If I give you my car keys, are you going to steal my car*, and I said, *I'm no thief, Gordon. You know that.*"

Gina looked down at her lap. She cleared her throat. "He, uh, he said, *we went to high school together. That only means I know you were the town whore and that you're now the town deadbeat. So, if I let you sit in my car to warm up, are. You. Going. To steal it?*"

Feather Anne cut it. "What an asshole. I hope you told him to f—"

Gina shook her head. "It was twenty degrees, and I had on a sweatshirt, jeans and sneakers. I took the keys, Feather Anne, and the backhanded charity. I hated myself even more for it, but that's what I did."

Feather Anne pictured the pathetic sight of Gina Byrd, probably no more than a hundred pounds, cowered before that arrogant, hawk-nosed jerk. If sweet, affable Pastor Thomas had been there, Gordon would never have dared behave so cruelly and condescendingly.

"Anyhow, about twenty minutes later, Gordon got into the driver's seat. I thought he was going to kick me out, but he said, *You may stay in the in-law apartment at my house for now. We can't have the likes of you lurking around the rectory and tarnishing Pastor Thomas's reputation.* I was too grateful and relieved to be out of the cold to be insulted."

Gina turned off the ignition and faced Feather Anne, a hard, angry glint in her gray eyes so like Feather Anne's own.

"Gordon expected repayment for his generosity, and he got it. That's all I'm saying about that. You're old enough now to read in between the lines, I think. Judge me if you want."

Feather Anne understood, and she felt sickened. Not by her mother, though.

"Mom, he took advantage of you when he was supposed to be helping you. He's the bad one here, not *you*."

Gina's heart squeezed at the *mom* slip—something that only happened when Feather Anne was distressed—gave a small head shake and made a sound of self-contempt. "Thanks, kid. But I had free will. It was a choice. A really, really, shitty one at that."

Feather Anne's frustration boiled over. "No, no. That's not true—I mean, yes, I know, you had a choice—but your choices were what? T-to freeze or starve to death or be his... whatever. That's like choosing between cutting off your right arm or your left."

She lifted each arm then slapped them down on her lap. "It's bullshit and he should be held responsible. Where the hell was his wife for all this, anyhow?"

"She knew I was there, in the in-law apartment. Anything else... I can't be positive, but I think she knew, and she was too afraid of him to say or do anything."

Feather Anne had a sudden, new thought. One that made her heart stutter and her stomach drop. "Gina? H-how long after that, was I born?"

Did she even want the answer? Now that it was asked, there were no take backs. She braced herself for the response she thought she already knew.

"Get that out of your head right now. Don't even—"

"Is Gordon Bourdreau my father, Gina? I deserve to know." Feather Anne felt like she might throw up. Or pass out. Maybe both.

Her answer came clear and direct. "Absolutely not."

Feather Anne slumped against the back of her seat and stared dumbly at the water stained concrete divider that marked their parking space.

"Gina, if you're just saying that, we need to find out for sure. I need to know."

"I swear on my life, he's not your father, Feather Anne. I-I'm not positive who is, but I am completely sure he is *not*."

25 Charles

December 1977

"Merry Christmas, darling wife."

Charles led Georgie into the living room where their tree stood tall, spindly, and heavy with white lights. Beneath it, a large, gaily wrapped box with a giant red bow on top.

"Oh, Charles. Please, can I open my eyes now?"

Her delight only matched her exasperation. Georgie Brightsider loved surprises, and Charles loved surprising her. They were perfectly matched.

"Hang on, hang on. Sit here. There you go. Okay. One more second. All right. Now. Open your eyes."

Georgie did as he told. She blinked several times, smoothed her hair, and when her gaze landed on the oversized box, she cocked her head.

"Charles Brightsider, I hope you are not trying to pass off a new bass drum as a gift."

He laughed. "Would I do something like that?"

"Why, yes. Yes, I believe you would, Mr. Funny Man. Now, I—did that box just move?"

Charles grin threatened to run all over his face. "It might could have. Open it up, Georgie."

Half fearful, half excited, Georgie skootched forward in her chair. The lid of the box fit loosely, and she lifted it off with ease.

"Oh," exclaimed Georgie, her hands to her cheeks. She said it again, this time tearfully. "Oh!"

She reached inside and lifted a floppy-eared, ginger and white bundle of silky fur. She reached in again, and pulled out another, this one with patches of black mixed in with the brown and white.

"Two, Charles? *Two*!" She nuzzled them to her face, and they lapped at her cheeks, eyes, and nose with pink puppy tongues as their long fan-like tails swept back and forth rapidly.

"I couldn't decide which one you'd love more, so, I got both. Boy and a girl. They're eight weeks old. Are you happy, darling?"

Georgie slipped from the chair onto the floor and laid down on her back, letting the excited puppies trample all over her as she giggled.

"Happy? *Happy*? Charles, I'm over the moon."

She laughed and warded off their exuberant kisses in vain. Charles laid down beside her, on his side with his head propped on his palm. He watched her laugh and play with their new furry family members with a relief that almost made him cry.

She'd not been herself in sometime. Since the last miscarriage, some eight months earlier. It grieved him to picture her there in the hospital bed, white as the pillow she lay on as the doctor told her they'd given her an emergency hysterectomy.

"I'm sorry, Mr. and Mrs. Brightsider, but your chances for having a child have expired."

Expired? What a stupid choice of words. That's what Charles had dwelled on in those moments post the doctor's abrupt exit. It kept him from feeling the weight of his wife's grief and disappointment. And his own.

As the months passed, Georgie returned to a superficial version of herself. But when she thought no one was looking, her facade dropped. Sure, she tried to hide it from Charles, but he knew his wife too well. Her sorrow for her own loss equaled her guilt at not giving him a family.

Charles damned himself for expressing his desire for a large brood in their dating days. Those conversations were probably etched and on repeat in her mind, if he knew her as well as he thought he did. He couldn't take them back or pretend they had never been said. Georgie was too bright to fall for it. All Charles could do, was assure her their life together was enough.

It had been Andrew van Bergen who'd given him the dog idea a few weeks prior. They'd been playing canasta at Jacob and Susan Waterman's while their little Stephen and Gloria's boys all played together in the living room—when the girls excused themselves to the kitchen.

They volleyed the usual small talk—Gerald Ford and that Jimmy Carter fella, Elvis's shocking death, what was all that fuss over a computer named after a piece of fruit—when Charles cleared his throat and glanced toward the kitchen.

"Say, fellas. I-I'm thinking of taking Georgie away for a little vacation. She's, uh, been—well, since—"

Andrew spoke around his fat cigar. "Get her a dog."

"A-a dog?" Charles frowned. "I don't—"

"I'm telling you, a dog's the answer. You take her away for what? A week? Ten days? Sure, maybe she'll be fine with all the distraction and what not. But what happens when you get back home?" He paused. "Boom. Right back where you were."

Charles warmed to the idea. "A dog, huh? You really think it'll help?"

"I know it will."

"I usually buy Susie some jewelry when she's blue. You could try that," offered Jacob.

"I think I may try Andrew's idea. Know anyone who's got some pups available?"

Andrew scratched his chin. "Matter a'fact, I do. My sister, Mary. Her bitch just had a litter not too long ago. Ready to go by Christmas, I believe. I'll put you two in touch."

Charles ignored the *coincidental* nature of the idea and the availability in Andrew's immediate circle and thanked him. "What kind of dog is it; you know?"

"Some kind of spaniel. Cute, if you like that sort of thing."

The women returned, and the subject dropped. But a week later, Charles stood in the kitchen of Mary and David Francis, staring down at a squirming basket of six puppies. By then he was so desperate to cheer his wife, he'd have taken them all then and there. Fortunately, all but two were reserved and couldn't go home until Christmas anyhow.

"I-I don't know which one to choose," said Charles, his chin in his hand.

"Well," said Mary, "the girl there, she's a bit feisty. But the boy—he's the only one sleeping, right there—he's a mellow little guy. Up to you. They're both same price, twenty-five."

Charles could see he was taking up too much of her time by the way she kept shifting her weight from foot to foot and glancing at the clock over the door. He looked helplessly at her. She smiled a thin smile.

He pulled out his wallet and counted the bills in his head. Fifty-three dollars and a linty penny. He extracted the cash, less the three singles, and handed it to her. She counted it, then her brow drew together.

"There's fifty here," said Mary.

"Yes. I-I'll take both."

"Both?" Her eyes widened. "You want both dogs? Does your wife know what you're up to? You can't bring em back, you know."

"Yes, I'm aware. She'll be pleased, don't worry, my dear."

At least I hope she will. A wave of trepidation passed through Charles and he almost snatched back the money. Just then, the little female grabbed a hold of his shoelace in her tiny teeth and shook it with a playful growl. He lifted her up to his face, so they were nose to nose.

"You're going to keep us on our toes, little one, aren't you?" She licked the tip of his nose and whined. Charles laughed and said, "See you soon, little troublemaker."

Now, with the two puppies prancing and rolling about on their living room floor, and Georgie laughing in sheer delight, Charles felt like kicking himself for not doing it sooner.

"Oh, Charles, what shall we name them?"

Charles pretended to ponder. "Hm, how about Frick and Frack?"

She swatted his arm. "They're much too lovely for such foolish names."

They took turns suggesting names, but none seemed to fit. Whether too short, too long, not pretty and masculine enough, *too* pretty and too masculine, each moniker got dismissed until they let out resigned sighs.

"Well, I'm sure the right names will come to us," said Charles.

"Yes, you're right, dear." Her voice was dreamy and relaxed as the pair lazily wrestled on her lap.

The telephone rang and Charles looked at his watch. "It's after eight. I wonder who that could be?"

"You answer it and I'll take these two out to do their business," said Georgie.

Charles helped her up—with a playful pat on her bottom for good measure—and whistled his way to the kitchen while Georgie pulled on her coat and herded the puppies toward the door.

"Brightsiders' residence. Hello and Merry Christmas," said Charles.

"Charles? It's Mavis, dear."

"Mavis," exclaimed Charles in delight. Georgie's parents were back in Chance for the holidays, on break from their sunny Florida retirement. "Bet you two are regretting coming back to cold New England. I think we got another foot of snow today. But don't fret, I'll come by in the morning to shovel the walk."

"Charles, it-it's Gene. H-he's had a heart attack," said Mavis, her voice quaking.

"Oh, my goodness. We'll come straight to the hospital. Everything—"

"No, no, Charles... he-he didn't make it. My Gene... he's gone."

Though her voice shook, Mavis Perri held her composure. "Don't come out in this weather, please. Just take care of Georgina. She's going to need to lean on you more than ever, dear."

"I—yes, of course, Mavis. Are you sure—"

"Yes. Positive. I need to be alone right now. Tomorrow. I'll be needing you tomorrow to help me with… the arrangements. Goodbye for now."

The rattle of the phone as she set it back on the receiver crackled in his ear. Georgie and the puppies burst back into the house by way of the kitchen's back door.

Georgie shook the snow out of her hair and the dogs did likewise. "Good gracious, it is nasty out there still. These two clowns managed to make a track around the house. I had to run to keep up with them. Who was on the phone?"

She still hadn't looked up from all her foot stomping and hair shaking. Charles couldn't bring himself to answer.

"Charles, I said, who was on the—"

"It was your mother. Sit down, sweetheart. I'm afraid I have some news."

Georgie looked up then, the look in her eyes changing from mildly curious to alarmed, to understanding.

"It's Daddy, isn't it?" She reached for the nearest chair back and gripped it tightly. "Is he…"

She begged him with silent anguish to tell her she misunderstood; that no, her father was fine, and he'd just taking a fall. But Charles sorrow ran deep for losing a man who'd treated him as a son, and he couldn't hide the redness from his eyes.

Like her mother, Georgie struggled for composure. She turned her cheek to her shoulder, away from Charles. Her body shook with silent tears and when he wrapped his arms around her, she buried her face in his chest. There, she allowed herself to sob and collapse.

When she'd exhausted the last of her grief for that moment, she pulled back and looked down at their feet.

"Look, Charles, they can tell we're upset."

Charles followed her gaze and had to smile. The pair sat on their tiny haunches and stared up at them with shiny black eyes and an expression that could only be called woeful.

"I believe you're right, darling. Why don't you lie down, I'll make you some tea and get the pups settled for the night? We've a long day ahead of us tomorrow, I'm afraid."

"Shouldn't we go stay at Mother and D-Daddy's? She'll be all alone and—"

Charles hushed her tears. "She was quite firm, I promise. Let her have time to grieve her husband before she has to share him."

Georgie sniffed. "You're very wise, husband."

"I'll remind you of those words the next time you call me a dolt, dear. Now, go on." He kissed her temple and sent her off.

When he heard the soft click of the bathroom door, Charles allowed himself a moment to tend to his own sadness. The two dogs had enough of the somber mood, however, and pawed and jumped at his ankles. So, Charles dried his eyes and blew his nose, then shuffled through the duo to make the tea.

In the wee hours of the morning, before the sun had yet risen, Charles awoke to something cold and wet on his cheek. His eyes, bleary and blurry, opened to see a black snout breathing warm air on him. He picked his head up, careful not to disturb the sleeping creature, and found his wife with the other ball of fur asleep on her chest.

She slowly turned her head to him, an apologetic smile twitching at her lips. "They were whining. I felt sorry for them. You don't mind, do you, darling? Can they stay?"

Her eyes were puffy from crying. How could he tell her no? "Just for tonight, dear. We don't want to spoil them, do we?"

"I think I've come up with names for them," said Georgie.

"In the middle of the night, have you? What's it going to be, then?" He propped himself on an elbow and pulled the warm little body closer.

He couldn't tell which one he had in the still dark room, but it chuffed and snorted once before falling back asleep against his chest and he couldn't help but grin.

"I was thinking and thinking—mostly about Daddy and all the wonderful memories I have of him—and trying to come up with something, I don't know, that honored him in some way."

She angled her body toward him and mirrored his pose, dog against chest, elbow under ribcage. "Do you remember the song he always had the band play for me? The one he changed the name—"

"From *Oh, Marie* to *Oh, Georgie*. Of course, I remember. Brought the house down every time. Louis Prima and Keely Smith." He knew instantly what the names were. A grin spread across both their faces. Charles tried it on for size, "Louis and

Keely. Hm. Yep, I like it. Your dad would've loved it, sweetheart."

Georgie nodded her agreement and rested back into the comfort of her pillow. Charles did the same. The dogs spent that night—and every one that followed—in the bed with them.

26 Ride OR DIE

Rosabelle locked the front door and tossed the car keys to Miles. "You drive. I'm too anxious."

"Sure thing, Rosie," said Miles. He opened the driver's side door and adjusted the seat to accommodate his much larger frame.

Rosabelle jerked the passenger door handle once, then a dozen times more in rapid succession. He'd forgotten to unlock the door and both her scowl and the attempt to rip it off its hinges showed her feelings on the matter.

"Sorry, babe."

"Just hurry and get us there, please," She whipped the seatbelt across her body and snapped it close. Once they pulled out of the driveway, she spoke again, forcing herself calm. "I'm sorry. I'm worried about Mae and I shouldn't take it out on you."

Miles reached across the console and patted her knee. "All good, babe. I know you're worried. Hell, I am, too. Baby Mae is my girl and William is my hombre. I'd hate to see anything happen to them."

They said nothing more the rest of the car ride to the hospital. Rosabelle for lack of desire, Miles for lack of anything useful to say. The traffic made her want to scream, but she changed the radio station repeatedly, searching for God knew what. Finding nothing, Rosabelle turned off the radio and threw herself against the backrest. An angry rush of words cut the silence.

"How does this even happen in this day? It's not the dark ages. I mean, she could actually *die*, Miles. Die. As in—"

"Yeah, I know what the word means, babe. You can't think like that, okay? You just gotta have faith."

She inhaled and exhaled several times. In through the nose, out through the mouth. Calm. Center. Control. She'd been practicing meditation to manage the chronic lower back pain she'd experienced daily since the accident. It helped.

"You're right. It's just so unfair, isn't it?" Miles nodded his assent, and she continued. "After my accident I said I'd never take anyone or anything for granted. I swore I'd live every moment like it could be my last. But that intense passion, it fades, you know?"

"It happens, Rosie. The business of life gets in the way."

"Yeah, I suppose. But this—Mae's situation— it brings it all right back again. How fleeting life is. Here today, maybe gone tomorrow. And what have we done with our time?"

"Oh, hey. Wait a minute, Rosie. Come on, we're living our best life, babe. Aren't we? We love our work, we're buying our dream home, we're in love… pretty good shit right there, if you ask me. You make it sound like we're just treading water or something. Are you saying you're not happy? With… me, I mean?"

She sometimes forgot how much reassurance he needed. "I'm completely happy with you… with *us*. But what did we do last night? I'll tell you. We watched tv. How about the night before? Same. We should be out *living*."

"Babe, three nights ago, we took the Essex dinner train on a whim. Last week we went zip lining. It's called balance. You can't be doing big things all the time. You'll burn out. Plus, we're planning a wedding."

He was right, of course. She knew this all intuitively. "I know. I do, really. I just want to make sure we're, you know, living our best life, or whatever."

"We are, babe. But if there's something you want to do—something wild and crazy—I'm game. I'm your ride or die, Rosie Posie."

Rosabelle laughed. "My *what*? Oh, my God, Miles. Please stop hanging around with Nora's son. He's eighteen. You're twenty-eight."

"Whatevs, yo."

She rolled her eyes at him but couldn't help but laugh. What he said about doing something wild and crazy stuck in her head, though.

"Miles? I know something wild and crazy we could do."

"Please don't say skydiving, babe. The zipline thing was great, but—"

"What if we elope? In Vegas. With... with an Elvis impersonator as the officiant."

Miles waited until they came to a stoplight before turning to look at her. He searched her face for a sign she was pulling his leg. Rosabelle was dead serious.

"But what about the wedding plans at the house? All our friends, the invitations. Shit. Our parents, Rosie."

She waited. He contemplated.

"Babe," he said, "our folks will freak. *Would* freak, I mean. *If* we did something like that."

The wheels spun in his head. Rosabelle nudged him. "I saw airfare really cheap."

"How cheap?"

"*Really* cheap. Actually, I had Jilly Jacobson—no, wait, it's Jilly Jarvis now—put together a travel package for us. Just for ha-has. And we couldn't go until we knew Mae was one hundred percent better, naturally."

He repeated, "Our parents will freak." This time he grinned devilishly.

Rosabelle bobbed her head and matched his smile. "Five nights, six days. We could have a reception at our new home for all our family and friends when we come back."

"You *really* want to do this?" He handed the keys to the hospital valet attendant.

Rosabelle took his hand. "Sure, why not? Our parents have been driving us insane with their requests, and opinions, and demands. It's supposed to be *our* day, not theirs."

"Well, Rosie Posie, it looks like we're eloping, then."

When they neared Mae's floor, their somber mood returned.

"Hello, we're here to see Mae Grant. Uh, Mae Huxley Grant?"

The nurse's face lit up. "Oh, you came at the perfect time. It's a party in there." She leaned forward. "But don't tell anyone I allowed it, you hear?"

Rosie and Miles exchanged confused looks. "But she's in serious—"

"Nope, she turned the corner this morning and everything is looking good. She'll be here a few more days, but that's precautionary. Down the hall, first room on the right."

Rosie squeezed Miles hand and yanked him along. As the nurse said, the room was full of family and friends. Balloons and flowers crowded every free surface and two empty hospital bassinet carts sat like sentinels at the foot of Mae's bed. Mae herself sat propped up by pillows, pale but beautiful with her babies swaddled in her arms.

"Rosabelle, Miles. Come in, come in."

William's careworn face showed the effect of the past days, but his joy shown through the enervation. He stepped aside to let them close.

"I'm gonna take a walk around, if that's okay?" Feather Anne hedged toward the door.

"I'll go with you," said Gina. She gave the girl a pointed look.

"Go on you two, I'm fine," said Mae. "Would you like to hold them?" She smiled up at Rosabelle and Miles.

"Oh, yes, please," said Rosabelle. She squeezed hand sanitizer into hers and Miles hands then reached for a snugly wrapped bundle. Miles took a step back. "Oh, no you don't," said Rosabelle, and deposited the bundle in his arms.

The moment the newborn was in his possession, his nervousness faded. "Hey, little football. What's your name, huh?"

Rosabelle tore her eyes from the pink blanketed baby in her arms and looked from William to Mae. "Please don't tell me they're still Baby A and Baby B?"

"Nope," said Mae proudly. "You're holding Evangeline Ruby. And you, Miles, are holding Thomas Keith."

Miles touched Thomas Keith's tiny nose. "Hey, TK. Uncle Miles is gonna teach you how to hold a football. How about that, buddy?"

"I think that's a job for Uncle Bruce," said Bruce from the doorway. He held a huge bouquet and two floppy teddy bears.

The two exchanged icy glares. William intervened. "I'm sure he'll learn plenty from *both* his surrogate uncles, won't he, Mae?"

"Yes," said Mae. "They both will, I'm sure. The first thing they'll learn is how to behave. Get in here, you." She extended her arms for a hug and Bruce hurried to put down his offerings.

"Scared the shit out of me, kid," whispered Bruce in Mae's ear. The hug lasted longer than what felt comfortable in Rosabelle's opinion.

Rosabelle thought she might've been the only one who heard the quiet words of suffering, but a glance at William told her otherwise. It wasn't anger or jealousy she read, but a sadness she somehow understood. What William knew and accepted, was that Bruce Grady loved his wife. And what made his tolerance more moving, was the sadness was for Bruce, not himself.

What a generous, gentle man. She'd always like William, now even more so.

Rosabelle handed Evangeline to Bruce, who took her with awe and reverence, and even a tear in his eye. She linked her arm through William's and tried to convey her understanding with just her eyes. He patted her hand and gave an almost imperceptible nod.

She also tried to give Miles a warning glare, but his enrapture with the newborn boy made it unobserved and unwarranted. He had no interest in his usual provocations of Bruce Grady. In fact, both men were so surprisingly engrossed in all things baby, that all she could do was exchange amazed and amused stares with Mae.

When it came time to pass back the twins, Miles did so with some reluctance. However, as soon as he did, the taunts began.

"So, Moose, where's the little lady? Don't tell me she dumped you already?"

Bruce's jaw clenched, and he addressed his answer to Mae. "She's busy getting the... spa place ready. She sends her love." He looked at Miles. "Hannaford, don't you have some over-priced houses to sell?"

"Oh, now don't be jealous you can't—"

"All right, time for us to head out," said Rosabelle. She mouthed sorry to Mae and gave Bruce a half-shrug. "Mae, I'll be back tomorrow. William, let me know if there's anything you or Mae need. Bruce, good seeing you. Miles, let's go."

She pulled him out and down the hall, not speaking until they crowded into the elevator. "Why must you go at him like that every time?"

Miles gave his most winsome, *who me*, shrug. "What, it was just a question. He's the one that got all butt hurt."

"I hate that saying, Miles."

"Sorry, babe. But hey, how about you being all Team William? Don't think I didn't notice." He wagged a finger at her.

They stepped out onto the main floor of the hospital "Shut up. I'm not team *anyone*, thank you." After a pause, she said, "You saw it, too, huh?"

Miles scoffed. "Please. Grady has been in love with baby Mae forever. He always will be. This him and Elise thing… it's a ruse. Maybe not a deliberate one but mark my words. It'll be a disaster."

A voice from behind said, "Excuse me. This is my floor." Rosabelle stepped aside and looked to the woman. It was Brittany Sheffield. "Oh, hello and goodbye, Miles, Rosemary. Off to see my uncle. Knee surgery."

She made a sympathetic face but her eyes glinted with mischief. As the doors slid close, Brittany smirked and gave a little wave to the frozen couple.

Too late, and not that it would matter, Miles said, "It's Rosabelle, not Rosemary."

"She knows that. She's just being a jerk, as usual. Do you think she heard what we said?"

"Oh, yeah. She heard," said Miles.

"Shit."

Of all people to have heard such talk, Brittany Sheffield had to be the worst possible. The woman inhaled drama the way the rest of the world inhaled the perfume of flowers or the ocean. It was her lifeblood.

"Yep. The only person who could do any damage control on that one is laid up in a hospital bed with two rugrats attached to her—"

"Yes, thank you, Miles. And I know, she's like the Hedda Hopper of the modern—" she saw Miles baffled expression. "The Perez Hilton before he became nice." Miles's confusion cleared.

"Yeah, she's a barracuda, that one. She's always had it out for Elise, too."

"I thought they were best friends?" Now Rosabelle felt confused.

"Yeah, they are... sort of. You know how the Fearsome Five are. When they don't have a target, they bite each other's ankles. Especially Brittany and Elise."

Rosabelle had a sudden recollection. "Didn't they get into a fight—like and actual fist fight—in high school once?"

"Ding, ding, ding. Yep, they did. Hair pulling, rolling around on the ground... it was hot. Sorry, babe."

Rosabelle rolled her eyes.

To change the subject he said, "How about them babies, though. Damn that little TK gave me all the feels. You know, like, baby fever or something."

"Baby fever? You? You're kidding," She laughed, then took another look at his face. "You're serious. Miles Hannaford, I'm shocked."

"I know, I said I didn't want kids for a while. But I don't know... maybe we could have one sooner instead of later. What do you think?"

"I—wow. I guess... I mean, well... yes! Of course. Sure, I was willing to wait until *you* felt ready, but I want kids as soon as possible. After we're married, though."

They stopped in the middle of the hospital lobby. "It's decided, then. Elope, then baby."

Rosabelle corrected. "Elope, a reception for the family and friends, then a baby."

Miles grabbed her into a bear hug and swung her around. They amused some passersby, others not so much. But Rosabelle, thanks to Miles, was learning how to care less about the opinions of others and she didn't resist his natural exuberance. Even when he shouted, "We're gonna have a baby," she merely shouted another correction. "Not until after we're married, though." A scattering of applause met the proclamations.

In the hospital parking garage, Rosabelle grabbed Miles's arm. "How mad would you be if I said I changed my mind again?"

Miles stared at her warily. "About what?"

"I think I may have behaved impulsively. I don't really want to elope, Miles. I want to get married in our English garden. The fear and worry about Mae… it made me—"

"Say no more, Rosie. Our English garden it is. However, I declare right here and now: No More. Changes. Got it?"

Rosabelle smirked and held her fingers up in scout's honor. "Got it."

27 C'est LA VIE

Mae winced at the eye-stinging jab of the needle as it pierced her abdomen and gave the apologetic nurse a wan smile. Once she left the room Mae sank back against her pillow.

"What was that one for?" William took his seat back beside the bed.

"To prevent a blood clot, I think. I can't remember what's what with all the poking and prodding day and night. I just want to go home with my babies and my husband, William."

He stroked her wrist. "I know, sweetheart. A couple more days."

She sighed, and they both gazed at the bassinets. "The pediatrician came in while you were gone," said Mae.

"And what did she say?" His hand stilled on her arm.

"So far, everything looks fine. She didn't seem too concerned about Evvie's weight loss. Apparently, it's normal, but they won't let her leave until she's gained enough back. As for Mister Little Man, he's a whopping 4 pounds, eleven ounces. A tank by preemie standards."

William's brow smoothed. "Have we a nickname for Evangeline already?"

Mae grinned. "Go on, try it on for size."

He went to the bassinets and placed a hand on each bundled, sleeping baby. "Evvie and… TK— isn't that what Miles called Thomas Keith?"

A chortle escaped Mae's lips. "Something tells me it's going to stick, isn't it?"

His eyes sparkled as he pulled a face and half shrugged. "I kind of like it, I think." William's gaze returned to his son and daughter. "While they're sleeping, get some rest, too. Right?"

William glanced up to see his wife had already fallen fast asleep. Her pallor still concerned him, yet she still took his breath away with her beauty. He dimmed the light over her bed and brought his laptop and chair by the window. Thanks to Gina's help, he would not have to leave Mae or the babies' sides for more than short durations.

The shock of nearly loosing his wife and the worries for little Evvie's health had prompted William to give his own health more serious consideration. There could be no escaping the reality of biology. He was considerably older than Mae. Noticeably so at that, as he reminded himself of by the double takes from some hospital staff and the one, "Are those your grandchildren," question outside the nursery.

He didn't mind it, mostly. However, sometimes he felt the sting of self-reproach for his selfishness. He wanted Mae, and he wanted those two perfect children, regardless of the higher probability that he may not live long enough to see them graduate college or marry. On the other hand, he just might.

Of all people, it had been his biggest detractor who'd set his mind at ease. Mae's aunt Katrina.

"Damn it, she gave us a hell of a scare," she'd spat just after the doctor's welcome news of her recovery. She sank down into the waiting room chair and looked up at William. "We just received good news. Why don't you look happy?"

William hurried to correct her. "No, no. Yes, I mean, of course I'm happy. Relieved and happy." He sat down beside Katrina and buried his face in his hands. After a moment he dropped them in his lap. Not looking up, he said, "You must hate me."

Katrina seemed perplexed. "Is that what you think? Jesus H. Christ. I don't—it's impossible to hate you, William. Not with the way you love my niece and the way she loves you. I mean, sure, I had my reservations and all. The age thing... but you know what? *C'est la vie*! Seriously, who cares?"

"You don't think it was—is—selfish of me to come back to Chance and marry Mae, then have children?"

"Why would I think that's selfish? Isn't that what most people want in life?"

"Yes, but at my age? Knowing that when they're twenty, I'll be seventy-six. *Seventy-six*." He shook his head.

"Big whoop. I mean it. Don't overthink it William. Our Mae says you have a tendency toward doing just that. I see she's right."

"But—"

"No 'buts.' Mae almost died, William. At *twenty-seven*. Just like mine and Keith's mother. Now, I don't know if that's irony or heredity, or whatever, but the fact is, you were almost about to be a widowed father of two."

She put her hand over his to soften her next words. "Your whole age theory is crap. Your time is your time, whether it twenty-seven or seventy-six or somewhere in between. So, live your best life for as long as the good Lord lets you."

She'd been right, of course, but he still knew he needed to make ready provisions and assurances for his wife and children should anything happen to him. *When* something happened to him. He typed the words, *Estate Planning Attorneys in Connecticut* and began the unpleasant task of planning for the event of his death.

28 Georgie

May 1985

"How long have we been friends now, Georgie?"

"Forty-two years," said Georgie without hesitation.

"Good heavens," said Gloria. "Impossible. I'm not a day over twenty." She sipped her gin and tonic. "Ah, to go back to twenty. Can you imagine?"

Georgie's face clouded. "I'll pass on twenty, thank you. Twenty-two or twenty-three is more like it for me."

The two women sat at a small bistro table set up by the country club outside the tennis courts. Andrew and Charles were in a doubles tourney and Georgie and Gloria, who'd already played that morning, now played the roles of proud supporters. TO each other, they agreed they were only there for the gin and tonics and canapes.

"I suppose," began Gloria, not looking at her friend, "I suppose you must still think about—" she gave a conspiratorial glance around them and dropped her voice to a whisper. "you know. *The baby*. Around this time of year, especially."

Georgie took another sip of her drink, her hand trembling ever so slightly now. Gloria had danced near the subject a few times over the years, always to be shot down politely by Georgie. She'd never pressed.

Perhaps it was the alcohol. Maybe that it was the birth month of the little boy she'd given up so long ago that it sometimes felt like a dream she'd had. Whatever the case, Georgie heard herself say, "It was a boy. Seven pounds, six ounces. I-I named him Matthew. In my heart, that was his name no matter what his… adoptive parents named him. He had wispy blond hair that looked like down. I never even got to hold him, Gloria."

Gloria, bless her dear heart, dabbed at the tears that had welled and spilled from the corners of her eyes. The women clasped hands across the table. Georgie didn't trust herself to say more, and Gloria let it be.

It was the first time she'd ever spoken of him. *Matthew*. What *had* his adoptive parents named him? Surely, they could see he was meant to be a Matthew. Mattie when he behaved, Matt to his little friends. That's what she'd imagined, at least. Oh, how she'd wondered about him. Not a day ever passed when she didn't think of him or see little boys that might possibly *be* him.

There had been one boy in particular who came through her third-grade class some years back. Blond and blue eyed, a bookish child with impeccable manners. Just the sort of boy she imagined her Matthew would have turned out. Christopher was his name.

At the first parent-teacher conference, Georgie, with an uncharacteristic loss of self-control and decorum, blurted to the child's parents, "Is Christopher adopted?"

Their stunned, wary stares were an immediate chastisement that was only rivaled by the one she received from the principal the next day. She could offer no explanation, only an apology and a promise it wouldn't happen again.

Days later in the teacher's lounge, Lydia McVicar—she was a fellow teacher then, and not principal until another seven years later—had raised her coffee mug to her in salute.

"Do you know how many times I've wondered where the hell these kids have come from? Bully for you, Georgie."

Georgie allowed the misunderstanding of her outburst. It was better for her to believe it came from an amazement that the boy—slight, blond, handsome, and tall for his age—came from those two short, dishwater-brown haired people. She learned the boy had not been adopted. From then on, Georgie better mastered her fantasies, though they never ceased.

Every May, Georgie celebrated and mourned the birth and loss of what would be her only child, and she did so in silence. On the day of his birthday, she planted a new perennial in his honor, rain or shine. If Charles ever noticed or wondered at what his wife was doing each May fifteenth with such ceremony, he never asked.

A waiter came to the table, startling Georgie from her memories. "Can I get you another?" He glanced at their empty glasses.

Gloria answered for them both. "Yes. And make them doubles."

Georgie caught and held her friend's gaze. "Thank you, Gloria. For everything, all these years. You truly are my dearest friend, you know. I-I'm sorry I can't tell you more about…"

"No thanks necessary. Just know, if you ever *do* want to tell me… you can."

"I know."

They spoke no more of it. Georgie knew she'd never tell her friend or anyone the hazy details of that night in New York. She would take the secret of Matthew's father to her grave if she could because it would devastate Gloria and perhaps even their friendship.

Your brother, Samuel Olsen, forced himself on me after the concert.

Those were the words that would never be spoken. It wasn't rape, she'd told herself many times after, no matter how dirty and violated she'd felt. They'd been drinking, all of them had. Gloria and James had gone to pick up pizza slices from the street vendors outside the hotel. Georgie—too loopy to get off the sofa—and Samuel—who claimed not to be hungry—had stayed behind.

When the door clicked Samuel dropped beside her, so close she had to yank the edge of her dress out from under his thigh. He laughed. Georgie did, too. Before she could say, "Scootch over, you ape," he was all over her. One hand squeezed her breast, and the other fumbled under the hem.

Shocked and alarmed, she'd said, "What are you doing? *No*, Samuel. *Stop*," but he didn't. Georgie didn't fight him or scream. She'd been too mortified and scared. All she could think was, *"What if Gloria and James come back and see us like this?"*

So, she let him do what he wanted, prayed he'd hurry and finish, and tried to forget it ever happened. It was simple, really. Good girls don't talk about such things, let alone do them. So, if Georgie told, no one would ever look at her the same way again.

They drove home the next morning, Sam behind the wheel, Georgie behind him in the backseat. She'd feigned a headache so she wouldn't have to speak much. But Sam? Sam acted just as he always had. Laughing, joking, singing along to the radio. Not a care in the world for Samuel Olsen, no sir-*rie*. He even had the audacity to wink at her in the rearview mirror when their eyes met.

Over twenty years later, even with those *Take Back the Night* rallies happening on college campuses, Georgie still questioned herself as much as—no, *more* than—she did Samuel. Why did he think she was that kind of girl? *She had been flirting with him, maybe a little*. He'd gotten the wrong idea. *She led him to getting the wrong idea.* Couldn't he tell she wasn't into it? *She stayed behind in the hotel room, alone with him.* Her dress was too short. She'd drank too much. She'd been flirting.

Oh, how she longed for someone to tell her it wasn't her fault, what happened that night. But this had to be a war she waged within herself. The other night, she'd watched those young women on television, marching around with their signs and their righteous anger. It was the very first time she'd considered placing more, if not all, the blame on Samuel.

As she sipped her gin and tonic by the tennis courts, beside her best friend who sat oblivious of the storm inside her, Georgie tasted the novel ideas in her mouth again. Samuel was older, meant to be their protector on that trip. He'd known Georgie since she was a little girl. She *said* no. She *asked him* to stop. He hurt her, physically and emotionally and he never even apologized. The bastard.

A sudden, loud crack startled her. Cold liquid sprayed all over Georgie's hand. "Oh." She stared down at her wet, dripping hand. Bright red blooms formed on her palm and fingers.

"Georgie," exclaimed Gloria. "Oh, my, God. What just happened? You're bleeding."

Gloria sprang up, grabbing napkins and calling for the waiter. Georgie stood too, dazed and perhaps shocked. In her mounting rage, she'd squeezed her glass so hard it shattered.

Charles, racquet in hand, sprinted over to the women. "Georgie, are you all right? What happened?"

Gloria answered for her. "Her glass, it must have been cracked or something. It broke right in her hand. Oh, dear, I think you'll need stitches, Georgie. Charles, you'd better take her to the emergency room."

Georgie roused herself. "No, no. None of that nonsense. It's fine. *I'm* fine. A bandage or two will do the trick. No need to fuss."

"Darling, that's a lot of blood. We're going to the emergency room."

Charles tone was firm and when he spoke like that, he meant business. Georgie allowed him to lead her away. Three hours and six stitches later, they were home. Her cuts throbbed and her head ached.

Sweet Charles tended to her with such care and concern that her eyes stung with gratitude. She watched him bustle about—propping a pillow behind her head, bringing her a glass of water and the big television remote control—as she languished on the sofa,

"Your soaps are on, I think," said Charles. He settled a blanket over her lap. "Should I keep the dogs away for a while? I think I should."

"I'm so grateful for you, you know?"

Charles paused in his ministrations and beamed down at her. "I know you are, dear. Now, rest. Let's prop that hand, too. Those painkillers should kick in about now."

As if his words held magic, Georgie's eyelids grew heavy and the throb in her hand dulled. Her last conscious thought was, "If God punished me with denying us children, he surely gave me redemption by sending me my Charles." Then she fell blissfully asleep.

29 *In Love* WITH LOVE

Bruce stepped back and admired his work. The Villeneuve's addition had been a Godsend, financially and emotionally. Getting Elise off his back? Priceless.

"Looks incredible, Bruce. Can't thank you enough for taking on the job," said Pedro, clapping him on the back.

"Nah, thank you, man. Felt good getting back into construction."

He meant it, too. Roofing was fine, but it was the inherited company, not the chosen one. Had his pop not crippled himself, he'd be heading his own company, doing his own thing. The resentment—one he shared with no one, save Mae's father, once—stayed below the surface most of the time but every so often, it rose to the top again.

"So, why don't you do it full time?"

Bruce took the proffered beer from Pedro—screw it, Elise was likely already mad he hadn't come home yet—and shrugged. "Eh, you know. I've got my dad's company to run, so—"

"Combine and subcontract, then. You get to do the parts you love and farm out the shit you don't love." Pedro clinked his bottle against Bruce's. "Boom. Problem solved."

It wasn't like the thought never crossed his mind. It had, many times. His old man shot it down—*can't spread yourself too thin, son*, then Elise did—*you're already gone too much of the time, Moose*. Somehow, hearing the idea come from someone else, shined a new light.

"I wish it were that easy," said Bruce.

"What do you mean? It is that easy. Grady Building and Roofing. Or, I know, Bruce Grady Contractor—"

"We've already got that new guy, Jason Marsdale, though."

"Marsdale only does new construction. Besides, he's a temp. As soon as new land opportunities dry up—"

"Or he gets tired of the town shooting his high-rise plans down," cut in Bruce.

"That, too. You handle the remodels. No competition, no problem. You know what? I handled his divorce last year, so I can put you in touch. It's good to make friends in the business."

Bruce couldn't deny the welling sensation of excitement at the prospect. He silenced Elise and his dad's voices in his head and said, "You know what, man. Yeah, set that up, will you?"

"Pedro, dinner's ready. Bruce, I've already made you a plate, so you can't leave," said Marisol from the door.

"Aw, thanks, Marisol. You know I can never turn down your cooking. I'll text Elise and let her know."

He did, then turned his phone off. He didn't want to see her response. Over dinner they discussed the logistics of Bruce incorporating the roofing business under the umbrella of the remodeling company. As it turned out, it was way less complicated than Bruce imagined.

"Okay, you two. Enough business talk. Tell me about Mae and her twins. I'm so excited to have another pair in Chance for Diego and Alejandro to grow up with," said Marisol.

"I saw them all the other day. Mom and babies are doing well, but they're keeping Mae and little Evangeline—Evvie, they're calling her—for a few more days."

"Such a relief after their scare. I'm waiting until they're home and settled before I visit. Ileana had a cold last week, so I was afraid I might spread the germs to them."

"Mae mentioned. She totally understood," said Bruce.

"That makes, what, the third set of twins in Chance, doesn't it?" Pedro laughed. "Better watch out, my friend. You and Elise might be next."

Bruce laughed along, but it felt hollow. All he and Elise seemed to do was fight. *Should* they bring another kid into the world? Doubt had sprung a leak in his head, and he couldn't seem to plug it up. He looked up to catch concerned glances between Marisol and Pedro.

"We're good." He reassured. "I mean, you know, sure we fight. Like, a lot. But that's… normal, isn't it? People argue. It doesn't mean they're not—"

Pedro jumped in. "Oh, yeah, no. Definitely. Couples argue. Very normal."

Marisol shot a dark look at Pedro that Bruce deciphered as a warning to him to not get involved. The smile she gave Bruce radiated warm as she offered him more rice. He suspected she wasn't Elise's biggest fan, but Marisol was too refined and gracious to say so.

When Pedro excused himself to take a call, Bruce jumped up to help Marisol carry in the dishes.

"Oh, you don't have to do that, Bruce. Relax. I'll put on some coffee," said Marisol.

"I can't let you do all the work. Here, I'll load the dishwasher while you make the coffee. Deal?"

Marisol laughed and shook her head. "Deal." She put a hand on his arm and squeezed. "You're a good man, Bruce. I hope she realizes that."

She blushed then, perhaps embarrassed she'd spoken out of turn.

"Thank you, Marisol. That means a lot. You and Pedro… man, you have, like, the perfect life. Exactly what I'd want. For me and Elise, I mean."

Marisol wagged the coffee pot at him. "Oh, now don't going throwing words like perfect around. There's no such thing. Pedro and I, we have our share of troubles."

She turned away to fill the pot. When she turned back, her eyes shone with feeling. "But we work them out. We work on our marriage, all the time. That is what it means to be married. Two people who put in the effort and the energy to—"

She stopped, smoothed her hair down and forced a laugh. "Anyhow, there's no such thing as perfect. Let's bring the coffee on the porch, yes?"

"I-ah, yes. Sounds perf—great, I mean."

They both smiled.

Later, on his drive home, he considered what she'd said. Were he and Elise the kind of people who could put the kind of work into a marriage to make it last? Just last week she walked out on an argument and didn't come back until he'd already gone to bed. Then there was him, that very night, doing everything he could to avoid going home. They weren't even fighting, so why didn't he want to go home?

Something else Marisol said over coffee stuck in his mind. She'd been talking about her sister, Ophelia and her erratic ways. She and Pedro bantered.

"Your sister is flighty, Mari."

"She's not flighty. She's just… free-spirited."

"She has a new boyfriend every other month."

"Well, Ophelia has a tendency to fall in love quickly, before she really knows someone."

"Because she's flighty," said Pedro.

"No, because she's in love with love. She'll grow out of it when she meets the right one."

It made Bruce question Elise's love for him. She'd always had a conveyor belt of boyfriends in high school and in college. Then she took off to Europe and came back married to a guy she barely knew… and who turned out to be gay. She also moved on to *him* pretty quickly.

According to Charlotte, Elise had always had a thing for Bruce. But maybe she only loved the *idea* of him, and the reality wasn't measuring up like she thought it would.

And what about him? He sure as hell wasn't *flighty*. But maybe he fell in love with the idea of being in a relationship. His last real girlfriend, Yarra, fizzled out shortly after he came back to Chance to help his dad. The thing with Mae didn't count. Neither did the string of brief hookups after her.

By the time Bruce pulled into the driveway, his heart had grown heavy with doubt and dread. He wasn't ready to pull the plug, but now the thought had wormed its way inside his brain and settled in for a stay.

Movement at the front door caught his eye. Elise stood, arms folded, leaning against the doorframe. The porch light cast her unsmiling face in a hard light. Bruce sighed and turned off the ignition.

30 *Golden* CHILD

Katie squinted at Brianna. "So, how are you feeling?"

"Me? I'm fine. You're the one who just had a baby. How are *you* feeling?"

Katie rolled her eyes. "Please, when you get to baby number five, they just slide right out."

"Ew. TMI, Katie. So, did you give her a name or are we just calling her Five?"

"Hilarious. Her name is Reagan Maura O'Brien."

"Cute, I like it," said Brianna.

"Have you guys started thinking about names?" Katie asked.

"I told you, I don't want to even think about it until... well, until I feel... oh, you know what I mean." Brianna stood up and began pacing.

"I know it's hard to relax after your scare, but you have to try. Have a little faith—" Katie winced.

"Sorry. I just mean you have to trust that all will be well."

Brianna adjusted the pink lilies in the vase by the window. Without turning around, she said, "Do you think I'm a good person?"

"What? Yes, of course. Bri, I've known you almost our whole lives. I don't *think* you're a good person, I *know* you are. Where's this coming from? I thought things were good?"

"They are. Really good, actually. It's just—I've been seeing that therapist, and it stirred up… stuff. I talked to Ricky about it but…" She trailed off.

Katie had the distinction of being one of the very few people who truly knew Brianna and what her life had been like growing up. Thankfully, she'd never made Brianna regret confiding in her. She went back to Katie's bedside and perched on the edge of the mattress and gazed helplessly at her friend.

Katie understood the unspoken words. "You want to believe him, but you can't quite get yourself to do it." She took Brianna's hand. "Brianna, you are a Bourdreau in name only. I mean, yes, you share the same DNA but that doesn't make you them. *Him*. You're you and you've built a life separate from all that."

Brianna nodded, her brow furrowed. "You're right. Do you think I was wrong to never report him?"

Katie hesitated. "I think you did what you felt you needed to do. Your father is a big deal in this town. I guess as long as Brandon isn't—"

"He's not. Gordon would never lay a hand on the golden child. I'm positive. I was positive." She bit her bottom lip. "The thing is, he's run off, it seems."

"Oh, Brianna. Do you think Gordon... could he have... what about your mother? Does she have any—"

"This is her fault, you know. *She* chose him. She chooses him time and again. I've tried to get her to leave. Instead, she let him chase me away and now her son. Brandon is a smart kid. I'm not worried about him. He's probably hiding out at a friend's house until the dust clears at home. He knows where to find me if he needs me."

She dismissed the conversation with a wave of her hand. "Anyhow. On to other topics. I hear your husband's cousin is dating none other than Gina Byrd. How scandalous for the first selectman and Mrs. O'Brien."

"Oh, hush, you. Billy and Chris might as well be strangers for as much as they see each other."

"Yes, but what about those big family gatherings? How will that look, him showing up with *her*?"

"Well, you said it right there—big family. No one will even notice. Or care, for that matter. The O'Brien's are not Kennedy's, for goodness' sake."

"Still, Gina Byrd is quite a step down for any family."

"Hello, Katie," said a voice from the doorway.

Katie's eyes widened and Brianna flushed. The both turned a guilty stare at Mae, who smiled at them. They needed not wonder if she'd heard, it was in the hard glint in her eyes.

"Mae," said Katie in forced cheer. "You look fantastic. I'm so glad to hear you're doing better. How are the twins? What did you name them again?"

She spoke so quickly, her sentences crowded. Brianna glared at her and mouthed, "Shut up," before turning her icy smile on Mae.

"Yes, congratulations, Mae. I-I'm sorry, I didn't mean—"

"No worries, Brianna. I know full well what some people in Chance think of Gina. I did to, before I took the time to know her. Anyhow, I just wanted to say congratulations to you, too. I saw little Reagan in the nursery. She's next to Evvie. Well, the doctor wanted me to keep my walks short, so I'd better get back to my room."

"Bye, Mae. Again, so glad you're doing better. We'll have to get the babies together soon." Katie called after Mae.

"Evvie?" Brianna hissed with disdain.

"Shut up." Katie hissed back. "You already got us in trouble with your mouth. Thanks a lot."

"I'm just saying the child's name. God. It's… cute." Her voice went up on the word *cute*.

"Oh, I remember now. Evangeline and Thomas Keith. They're calling the boy TK. And I *do* think the names are cute, so don't be mean."

"Fine, whatever. I apologized. What more can I say?"

Brianna wanted to mask her embarrassment, but mortified she was. She had no beef with Mae

Huxley. In fact, she quite liked her. That husband of hers was yummy, too. And the woman had almost died, for fuck's sake. She felt worse by the minute. Later she'd have to send a basket from her and Ricky.

When Billy and their brood returned to the room wreaking havoc as the O'Brien clan was wont to do, Brianna made her escape. At the elevators she pivoted and strode to the nursery instead.

She peered through the glass at the clear bassinets with swaddled, squirming pink and brown babies. The girls outnumbered the boys by her count. Brianna allowed herself a moment to think about the little alien in her belly. Her next appointment was in less than an hour and would tell them the sex of the baby if they wanted to know.

Ricky wanted to find out, Brianna did not. Knowing would make it feel even more real, and the loss that much greater should she miscarry. Brianna looked down at the small swell of her abdomen to see that her hand had floated and rested there against her conscious will.

"Stay with me, little one. Just… hang in there, okay?"

She brushed a tear from her cheek roughly and darted her gaze around in hopes no one saw or heard her. Since karma seemed to always be her enemy, none other than Miles Hannaford stood awkwardly at the edge of the nursery.

"Ah, hey, Sorry. I, uh, came to visit Mae but the doctor is in with her right now. We forgot to bring something last visit, so… I thought I'd come down and see… are you, uh, all right?"

He looked down at her stomach. The wrapping on the bouquet crackled as he switched hands. He looked so stupid and uncomfortable that Brianna half wanted to punch him and half laugh.

"I'm fine, Miles. Shut up and come see the babies. Katie had hers, too." She pointed a finger against the glass to show him Reagan,

"Ah, shit. Cute. Wow, they're so damn tiny."

"Well, they're newborns, Miles, so yes." Brianna's natural tendency toward sarcasm always bubbled over around him. She forced a neutral tone. "So, you and Rosalind plan on having kids?"

"Rosa*belle* and I have discussed the idea, yes." He side-glanced Brianna and matched her tone. "Looks like you and Ricky are back on track. Good for you."

"Yes, thank you. Well, I've got to get going. Take care, Miles."

"You, too, Bri."

There was a time when Brianna would've added an extra swish to her step in rightful expectation of his rapt attention. That time had passed. She was as certain of his disinterest as she was her own. It reminded her of her morning runs on the beach—that moment when the sun burned the fog from the ocean, and everything became clear and bright—and it made her smile. Her phone buzzed and her smile grew when she saw Ricky's name on the screen.

"Hello, handsome. Are you in the lobby already?"

"Hey, babe. Two more minutes, Just looking for a parking space."

"I'm on my way down. Meet you in the lobby."

"Great, see you in a few."

She dropped the phone in her purse and stepped out onto the main floor. The smile that hovered on her lips fell at the sight of Gordon Bourdreau striding toward her, his laser beam eyes boring into her with a menace only she could see. How could no one see the coldness in his eyes?

"Hello, Dad. What brings you here?" She spoke coolly, looking everywhere but at him.

Instead of answering her, he said, "Where is he?"

"Who?" Asked Brianna.

His temple pulsed and his jaw clenched. Gordon stepped closer, and he spoke in a deathly low tone. "You know God damn well *who*. Where is your brother, Brianna?"

"Careful, Dad. We're in a public place," warned Brianna. A slight tremble belied the glacial flow of her words.

"You're right. Let's go talk in private."

Gordon stepped close so he could grab her arm. His hand gripped vise-like above her elbow, his fingertips digging hard into the soft flesh of her inner arm. Brianna winced. What happened next transpired so quickly Brianna struggled to process it.

One second, Gordon stood beside her, hissing something threatening she only half heard. The next, she was abruptly released, staring down at

Gordon on the floor and up at Ricky, who towered over him. His fists balled at his sides and his eyes blazed.

Quietly, Ricky said, "I warned you, Gordon. Didn't I? I fucking warned you. You keep your hands off my wife."

A loose crowd had formed. Gordon got up from the floor with slow, awkward care. He gave a blustering laugh and spoke loud enough for those closest to hear.

"Nothing to see here, folks. My over-exuberant son-in-law forgets his strength. Just playing around, aren't we, son?"

Ricky ignored him and looked at Brianna. "You okay, babe? He hurt you?"

She moved to his side, rubbing her arm where she still felt the phantom grip of her father's hand.

"I'm okay," she said.

Brianna looked into his eyes to reassure him and saw how hard he was fighting not to give into his rage and pummel Gordon. She took his arm and turned him away from her father and said, "He's not worth it. Let's go."

Ricky resisted for the briefest of moments, then the fire in his eyes mellowed and he let his wife pull him away. They ignored Gordon's calls.

"Brianna," he said.

She flinched. Ricky wrapped his arm around her waist, kissed her temple, and they stepped out into the sunshine. A new resolution formed in Brianna's mind. He had no power over her. Not anymore. Not ever again. And what's more? She planned on ruining him.

Twenty minutes later, she and Ricky stared at a very bouncy, active image on a monitor.

"All right, you two. Moment of truth. To find out, or not to find out?"

Ricky looked down at Brianna. "What do you think, babe?"

He looked so hopeful, so excited. She wanted more than anything to please him. So, despite her trepidations, she looked to the sonographer and said, "Spill it. Boy or girl?"

The woman grinned. "This part never gets old. Congratulations, Mr. and Mrs. Baker. You're having a… boy!"

"A boy? We're having a boy?" Brianna repeated it in amazement. "Ricky, we're having a boy."

Ricky wiped tears from his eyes. "A boy. Holy shit, I can't believe it."

"Well, it was a fifty-fifty shot, so…" Brianna couldn't help herself sometimes.

"Little Ricky, a chip off—"

"Whoa, slow your roll there, big guy. Little Ricky? What are we, the *I Love Lucy* show?"

"Okay, you two. I think we are all set here," said the sonographer, handing Brianna a cloth to wipe away the gel from her stomach. "Everything looks lovely and baby boy Baker is growing right on schedule."

"Thank you. September twenty-second can't get here fast enough," said Brianna.

Ricky helped Brianna sit up. When the woman left the room, he lifted her off the table and spun her around. Fresh tears sprung to Brianna's eyes. Since the scare after the memorial, Ricky had been coming back to her little by little, but the wariness had lingered underneath. Until now. The old Ricky, the one who loved Brianna with abandon, was back. It might only be for the moment, but it furthered her hope that they could recover from her transgression.

He seemed to accept the marriage counselor's assertion that knowing who it was with would be counter-productive to healing their marriage and had stopped asking her. Brianna's relief had been palpable. However, it came not from a desire to protect Miles, but her own dignity.

If Ricky knew, he'd have to ask, "Why *Miles*?" It was an excellent question. In retrospect, she'd latched onto him simply because she knew he'd never want or expect something more from her. It didn't take a counselor to tell her that, she understood it intuitively.

Miles Hannaford was a sleaze, and no amount of time with Rosabelle Waterman would change that. Not in Brianna's eyes. She just wished *she* hadn't been the sleaze who slept with him. Alas, there was no turning back time. All she could do was hope that secret stayed buried.

But what about her other secrets? The family ones? The ones she'd lived with her whole life in shame and fear? Suddenly, Brianna wasn't so resolute in her dutiful compliance. A change—an axis tilt—occurred when she saw him on the hospital floor after Ricky pushed him. The man who'd always loomed larger than life in her eyes now looked small. He looked *weak*.

She'd spent her whole childhood in fear of that man. One look from him could send both her and her mother cowering. But today, she saw a man who could be taken down. How had she, Brianna the Ice Queen of Chance, not have seen him for what he was? A coward. Gordon Bourdreau was nothing but a coward and a bully and it only took her twenty-eight years to know it.

"Ricky?"

Ricky pulled into their driveway and put the car in park. "I know that tone. Are you going to yell at me for that thing with your father? Listen, babe. I know how you feel about—"

"I think we need to get Brandon out of that house and into ours."

Ricky blinked. "Brandon? Your *brother*... Brandon? Wow. I did not see that coming. What's going on over there now?"

"Well, apparently, Brandon's run away. Gordon seemed to think he was with us."

Ricky's eyebrows went up. "*Is* he with us?"

"No." She almost added, "*don't you think you'd know if there were another man in the house?*" But thought better of it. "That's the thing, Ricky. It must've gotten bad for him to run away, and he didn't come to his own sister for help."

She bowed her head and massaged her temples. "I've been a really shitty sister to him. I'm so caught up in my own stuff, I forgot how awful it must be for him to watch those two and their sick, toxic fucking relationship."

"Babe, Brandon is a great kid. He's always welcome in our house, not even a question. But, back up a minute. Why hasn't Gordon reported him missing? Shouldn't there be, like, an Amber Alert out?"

"You know how he is. Appearances must be kept at all times." She shuddered recalling the scene at the hospital, then reminded herself she didn't care anymore. "He told Joel that he knows where Brandon is and that he just wants him to come home."

Ricky seethed. "What a dick. And what if the kid *didn't* run away and got kidnapped or something? He'd probably want that kept quiet, too."

Brianna looked up sharply. "Jesus. I hadn't even thought of that. Do you think that's possible?"

"Ah, shit. Sorry, babe. Nah. He's hiding out at a buddy's house, mark my words. Listen if it'll make you feel better, I'll ask around. Who does he hang out with?"

Brianna thought for a moment, then blanched. "Oh, hell. I think I know where to find him." She closed her eyes and let her head fall back against the headrest. "Mae's house. Feather Anne is the only kid he hangs out with."

"All right. You rest. My mom is bringing Cassidy home in a couple hours, so take advantage of it. I'll swing by the Huxley's and see what I can find out."

Brianna made a couple weak protestations before doing as he suggested. It would be better if Ricky found and talked to him, rather than Brianna.

They had an easy way with one another, bonding over football and cars. For the siblings, it was more of a challenge. They'd never been close—Gordon saw to that—and they had little in common except for family shame. It didn't facilitate closeness.

Once changed and into comfortable clothes, Brianna stretched out on the sofa and closed her eyes. The images that played like vignettes discouraged her sleep. Gordon's eyes filled with simmering rage. Gordon on the hospital lobby floor, humiliated and weak looking. Ricky towering over him, his face a mask. Sonogram. Baby Boy. Gordon's hate.

The scenes replayed, Gordon's steel grip on her arm. Ricky threatening him. She saw herself, seeing Gordon anew. Sonogram. Boy. The sliding doors. Gordon on the floor. Repeat. Long ago memories pushed their way forward. Her father's coldly calm expression as he sent her to the basement. Her mother's tear-streaked face as she pleaded with him to stop. Her own whimpering appeals.

She bolted upright, cradling her forearm as if the candle flame burned her flesh right then instead of years before. She looked at the scar. There were dozens more like it, all hidden by clothing or excusable with clumsy cooking or ironing accidents.

After one of their *behavior adjustments*, they'd gone to the annual picnic in the park. Brianna wore long sleeves even though the temperature reached eighty-five degrees that day. Her mother never removed her sunglasses. They clapped and smiled when Gordon received a plaque for his service to the community. Brandon hadn't been born yet.

By the time Brandon came into existence, Brianna Bourdreau had been plotting her escape. She had nine hundred dollars hidden in a tampon box—the one place spared from Gordon's weekly inspections—and had the bus schedule to New York memorized. She already loved Ricky, but even he couldn't convince her to stay.

It was Brandon who changed her mind. Not with words, but with tiny flailing fists and wide trusting eyes. Martha Bourdreau had done nothing to protect Brianna from Gordon, so it seemed a matter of course she'd not protect this child either. It would be up to her.

That was the plan, at least. Only Brandon hadn't needed her protection. Not in the way she'd expected. Gordon never laid a hand on the boy. However, if Brianna or Martha failed to keep him quiet and well behaved—especially in public—they were the ones to pay.

Fortunately, Brandon was a reticent child. Even as a baby. To Brianna, it was like he somehow knew what Gordon would do and tried to protect them in his own way. It was silly to think such a thing, but Brandon never gave her reason to doubt it.

Such an unexpectedly great kid, and she'd neglected him from the moment she finally got out of that house. Brianna was going to fix that, though. Even if it meant going up against her father.

31 Charles

September 1992

"Did you hear the news?"

Charles looked up from his newspaper. "What news is that, my darling bride?"

Georgie gave him a look that said, *I know you're patronizing me, and I don't care.* "The news about Keith Huxley."

"Keith Huxley?"

"Yes, Charles. The same Keith Huxley who's lived up the street from us for many years."

Charles folded his paper and set it on lap with deliberate slowness. He removed his reading glasses and set them on the coffee table. After he'd angled his body toward Georgie, he said, "If you're going to tell me he's a homosexual, that's old news, dear."

"Oh, Charles. Honestly. No, that is *not* what the news is. The news is that Keith Huxley has a baby. A little girl, I'm told. Can you imagine?"

"A baby? A human baby? How'd he manage that?"

"Well, I don't know the details yet. But I'm sure—"

The doorbell rang, setting the dogs in a frenzy. Charles rose to open the door and Georgie shushed the rambunctious duo. Milly and Marlon were more a handful than her beloved Louis and Keely had been, but she loved them dearly just the same.

"Keith, we were just talking about you. Come on in."

"Thanks, Charles. Hello, Georgie. I wanted you two to be the first to meet my daughter, Mae Scarlett Huxley."

He turned the carrier around to present the most perfect, pink-cheeked, round-eyed baby they'd ever seen.

Charles watched his wife move slowly toward their neighbor and his child. His heart ached for her. He knew her thoughts surely as he knew his own.

Her voice was wonderous and awestruck, but also confused. "Us? That's so thoughtful of you, but… why us?"

Charles wondered the same. Keith had always been a friendly, hospitable neighbor and they got on quite well. Still, their friendship was more an acquaintanceship than anything deeper.

Keith cleared his throat. "Can we sit?"

"Of course, of course."

Charles motioned him to the sofa. Georgie sat beside him and he took his lounge chair. They watched and waited with curious anticipation, exchanging a baffled glance as Keith situated the infant.

After a moment, he explained. "I know it seems a little odd for me to come here and—well, I suppose everything seems odd about my situation—but I've been thinking a whole lot since this little person came into my life just three days ago. The, uh truth is, I don't know what the hell I'm doing. I'm, uh, flying solo on this one. I've got my sister, naturally. But I—oh, hell. I'm making a mess of this."

"Now, now. You just take your time, Keith. Charles, get the man a glass of wine, will you?"

Charles decided they all could do for a glass of wine. When he returned, it seemed Georgie had gotten most of the story behind the arrival of little Mae Scarlett. He expected she'd fill him in on the details later, and let the conversation go uninterrupted.

"And, so you see," said Keith, "I thought, well, I thought maybe you two would be willing to be sort of, like, honorary aunt and uncle to Mae. Or something like that. This sounded so much better in my head," confessed Keith.

"It sounds just lovely to my ears," said Georgie. "Doesn't it, Charles?"

"Oh, oh, yes. Certainly. We're honored."

Truthfully, Charles wasn't sure what to make of the whole thing. Was the man just buttering them up to be free—

"I do hope you'll let us babysit her whenever you need help," offered Georgie.

"Oh, you're very kind. I wouldn't want to impose—"

"Nonsense," Charles heard himself saying, "we'd be delighted."

It was that tiny sigh from the carrier that sucked him in, not the handsome, earnest fella giving them wide, *what have I gotten myself into* eyes. Although Charles did feel sympathy for the guy. Raising a child on ones own would be a challenge. But he'd heard a saying about it taking a village to raise a child, and it resonated.

He watched his wife lift the child and cradle her as she and Keith chatted about sleep habits and feeding. It came so naturally to her, this motherly way. It was clear the little bundle already managed to enrapture her. Perhaps it would be good for Georgie, having a baby around to love and cherish. So long as Huxley planned on staying around.

"So, do you plan on staying in the area or moving away, Keith?" For Georgie's sake, he needed the answer.

"Oh, yes. I left Chance once, but never again. I want to live here, raise my little girl here, and die here in Chance. That's how much I love this town."

He went on to paint them a picture of how he envisioned his and his daughter's life. A house filled with music and laughter. A chicken coop in the backyard. Endless days on the beach. By God, he painted it so well, Charles couldn't help but want to be a part of it, too.

"Now, listen, Keith," said Georgie in her teacher's voice. "I want you to know we are here for you whenever you need us. However, we are not the meddling type, so we won't be popping over unannounced or giving you unwanted advice."

Keith grinned at Georgie in a way that Charles suspected she thought dashing. "I appreciate that, Georgie. You and Charles are my kind of people. Mae's going to love you, I just know it."

Later that night, Georgie seemed to teeter from elation to trepidation. Charles sensed her shifting moods under the current of their conversation. At last he asked her what played so contrarily on her mind.

"Well, that's the thing, Charles. I can't pin it down. I'm overjoyed about that sweet baby coming into our lives, truly, I am. Yet, the circumstances… that woman. I fear trouble ahead."

Georgie had filled him in about the… *tête-à-tête* between Keith and Gina Byrd, the girl who'd grown up to be a woman of questionable character, and the resulting agreement between them at the discovery of her being with child. It raised Charles's eyebrows, but ultimately, he figured it wasn't any of their business. Now it seemed his wife only half agreed.

"If there is trouble ahead, might I suggest we stay out of it, dear?"

She waved him away. "Yes, yes. Of course. We'll just play our role and not get involved otherwise. Why are you looking at me like that, Charles?"

"Oh, no reason, darling." Charles put on his reading glasses and picked up his book. Fella by the name of John Grisham. Charles read his first two books and this third was just as gripping.

"Whatever. You just read your… whatever it is, and I'll grade papers." A few minutes later. "I just think that a child should—it would be so nice for her to know her mother. Don't you think?"

Charles set his book on his lap. "I've no idea, really. Put yourself in her—Gina's—shoes, I suppose? If you gave up your child, would you want to be hanging around in the peripheral like some kind of lurker? Always on the outside, never in. Then there's the girl herself. What'll she be thinking about all this when she grows up? Has he thought of that, you think? Georgie?"

She'd gone quiet, a million miles away. In a strangled tone, she said, "When you put it like that…"

Charles patted her knee. "Oh, now. I didn't mean to upset you. The girl will be fine, I'm certain of it."

"But what of Gina? How will *she* be?"

"Oh." Charles considered. "Well, I can't say. How does one deal after something like that? That's quite a burden to bear."

"Indeed, it is."

They said nothing more on the matter. Charles resumed his book and Georgie graded her students' papers. Knowing his wife as he did, he suspected she'd not be letting it go and was merely humoring him with her silence. He'd expect no less, either.

32 ~~Father~~ LIKE DAUGHTER

Gina's eyes darted back and forth between Feather Anne and Chris as they fed Mae's goats. They were laughing and bantering, like old friends. Or like father and daughter. They looked nothing alike but still…

"Hey, Gina. You didn't tell me you and Chris dated before," said Feather Anne over her shoulder. She turned around, looking between them. "When exactly? No offense, Chris, but I don't remember you coming around."

Chris and Gina said, "It was before you were born."

Under her breath, Gina added, "And I wouldn't call it dating, either."

She watched the color of Feather Anne's eyes change as she cocked her head. The mental wheels were spinning. The damn kid was too smart for her own good. Gina braced herself for the next question.

"*How* long before I was born?"

There it was. The million-dollar question.

Chris—slower on the uptake than the twelve-year-old—said, "I dunno, like a year before? Sound bout right, Gi?"

Feather Anne's laser beam stare locked on Gina's matching eyes. "*Does* that sound about right, *Gi*?

Gina busied herself with feeding the chickens. "Something like that." She tried changing the subject. "Hey, are we supposed to check for eggs, too?"

"Already did it earlier this morning. So, you two went out a year before I was born, huh? For, like, how long?"

Chris set down the bucket of feed and looked skyward. "Well, let's see. Your mom and I hook— went out in the spring of—no, winter, I think. What year was that, Gi? O-seven, maybe?"

Gina rubbed the middle of her forehead. "February through March of two-thousand-seven."

"Good memory," said Chris. He picked up the bucket again and fed a handful to Gracie.

"Yeah, good memory, Gina. So, you two *dated* in February, and I was born in November. If my math is—"

"Feather Anne," said Gina. She gave her a pleading look.

Feather Anne looked at Chris, happily, obliviously petting the goats. Or maybe not so obliviously. He looked up, eyebrows pulled together.

"February to November is nine months." He looked from Gina to Feather Anne. The bucket slipped from his hand and the goats crowded around his feet.

"Is he—" said Feather Anne.

At the same time, Chris asked, "Am I—"

"Ah, shit," said Gina, sitting down hard on a stump. "Yeah. He is. You are, Chris. I-I wasn't sure until today. But, yeah. You two are…"

"Father," said Feather Anne.

"And daughter," said Chris.

The two looked at one another with new interest. Chris's blue-green eyes, blond-tinged lashes and ruddy Irish complexion was in stark contrast to Feather Anne's dark lashes, hair, and smooth skin. Yet, they stood in mirrored stances— one knee bent, hand on hip, head tilted.

"My Dad's side of the family has your coloring. My mom's side calls them the Dark Irish. Shit, wow. Those are your grandparents."

"My—holy shit. I have grandparents. Living ones?"

"Oh, yeah, yeah. They're alive. They live in Rocky Hill. Plus, you got aunts, uncles, cousins… there are a shit ton of O'Brien's in Connecticut. Massachusetts, too."

Gina still sat on the stump, her elbow on her knee and her hand over her mouth as she watched the pair process the news. *She* still had to process it. Sure, she'd suspected he might be the one, but there'd been others back then. More than she remembered. But if Chris asked for a paternity test, it would only confirm what she saw in front of her. These two were kin.

"Wait, so that means Billy O'Brien—the town's First Selectman—is my... what is he to me?"

Chris thought for a moment. "Ah, your cousin. Yeah, he'd be your second cousin, because me and him are first cousins. His kids are your third cousins."

"Holy shit. This is insane."

A grin spread across her face. A matching one spread across Chris's. The only one not smiling, was Gina. These people would take away the already tenuous hold Gina had on the girl. She'd be pushed another step away, another increment outside the bubble of happy, normal people.

The O'Brien clan might balk initially at the child's connections, but they wouldn't reject her. Gina had no place in their scene. Chris, however, didn't seem to realize it.

"Gi, you and Feather Anne gotta come to our annual family fest. It's next week in Kennebunkport, Maine, at my uncle's cottage. It's practically on the beach. You'll love it."

"Oh, I don't think—"

"Hell's yeah," said Feather Anne, giving Chris a high five. "I can't believe I have such a cool family."

The shock and euphoria still coursed through Feather Anne's mind, but Gina expected the girl's thoughts would soon turn from elation to resentment. Not at Chris, he fell blameless in his lack of prior knowledge. It was Gina who'd endure her daughter's anger.

Father and daughter quizzed each other on likes and dislikes, unaware of Gina's inner turmoil. They discovered the both hated spinach but loved broccoli. Their shared favorite color was teal. Neither had ever watched Game of Thrones but wanted to. Both preferred their ice cream mostly melted and with peanut butter topping. All the while, Gina's stomach churned.

When Chris left an hour later, it was with Feather Anne in tow. They were going fishing off the jetty together. Gina had been invited, but she declined.

"I have to get the house ready for Mae and the twins. They'll be home in the morning, and I want everything to be perfect."

Feather Anne hesitated at the door. "You want me to stay and help? I can…"

"No, no. You two go on. Get some, you know, bonding time. Just the two of you."

Chris, bless him, beamed from ear to ear. Gina marveled again at what a sweet, unassuming soul he was. The proverbial good guy. He was the same guy now as he was then. Gina had tossed him and his good intentions aside all those years ago. Shrugged him off when he offered to help her get clean. She'd assumed—wrongly—he was just another guy trying to get a piece of ass.

When Chris approached her at the memorial luncheon, she recognized him instantly. Older, thicker around the middle, but still the same open, kind face she remembered.

"Uh, you probably don't remember me, but I—"

"Hello, Chris. It's nice to see you again."

Chris blushed and grinned. "Hey, Gina. You're looking really great. I mean, like, you look—"

"Chris, it's fine. I understand. You, uh, you look good, too. I heard about—"

"The accident? Yeah, it was… it was awful. I had a hard time after." He'd been staring down at the floor but jerked his head up. "Not, like, compared to what Rosabelle went through, though. I-I'd never compare the two. I mean, I didn't even have a scrape and she—"

"Chris, I know for a fact she doesn't blame you at all for that accident. She never has. It was an *accident*. Stop beating yourself up over it."

He picked at his cuticles. "She said that? I haven't been able to—I'm afraid she'll—"

"Come with me."

Gina grabbed his hand and pulled him through the crowd toward Rosabelle. She stood by the stage with her boyfriend. When she saw Chris, her face lost its anxious tightness and broke into a warm smile.

"Chris," said Rosabelle as if he were a lost child found. "I've been hoping we'd run into each other. Come here."

She spread her arms and welcomed him for a hug. Chris turned an uncertain look to Gina, who nudged him forward. He shuffled over and hugged her gently. She squeezed him tightly and whispered something in his ear that made his eyes water.

Whatever she'd said transformed him. His shoulders dropped and the tightness around his eyes disappeared. He looked like the Chris she knew back when, and she remembered all the things she'd liked about him. In those days, Gina couldn't appreciate a guy like Chris. But now…

"Gina, just the person I wanted to see."

William came up the sidewalk from the driveway, car keys jangling in his hand and a bounce in his step. Gina hadn't noticed him pull in.

"Hey, William. How is Mae and the twins? We took care of the goats and chickens and I think the house looks Mae-ready."

William chuckled. "Mae-ready," he repeated. "Wonderful, thank you and Feather Anne, too. Say, where is Feather Anne?"

"She, uh, went fishing with Chris," said Gina.

"Well, that's nice. Isn't it? You seem… not as happy about it as I'd have thought."

Gina wasn't going to tell him the news, not until she had both him and Mae together, but she couldn't stop herself. "He's her father. Her real father. Chris is."

William pulled his head back and blinked. "Chris O'Brien? He's Feather Anne's biological father? Huh. I didn't see that coming, Gina. Does she—do they know?"

"Yes. I told them this morning. I only figured it out myself when I saw them together."

He winced at her. "Forgive me for asking, but… you haven't had a paternity test done?"

Gina set her jaw. "I know what I know. It's plain as day those two are father and daughter. If he wants one done, we'll do it. But I'm positive Chris is her dad."

William mulled over the news. Then he said, "Well, he's a welcome addition to our suddenly big family." He paused a moment. "Are you happy about this? You seem… off."

Gina tipped her head to the door, and they went back inside the house. They sat across each other in the kitchen. It felt weird talking about feelings, but William had a knack for drawing them out.

"It's just… I don't know. I thought it would be… shit. I can't explain it."

"Sure, you can." William smiled patiently.

Gina took a deep breath. "I guess I didn't think about what it would mean for Feather Anne. That she'd get, like, this whole new family. If they're decent folk—and the O'Brien clan is—they'll want to get to know her. Which is great, but…"

"But it makes you feel like the odd man out? Like Feather Anne will get pulled further away from you? Like you can't compare with what they bring to the table?"

Gina exhaled and slumped. "Yes. Exactly. What do I do, William?"

He patted her hand. "You already know what you'll do. You'll let her spread her wings and give her room to fly. Hearts are ever expandable things. Just because she'll come to love new people, doesn't mean she'll stop loving the ones she's had all along."

Gina nodded and smiled up at him. "Wise William. That's what Mae calls you."

"Among other things, I'm sure. Now, can we discuss another pressing matter? Like the boy living in our garage, perhaps?"

33 It's BAD

"Seems I've arrived at just the right time." Gordon Bourdeau leaned against the kitchen entrance. The smile he gave them appeared benign, jovial even.

"Gordon? What are—"

"Forgive me, but your front door was wide open. I followed the sound of your voices, and…" He spread his arms as if to say *and here I am*. As if he were a welcome and expected guest.

"How long have you been here," asked William. He glanced at Gina. She'd gone white but for two spots of red high on her cheeks. Her expression looked defiant *and* defeated.

He'd no idea what their hostilities were or from where they came. All he knew was that the man had the audacity to walk into another man's home uninvited. At least one of Gina's assertions were confirmed for William—Gordon Bourdreau was a smug prick.

"Oh, long enough," said Gordon. He directed his words to Gina. His smile widened but never reached his eyes. "So, Gina. Adding kidnapping to your resume, are we?"

William—who had no strong opinion of Gordon prior—concluded in those short minutes he did not like the man. This, he noted with interest, was a very different Gordon than the one he'd seen out socially. The veneer slipped in his blatant contempt for Gina.

William didn't hide the scorn from his tone. "Hold on a second, there. That's a hefty accusation, wouldn't you say? The way I understand it, your son's run away. No one *kidnapped* the boy."

Gordon turned his laser beam stare at William. His attempt at a lazy appraisal faltered when he met William's unwavering, cold gaze. That gaze told Gordon he'd barked up the wrong tree, walked uninvited into the wrong home, and challenged the wrong person.

In the time it took for Gordon's confidence to waiver, William made his own appraisal. He'd know many men like him in his lifetime. Brandon Bourdreau's father was a tyrant. A bully who picked on the weak and wore false bravado like armor. All it took was someone equal or stronger to put him in his place.

Gordon pointed a long finger at Gina. It shook ever so slightly. "She and her daughter are trying to poison my son against me. I know he's here, and she's hiding him. It's kidnapping in the eyes of the law, and you are an accomplice. I'll have you both arrested. Your wife, too. All of—"

"Dad, stop." Brandon stood pale-faced and trembling behind Gordon. He'd come in from the garage. "Leave them alone. I ran away and I'm not going back."

"Son, get in the car. You don't know what you're saying. These people have brainwashed you."

"No one has brain—"

Gordon thundered. "Get in the car, damn it."

Brandon jumped. Gina flinched. William took a step forward, in front of the boy, and put a protective hand out. "How about you let him stay just one more night? Until things… cool down."

"You don't seem to understand, pal. That's *my* son. You people are kidnappers. You… indoctrinated him into thinking this—" He looked around the kitchen with disgust, "this house of sin is *normal*. I'm calling Joel Asheby right now. Gina Byrd is no stranger to jail, so—"

"Put your phone away, Bourdreau." The hulking figure of Ricky Baker stood in the front doorway. "May I come in, Mr. Grant?"

"Of course, Ricky. Please do," said William.

The new arrival to his suddenly full house caught him by surprise. Not as much as it did Gordon, though. He bore the look of a cornered rat. Taking several steps back, away from Ricky's approach, he sputtered, "What are you doing here? This is none of your—"

"Actually, it is." He looked around William at the boy. "Brandon, would you like to come stay at me and Bri's? Cassidy misses her Uncle Bam Bam."

"Now, you wait a damn minute—"

"No. Unless you'd like me to tell these good people here everything I know about the Bourdreau household? Then, I'd definitely have a minute for you."

Gordon turned a violent shade of red but said nothing. Brandon looked from his father to Ricky, then up at William. He questioned him with only his eyes.

What should I do, Mr. Grant?

William ruffled his hair. "Go on with Ricky. Your sister is probably worried sick about you by now."

Ricky confirmed. "She said if I didn't get you home with me by dinnertime, my ass is grass, man."

Brandon grinned and bobbed his head. He came out from behind William and walked past his father without glancing his way. Ricky threw a casual arm around the boy's shoulders.

"Thank you, William, Gina, for being a safe place for Brandon. Thank Feather Anne for us, too. She's a great friend."

"Sorry for any trouble I've caused, Mr. Grant. Especially for you, Gina," said Brandon.

Gordon found his voice. It was with only half the authority of earlier. "And what about the trouble you've caused your mother, son? She's been worried sick. You need to get on home to her and—"

"Brandon will stay with us indefinitely. Martha can come to the house to see her kids if she'd like."

They turned and walked toward the door.

"Son, if you walk out that door with him, I swear to God I will burn all of your belongings. Every last one."

Brandon paused. He faced his father and said, "I think you need God more than anyone else here, so I wouldn't go swearing at him if I were you. Goodbye, Dad."

As they passed across the threshold, Feather Anne came bursting through. "Brandon, hey— what's—"

Ricky patted her shoulder. "Your mom will explain everything. Glad I got to see you before we left."

"Am I in trouble?" Feather Anne looked around the room.

"Not at all. Thank you for being a great friend to Brandon. He's a lucky kid."

"Yeah. Thanks, Feather Anne," said Brandon. After a brief hesitation, he hugged her and whispered something in her ear. She looked too stunned to reply.

Gordon, too, appeared stunned. And out of place. All remaining eyes turned to him. The scared rabbit expression had left Gina's face. William's returned to its impassive state. Feather Anne, quick to deduce something major had transpired, folded her arms across her chest and cocked an eyebrow at Gordon.

His slack jaw snapped shut, and he slicked back his hair. He cleared his throat. "W-Well. I'm glad that's resolved. If you'll excuse me, my wife is at home waiting for news of her son."

No one spoke as he strode out the door, down the steps, and into his car. The loud slam and gunning of the engine assured them his calm was only superficial. Feather Anne faced her mother and William, shifting her gaze from one to the other. Then she spoke her mind.

"I'm starving. What's for dinner?"

William laughed. "That's our girl."

Gina released the breath she'd been holding for God knew how long. "Go wash up. You stink like fish."

"Fine, whatever. When I come back, I'll tell you all about the fish I caught with Dad."

William's eyebrows lifted high. Gina's face mirrored his. When Feather Anne bounced off merrily down the hall, Gina exhaled again and slumped into a chair. "Holy shit. That was—"

"Intense. Yes, I agree. That could've gone differently had Ricky Baker not shown up."

"Yeah, no shit. Man, Gordon must be fired up big time now. He just got humiliated, rejected, and schooled." She bit the inside of her cheek and looked toward the front door. After a hesitation, she said, "That wife of his will get the brunt of this."

William exhaled. "Just how bad is it in the Bourdreau house, Gina? I get the idea you know much more than you've said."

"I do and it's a long story. Suffice to say it's bad."

"Then we have a responsibility to do something. I'm going to call Joel Asheby. See if he'll take a ride over there."

"Oh, boy. That news will be across town in an hour," said Gina. She let out a long whistle.

"This town hordes secrets like… like a hoarder. It's unhealthy, and in this case, it might be deadly. I'm calling."

Gina made no move or sound to stop him. She looked relieved, even. William dialed the direct line to Joel's office. A recorded message played.

"Hello, you've reached Sergeant Joel Asheby of the Chance Police Department. Please leave your name, number and a brief message. If this is an emergency, hang up and dial 911."

William debated. Was this an emergency? He couldn't know for certain where Gordon had gone or what he planned to do. However, if Martha Bourdreau was in danger of domestic violence, he had a moral obligation to help her.

He knew enough about the perpetuating cycles of abusive relationships to understand the complicated layers as to why a person would stay in such a toxic situation. It seemed unfathomable to him, it frustrated him, and it made him want to give that coward, Gordon, a taste of his own medicine. A man who abused a woman, or child, or an animal didn't deserve to be called a man.

"Joel, this is William Grant. I'd appreciate a call back when you get this. It's not an emergency, but it may be urgent."

William ended the call and set the phone on the kitchen island with a frown. It was something, the call, but it wasn't enough. To Gina he said, "I think I'll take a ride over there myself."

"And do what? *Say* what? I don't think that's such a hot idea, William," cautioned Gina.

"Keep Feather Anne occupied. If she knows where I'm going, she'll want to—"

"I'm coming with you," said Feather Anne from the hallway. "You suck at whispering, by the way." She tossed his keys at him and turned away.

"Young lady, you are staying here with your mother. End of discussion." William used his *I mean business* voice and hoped it would work. It did.

"No *fair*. Can I at least go to the Baker's house?"

Gina piped in, "Sorry, sport. Need ya here to help make some meals for Mae."

Feather Anne stomped back to the kitchen and glared at them. Both were too relieved that she'd listened to say another word.

William's car nosed out of the driveway when his phone rang.

"Joel. Thanks for calling back so quickly." He spoke a little louder than what was probably necessary for the bluetooth connection—a habit Mae had tried to break him of many a time.

"Sure thing, buddy. What's up? You said urgent?"

William hedged. "Potentially urgent. I may be over-reacting. I just had a run in with Gordon Bourdreau."

William detailed the events leading to the call, excluding, at first, the part about Brandon staying in their home. He realized it would be the first thing Gordon would say when cornered, though. Though it was against his nature to lie, William also knew he had to protect Gina from repercussions.

"There's more to it, actually. It seems our little waif has been in cahoots with Brandon. I'm afraid he's been here, under our noses this whole week."

There was a pause. "Did you all know about this when I asked you?"

"No, no. Of course not. However, I think Gordon may want to press charges against us. For *kidnapping*. Can he do that?"

Joel exhaled into the receiver. "Well, he could try, I suppose. But technically, he never reported the kid as missing. He kept saying, *I know the boy is over a friend's house and he's fine*, so, he'd have some explaining to do."

William's grip on the steering wheel loosened. "Well, that's a relief. It's the last thing Mae needs going on as she brings the twins home."

"You can say that again. So, why do you feel like we need to go to the Bourdreau's, William? Something you're not saying?"

Again, William hesitated. He didn't really know what went on in the Bourdreau house. If Gordon was only verbally abusive and not physically, would it merit a visit from the police? No matter how harmful verbal abuse was, did they even have the right?

"It's been implied that Gordon is... abusive to his wife and kids. Gina seems to think he's going to take out his anger on Martha when he gets home. He was—it was a rather humiliating scene for him here earlier."

"Let me get this all straight—wait, is that you, turning onto Cardinal?"

"Oh, yes. I see your cruiser."

"Pull over and wait for me. Easier to talk in person. I'll send a guy over in the meantime."

William pulled over across from Elise Martino's house and waited. A moment later, Joel's SUV cruiser rolled to a stop behind his car and he climbed out. He paused, angled his head to his shoulder, and spoke into a mic clipped to his uniform's epaulet. On his hip, a portable radio crackled to life with a response. He finished and then shook William's hand.

"Denny and Marlene are taking a ride over there now. Tips are anonymous, by the way. He'll never know it was you."

"Appreciate that and I hope we're wrong."

"Between me and you, I never liked the guy. And you know Ricky hates him. Never said why, but I always had my suspicions. Son of a bitch never gave us a reason to knock on his door, though."

"Interesting. I always thought the Bourdreau's were so well respected in town."

"Oh, they are. There's a handful of us though that don't hold him in such high esteem. Charlotte and them never used to go over the Bourdreau's house when we were growing up. Those five had sleepover's every single week, but never there, It raised eyebrows."

Joel adjusted his belt and scoffed. "Hell just knowing the two sweetest people in the world don't like him is enough for me."

William's brow creased, then he looked at Joel in surprise. "You mean the Brightsider's? They don't like Gordon and Martha?"

"Eh, they don't say much about Martha. Who could, really? But I've caught them—Georgie in particular—giving him the evil eye on more than a few occasions."

"Did you ever ask her why?"

"Nah, never had the opportunity to bring it up. But I—" his radio crackled again, and a female voice spoke out in a mix of code and regular speech. Joel's face tightened and his lips pursed as he listened.

He glanced at William then away. "Roger that. On my way." To William he said, "Gotta go," and he sprinted to his SUV.

William called out, "She said Maple Street. Isn't that where—"

Joel swung open the driver's door and climbed up. "You made the right call, William."

Seconds later, Joel peeled out and around William's car, lights and sirens flashing and blaring.

34 Georgie

September 1988

Georgie set her bag on the floor under her desk and faced her fresh, new class of eighth graders. They weren't the sweet, still innocent faces of her third graders, but ones of children who bore hints of the adults they'd one day be.

She recognized all but two newcomers to town, although their five-year older and taller selves jarred her. Did she look older to them? Georgie dismissed the question. Mrs. Brightsider was the least of interesting topics in the minds of twelve- and thirteen-year-old boys and girls.

Hormones had kicked in the year prior and the same children who'd stood at opposite sides of a school dance, now had to be pried apart by chaperones. As she looked over the small sea of twenty-three sun-tanned, freckled, and pimpled faces, she acknowledged once again how different it would be teaching these children.

"Good morning, class. Welcome back to school. As many of you know, I'm Mrs. Brightsider. For those of you I taught back in third grade, it is lovely to see you again. I see many of you have spent a great deal of time at the beach this summer, yes?" Murmurs and mutters of, "yes," rippled through the room. "Excellent. Your first assignment will be an easy one, then. Two pages about your summer vacation, please."

Over the groans, she added further instructions about complete sentences, grammar, and punctuation. What she didn't tell them—and wouldn't until the end of class—was that she would not be grading their work.

For two weeks before the start of school, Georgie had planned her strategy for teaching these burgeoning young adults. The days of sticker rewards and behavior charts were over. Now was a time for establishing a standard and a code of behavior... without looking like a total stick in the mud.

First, an assignment right off the bat to show she was tough. Then, she'd surprise them by not judging them on their work. After they'd turned in their papers, she'd explain her expectations in a firm but kind way. They would be respectful and attentive, work hard and give their best effort.

In return, she'd be fair, compassionate, and as helpful to them as possible. She'd end her speech with, "I believe in each one of you. Your potential is limitless." She imagined beaming, relieved expressions and a satisfying first day. It did not go as planned.

"Mrs. B.? Can I move my seat?"

Georgie looked up from her planner for the source of the voice. "Gary... no, Gordon, right?"

"Yeah. Can I?"

Twitters and snickers fluttered around the room like feathers.

"Why do you need to move your seat, Gordon?" The request perplexed Georgie.

Gordon shifted his gaze to his left, then slid it back to Georgie at the front of the room. All eyes volleyed back and forth. There was a sensation in the room that made Georgie feel the way she did when watching someone over inflating a balloon, but she didn't understand why.

"Because, Mrs. B.," said Gordon, "it smells like someone dropped a turd over here."

Laughter erupted around the room. Everyone but Martha Lemont in the back row and the skinny girl to his left found this to be hysterical. The girl's skin—barely visible through the curtain of black hair—turned pink, then red. Her bony knee bounced up and down like a jackhammer and she bit on her thumbnail. Gina Byrd.

They'd forewarned Georgie that the girl was disruptive and problematic in her student assessments meeting. What she hadn't been told, was that the girl was being bullied. Another glance at the smug, smiling boy beside her told Georgie everything she needed to know about him.

Her voice neutral, she said, "And where is it you'd like to sit, Gordon?" Meanwhile, Georgie's knuckles shown white as she gripped the edge of her desk.

Gordon rolled his head around the room, scanning the chairs. Two were empty—one beside Martha, and one dead center of the rows. As expected, he thrust his chin at the one in the middle.

"I'll take that one, Mrs. B."

Not, *can I take that one? I'll take that one.* The little shit.

Georgie smiled thinly at him. "You can take the one in the back, thank you."

"No, I—"

"In the back or in the office, Gordon. Your choice."

They locked eyes, and the room went silent. Both Martha and Gina looked up to watch the battle of wills.

Gordon glanced around the room. His confidence wavered and a tinge of red colored his cheeks. With an exaggerated show of nonchalance, he swept his book under his arm and stood.

"No problem, Mrs. B. Don't have a cow, I'll sit in the back. Better view, anyhow."

By the look he gave Jeannie Schwartz, hers was the view he anticipated. Georgie regretted her offered choices almost immediately. She should have made him sit at the front of the room. She couldn't change her mind now though; it would make her appear indecisive.

Despite achieving her goals as a teacher, Georgie's first year with grade eight served as her least favorite. Gordon Bourdreau remained a sliver just under her skin—enough to irritate her, challenging to be rid of. He spoke in a patronizing tone that, when called out for it, became conciliatory.

Many a night she went home to Charles to rant about *that insolent twerp* as she called him in private. The parents were no better—the father, condescending and rude, the mother, a mouse—and she gave up on them after the first parent teacher conference.

As for Gina Byrd and Georgie's hopes to help the girl, those were dashed as well. Gina proved to be prickly and sullen and rejected Georgie's efforts with little more than blank indifference in her unusual gray-green eyes. To only Charles and Gloria did she admit her difficulty in liking the child, even though she pitied her.

"Perhaps *that's* the trouble, dear," said Charles one evening. He was in between music students and Georgie had unloaded her frustrations about the girl again.

"*What's* the trouble," asked Georgie, annoyed.

"You pity her, and she knows it."

"She's just a child."

"Children have pride and egos, too," said Charles with a smile to soften the rebuke.

"What do you suggest I do, then?" It came out sounding both insulted and curious.

Charles scratched his chin and gazed up at the ceiling. "Why not suggest her parents sign her up for music lessons?"

Georgie snorted. "Have you seen where those people live? Their property is a blight on the town. They should condemn the house. They can't afford music lessons and if she's as proud as you suggest, she won't take a handout either."

"True, true," agreed Charles. "Then create a contest. A rigged one that she wins. The grand prize: music lessons with world famous jazz musician Charles Brightsider."

"World famous?" Georgie's eyebrow lifted, and a smirk pulled at her lips.

"World known, at least. I played on a Grammy award winning album, my dear."

"Oh, I know. Believe me, I know." She looked away as she muttered, "It's a great idea."

"What was that? I couldn't hear you, sweetheart." Charles cupped his ear and leaned closer to his wife. His eyes twinkled.

"You heard me perfectly fine, smart ass. Last week Carol Baker—our science teacher—caught her in the music room tinkering on the piano. Maybe start there?"

"Piano it is."

The contest was easy enough to create. They were to write an essay about one thing they loved, and why. The best essay would win a six months' worth of free music lessons from Mr. Brightsider. Georgie already knew Charles was well known and beloved in town by all the children he taught, but it still warmed her heart to see the excitement buzzing about the room.

She slid her gaze to Gina Byrd to see her reaction. There was none. Her expression remained impassive. However, she was also the first to pull out a sheet of paper and begin writing, her arms arced around her paper and her torso curved over her desk.

At the back of the room, Gordon Bourdreau leaned his chair back on two legs and yawned. When he realized he had no audience for his display of disinterest in winning, he dropped the front legs back onto the floor and whisked Martha Lemont's blank paper off her desk and onto his with a chortle.

"Hey," said Martha softly.

"I'm out of paper. You don't mind, right?" He flashed a smile at her, and Martha blushed.

Oh, no, Martha. Don't fall for a boy like that. Georgie blanched.

"I'll announce the winner on Friday. Best of luck to each of you," said Georgie. She felt only a little guilty at her deception.

Three days later, as promised, Georgie called the class to attention. When all eyes were on her, she announced the winner.

"Thank you all for taking part in our little writing contest. I had a challenging time picking a winner from all your insightful, funny, and even unusual—I'm talking to you, Victor Fuentes—topics. But the winner is—" She paused for effect. "Gina Byrd."

Silence greeted her. Then, from the back of the room, a sound that could only be described as a guffaw.

"Gina Bird-Turd? Seriously? Can she even spell?"

Gordon laughed at his own joke and a few of his cronies joined in. Jeannie Schwartz and a few other girls giggled then halted when Georgie made eye contact with them. Gina Byrd had yet to look up.

"Get out of my classroom, Gordon."

"*What*? Oh, come on, Mrs. B. It was a joke, God. I'm just teasing."

"Get. Out. Now. Go to the principal's office." Her voice shook with fury.

At first, she thought he'd refuse. Slowly, casually even, he stood and gathered his belongings. He smiled as he strolled down the aisle and when he reached the front of the room, where only Georgie could see his face, the smile dropped. The expression that replaced it made her want to step back, but she held her ground. She'd be damned before a child intimidated her.

"Close the door on your way out," said Georgie in her most controlled tone. He left it open.

An awkward silence followed. Someone clapped from the front row and called out, "Congratulations, Gina." It was Keith Huxley.

35 Unhinged

"Bri? We're home," called Ricky. "Brandon is here, babe." He shouted up the stairs.

Mrs. Teccio came out of the kitchen, a stack of dinner plates between her hands. "Missy Brianna said she had to go out. I make dinner for you and the children."

She set the dishes on the dining room table and hugged a bashful Brandon before sending him to the kitchen to find Cassidy. When he was out of earshot, she whispered, "Your wife got a call from her father. I could hear him yelling—oh, my goodness, he yelled and yelled—but Missy stayed quiet. When she hung up the phone, she say, *I have to do something*, and she make a lot a noise in the closet and left."

She clasped Ricky's arm and added, "I no like the way she look, Ricky."

Ricky paled and his heart thudded against his ribs. "Which closet, Mrs. Teccio?"

"The upstairs. Spare room."

The gun closet. An icy finger of fear and dread slid down his spine. Could he hear sirens in the distance?

"Stay with the kids, Mrs. Teccio. I'll be back."

She wrung her hands. "Yes, yes. Go ahead, I stay."

He was already out the door and in the car. The whole ride—a mere eleven minutes—he dialed and redialed Brianna's cell phone. Each time, it went to voicemail.

"Fuck. Fucking shit. Jesus, Brianna. Don't do what I think you're going to do. Please, please, please, God. Don't let anything happen to her."

On the Bourdreau's street several cruisers with flashing lights jutted out at different angles in front of Gordon and Martha's house. An ambulance sat in the driveway, nose facing the street, back doors open.

Neighbors stood in clusters outside their houses and on the sidewalk, murmuring behind their hands. Ricky had to park two houses back. He jumped from his car, leaving it running and the driver's door open, and ran toward the house. Joel intercepted him at the gate.

"Whoa, whoa. You can't go in there, buddy."

"Brianna—is she... did she—" He couldn't say it. The words stuck in his throat.

"She's with her mom. Over there, in the ambulance. She's banged up pretty bad—" He saw Ricky's face and blurted, "Martha, not Bri. Jesus."

"Is he—did she..."

Joel frowned. "My officers are arresting him. They're questioning him now. What did you think happened here? Wait—don't tell me, man. I have a feeling I don't want to know."

"Yeah, no," said Ricky, shaking. "You don't. I gotta go see Bri. I can go over there, right?"

"Yes, sure. They're being questioned, too. Routine stuff. Go on."

Marginally calmer, Ricky jogged over to the ambulance. The moment Brianna's eyes landed on him, she crumpled. He pulled her tight against him and kissed her hair, her face, her shoulder. The relief made his eyes sting. Then he saw Martha. His stomach dropped.

"Jesus," hissed from his lips.

One eye had swelled shut and bruised scarlet and purple. Her bottom lip was split, and her right cheek bore a welt. Her throat had blotchy red marks and one shoulder of her blouse had been ripped at the seam.

"The bastard got here first," said Brianna. Her voice was raw, but calm. "I was almost too late. But I got him. I got the son of a bitch good."

Ricky moved her away at arm's length to better see her face. "Bri, baby? What happened? What do you mean you got him?"

Had she brought the gun? Joel had said nothing, no one seemed interested in arresting her. His confusion mounted. There was a commotion at the side door of the Bourdreau's. They all turned to watch two uniformed officers walk a handcuffed, swearing, and disheveled Gordon down the steps.

There was a dried smear of blood under his nose and on his chin.

Gordon looked around wildly until his gaze landed on his wife perched on the end of the ambulance next to Brianna. She'd been silent and withdrawn until then. She stood and Brianna took her arm to steady her.

Gordon shouted, "Martha, call my lawyer. You call him right now."

Martha stood straighter. It seemed to take every ounce of courage, but her response came out firm. "Call him yourself."

His stunned expression turned livid, and he tried to take a step toward her. Martha flinched and Ricky took a step forward, but it proved unnecessary.

Officer Denny Hammock—affectionately known as Ham Hock back in high school—weighed in at a solid two-hundred and eighty pounds of farm-raised, God-fearing, mother-loving man and his none too gentle arm tug jerked Gordon back to the reality of his situation.

He called out to the nearest neighbors. "Did you see that? Police brutality. I'll have your badge, Ham Hock. I pay your damn taxes. I—"

His head was pushed down into the waiting cruiser and the door slammed, separating him from the free world. Martha sagged against Brianna and she wrapped her arms around her mother. It was the first time Ricky had ever seen a show of affection between the two.

"Mom, why don't you come stay with us. At least for a little while?"

Ricky chimed in, "Plenty of room, Martha. Brandon is already there."

An officer who'd been standing off to the side approached. "Sorry, folks, but Mrs. Bourdreau really needs to get a full check up at the hospital. They'll want to photograph the… evidence for the court." She cleared her throat and nodded at Brianna's hand. "You, uh, might want to get that hand looked at, too."

Ricky could swear the officer smirked as she turned away. He lifted Brianna's hand and saw that the knuckles were an angry red and puffy.

"Bri," said Ricky slow and drawn out.

Brianna cleared her throat and made a split-second eye contact with Officer Marlene Nikolopoulos before blinking up at Ricky. She shrugged one shoulder and said, "Clumsy me, I stumbled and banged my hand against the wall."

"I see," said Ricky.

Officer Nikolopoulos spoke in a way that sounded suspiciously coaching. "And just to confirm, Mrs. Bourdreau—did *you* see your daughter… stumble?"

Martha grinned, then winced at the pain from her lip. "Yes. I saw her trip and bang into the wall."

"And last question. The bloody nose Mr. Bourdreau sustained occurred when…"

Both mother and daughter recited, "When he, too, stumbled over the same rug and banged into the same wall."

Satisfied, the officer shook Ricky's hand and winked at the two women. "I can't force you to go to the hospital, but I highly recommend it, ladies. Your husband will be held over the weekend until a hearing on Monday and a restraining order will be in place. So, if you'd like to stay in the home, you'll be safe."

Martha thanked her and turned to Ricky and Brianna. "I-I'd prefer Brandon and Cassidy didn't see me like this. It's never been this—he's never been this bad."

"That's fine, if it's what you really want. But we need to get you to the hospital, like Officer Nikolopoulos said."

"Oh, honey. I don't think—I don't want everyone knowing—"

"Mom, this has to stop. Right here, right now. None of this was our fault. *He's* the monster, not us. I will not be ashamed anymore for something that was *never my fault*. Fuck him and fuck his secrecy."

She spun around to face the dwindling clumps of neighbors. "Hey! Guess what? My father, Gordon Fucking Bourdreau, is a mean, abusive son of a bitch. He beat my mother and me my whole life. And I am not keeping it a secret any fucking more."

If Ricky had any expectation of those people and their gawking faces, it would be that they'd scurry off to their homes and pretend they hadn't heard a thing. Some did. But some didn't.

A cluster of four women approached, compassion and sadness in their eyes.

"Oh, honey," said one. Ricky recognized her from church. Gladys was her name. "We had no idea what you were going through. I am so very sorry."

Another—Jaleesa Johnston—chimed in. "I'm so ashamed I never reached out to you. I-I wanted to so many times, but…" she trailed off. They huddled around Martha and offered words of encouragement and apology. Despite the ugly bruises, Martha bloomed under their attention.

Brianna leaned against Ricky. "She's never had women friends. I never noticed it."

The woman called Gladys said, "You kids go on home. We'll take your momma to the hospital and stay with her, won't we, girls?" They all heartily agreed.

Ricky led a reluctant Brianna away. Inside his car she said, "Oh, my car is here, too."

"I don't want you driving, okay? We'll get it tomorrow, babe. Now how about explaining to me what the hell went on here? He could've… you could've—"

"I didn't bring the gun, Ricky. Not because I didn't want to, but because I *did* want to. I wanted to kill him. He called, screaming at me about what a piece of shit I am, my mother is. He sounded insane. Unhinged. I don't know what set him off, but—"

"I might have something to do with that. I'm sorry, babe. I feel like this is my fault. I shouldn't have provoked—"

"No. Oh, no you don't. No more excuses for Gordon's monstrous behavior. No one made him do anything. It was a choice he made and kept making repeatedly. Fuck him."

He patted her knee. "So, what happened when you got to the house? If he laid a hand on you—"

"He never had a chance." She smiled with vicious glee. "I could hear them from the front door. She was crying, and he was... I could hear the slaps. I followed the sound to Brandon's room. I walked in as she fell to the floor."

Brianna gulped and looked straight ahead. "She looked up at him—she had her hands up to shield her face—and saw me behind him. He turned. That's when I punched him. Square in the nose."

She lolled her head in his direction. "You'd have been proud, babe. Perfect shot. He kinda staggered back, his hand over his nose. I stunned him." Her gaze fixed out the windshield again. "Anyhow, I couldn't let him get his senses back, otherwise he'd come after me, too. So, I kicked him in the balls. He crumpled to the floor, and he kept saying, *you bitch, you stupid bitch*,"

Her chin quivered, but she clenched her teeth. "I kicked him again. And again, and again. Anywhere I could land a shot, I kicked. Marlene— you know, Officer Nikolopoulos—she was the first one in the room. Strong girl," Brianna chuckled. "She basically lifted me and carried me out."

"Jesus," swore Ricky.

"After, when she got the full story, she said to me, *my old man liked to knock us around, too. Until*

I became a cop, that is. Nobody fucks with me anymore."

"Badass chick, right there."

"Yeah, she is."

"I meant you, babe. Her, too, sure. But I meant you."

There was a lot he wanted to say. He wanted to rant about endangering herself and their baby. He wanted to make her promise she'd never do something so fucking insane ever again. But he bit his tongue. There would be time for those words later. Now, he wanted to get his wife home and keep her safe.

"I'm okay, Ricky. The baby is okay, too. I can feel him moving."

"Holy shit. Really? You can?"

She took his hand and rested it low on the small swell of her stomach. With both eyes on the road, he waited. "Hey, little dude. It's your daddy."

Whether he heard him or by coincidence, Ricky felt a small ripple in Brianna's abdomen.

"Was that—did he just—"

"Yes," laughed Brianna. "Baby Baker just said hi, Daddy."

"Holy shit," said Ricky again.

"Holy shit," agreed Brianna.

36 Drunk CRYING

Elise watched and waited as Bruce hung the last zebra-print light fixture from the ceiling, wiped his brow, and climbed down the ladder before speaking.

She said, "Looks great. Thank you for putting them all up."

He turned around and offered a tired smile. "That was the last of them. Every room now has lights to match their themes."

They both looked around the boutique room she'd named, "The Jungle Paradise Room." Faux exotic flower garland and green ivy vines roped every which way, papier mâché monkeys and birds dangled and perched on artificial branches, and paper-winged butterflies appeared to glide through the air.

The walls all had jungle murals, the chairs had animals for backrests, and—when the Enchanted Oasis Girls Boutique opened in less than twenty-four hours—the jungle sounds of macaws, gorillas, and tigers would play through the built-in speakers in this room only.

"Do a room check with me?"

Bruce stuck his screwdriver in his belt and nodded. "Sure."

The decorators and Elise had worked at warp speed to meet the July thirty-first grand opening deadline, but the workmanship appeared top-notch. Each themed party room—from Pop Star for A Day to Princess Palace, and everything in between—exploded with color and glitter and teeth-aching sweetness.

"Looks good, right?" Elise looked up and back at Bruce.

He rested a hand on her shoulder. "Looks, great, kid. You should be proud."

Elise's ear caught the *you should be proud,* and her mind got stuck on it. *We* should be proud. It sat on the tip of her tongue, yet she bit it back. It wasn't like her to bottle her thoughts, but they'd crossed over into a weird space in their relationship. No, it was worse than weird. She was losing him, and she didn't know why. Or how to pull him back.

Instead, she said, "Yeah, I am. Over a hundred people Rsvp'd for the grand opening festival tomorrow."

"Awesome. The tents are coming in the morning?"

"Seven a.m., sharp. I'll be here for six, though. Lots to do. Are you…"?

"Not till after one-thirty. Sorry, I wish I could help for the whole thing, but—"

"But Mae needs your help at the café." She said it flatly.

He made a sound—a cross between a groan and a sigh—and said, "Please don't start, Elise."

"Sure. Whatever you say."

She heard the words and the tone of her own voice and wanted to kick herself. The topic of Mae brought it out in her, and she couldn't seem to stop herself.

"Right," said Bruce. "Well, I gotta roll. Skinny Chris and Not Fat Chris will be here to finish up the stuff on your list. I'll see you tonight at home."

Elise tipped her head for a goodbye kiss that didn't get planted on her lips. He'd already turned away. Any other time, she'd have called him back. She wanted to but, again, the words lodged in her throat.

Maybe he'll realize his mistake and come back. He'll say, *Sorry, babe, I almost forgot*, and kiss her like he used to. Elise kept thinking this until the sound of his truck grew distant, then gone. With a sigh, she flicked off the lights in each room.

In the front room—which would serve as both the reception area and store where nail polish, jewelry, stickers, candy, toys, and tons of random goodies could be purchased—Elise began filling the greeting card rack with Rosabelle Waterman's cards. When the last card fell into place, her phone rang.

Bruce, calling to apologize.

It was Charlotte Asheby.

"Hey, how's everything going?"

"Good, good. Everything's coming together," answered Elise.

"I know that tone. What's wrong? You two have another fight? Joel's home, so I can come over now."

In her head, Elise said, *No I'm fine*, but what came out of her mouth sounded more like, "Yes. Bring wine."

Twenty minutes later, they sat on the floor of the Fancy Fairytale room, leaning against giant stuffed unicorns and drinking Pinot Grigio from mermaid glasses.

"This is my favorite room," breathed Charlotte. "I want a room like this in my house."

"Well, have a little girl, and we'll have a perfect excuse," said Elise. Charlotte's wistful expression turned sad. "What? What'd I say?"

"Nothing, no. It's just... I had a miscarriage last month. It-it was my third one since we started trying for another baby."

"Oh, Char. I'm so sorry. I-I had no idea. Why have you kept this to yourself? Fuck, I've been whining to you about my stupid problems and you've had this going on?"

"Stop, please. It's fine, really. I guess, I don't know, I was embarrassed? No, that's not it exactly. I can't explain. Besides, we knew it would be difficult."

"Why is this the first I'm hearing about any of this? Why would it be difficult?"

"After I had Benjamin, I was having some… pelvic issues. The doctor found pre-cancerous cells, and they cut out basically a pie slice of my cervix. She said carrying a child to term would be improbable, but not impossible."

"Oh, honey." The news stunned Elise. None of them knew.

Charlotte's chin quivered. "We always thought we'd have a big family." She looked up at Elise's stricken face. "It's okay, really. *I'm* okay. It's been hard seeing all the pregnant bellies around town lately, but…" She hedged and a small grin tugged at the corners of her mouth.

Elise squinted at her. "But what? You have news. Spill it."

Charlotte squirmed forward. "Okay, but you have to keep quiet. Swear on it."

"I swear. Jesus, I swear. Now spill."

"We're going to adopt. There's a little girl, her name is Brooklynne, and she's three years old. She's been in the system since she was ten months old."

"Poor baby," said Elise, heartbroken for the child. "How has no one adopted her yet? That's insane."

"Well," said Charlotte, "she has Down Syndrome." She waited for Elise's reaction.

"Down Syndrome," repeated Elise. "Okay. Are you prepared for everything that comes with having a child with special needs? Don't get me wrong—

I'm not discouraging it. The opposite, actually. My cousin Danny has Down Syndrome. Coolest guy on the planet and probably my favorite human ever."

Charlotte squeezed Elise's hand. "Thank you for that. My mother has been beside herself over it. She actually said, *Do you really want to be saddled with that kind of burden*?" Charlotte growled in frustration.

Elise cringed. "Oh, you know, different generation. I'm sure she'll fall in love with little Brookie. We all will. When will she come home?"

"Well, that's the thing. It's not one-hundred percent definite yet so we want to keep it quiet for now. I'm afraid to get too excited."

"Well, I'm excited for you. And Joel, and Benjamin, and Brooklynne. She's the perfect age for Gianna, too. They'll be best friends, I know it."

"I freaking love you, Elise."

And then they were both drunk crying on the floor of the Fancy Fairytale room.

"Well, isn't this a sight," said Brittany from the arched doorway.

"Looks like we arrived just in time," added Brianna.

Behind them, Katie hollered, "I've got exactly one hour before I have to nurse. Get your drunk asses off the floor and let's get this place ready."

They pulled the two women up off the floor and the five friends tidied up, inflated balloons, hung streamers and banners, and anything else Elise thought of.

"We never talked about you and Bruce," whispered Charlotte in Elise's ear.

Elise gave her a squeeze. "No worries, chickie. All good. Thanks for coming so quickly."

From across the room, Brianna called, "I smell secrets over in—what in fuck's hell is that you're standing in?"

Elise looked around at the faux bubbles of varying sizes suspended from the ceiling. "Uh, Bubble Blast Bonanza, duh."

Charlotte replied, "No secrets here, unless you feel like sharing the reason your hand is in a cast?"

"Yeah, two weeks and still no explanation. And don't give us that *I tripped* bullshit," said Elise.

"If she says she tripped, then—"

"Shut up, Brittany," said the group.

"Oh, fuck your faces, all of you," said Brittany with a scowl.

"Wow," said Katie. "Your language, ladies, is fucking appalling."

The tension broke, and they all laughed. But Charlotte, against character, wasn't relenting. "Seriously, though. What really happened? And how is your mom doing?"

"How are *you* doing," added Elise.

Brianna had laid low the first few days after her father's arrest. The news spread and the versions of what happened varied. Brianna's role in the events ranged from *she wasn't even there* to *she gave Gordon a bloody nose and three fractured ribs*. Between the friends, they had little doubt of Brianna's ability to inflict such damage.

Brianna stared down at her hand a moment. "All right. Sit down, bitches. Mama has a story for you."

Like obedient children, the four sat on the floor and Brianna sank into a chair. "Fuck it this feels ridiculous." She got down on the floor with them. "Here goes…"

Each took her news with varying degrees of surprise, but equal horror. They'd all known a tyrant ran the Bourdreau household. A couple times they'd secretly wondered if there was physical abuse and had even asked Brianna. She'd always made it clear her home life fell under the category of non-topic. The extent of what her childhood entailed floored and sickened them.

"I realize now how insane it was to hide our family's—no, I realize how insane it was to protect Gordon. We were afraid of him." She half shrugged and spread her hands wide. "He made us think it was *our* fault. My mother's blouse was too tight. I behaved in a way that embarrassed him. It was always us, never him."

"Bri, I can't—" began Elise.

"No. Don't. It wasn't your fault. You never knew because I didn't *want* you to know, okay? Don't blame yourselves. Jesus, we were all just fucking kids, anyhow."

"Still—" said Katie.

Brianna shook her head. "Nope. Done is done. I'm not living in the past, but I'm also not hiding it anymore. And to answer everyone's question, yes. I beat the shit out of Gordon, and I'm not even a tiny bit sorry."

"Cheers to that," said Elise, holding her mermaid glass high in salute.

"All right. Enough of that, now. Elise, what do you think? Ready for tomorrow?"

Elise took a slow spin around, scrutinizing every inch of the room. "As ready as I'll ever be."

37 The Secret GARDEN

At about the same time, Mae also spun slowly around in the new addition of Mae's Café. Bruce and his crew had built and office-slash-nursery where her garden had stood in record time.

"How did you finish this in just three weeks?"

Bruce ducked his head and shoved his hands in his pockets. "Eh, it was nothing. Once William secured the permits, we got right to work. Easiest job of the summer—three walls and a roof. Boom. Done."

"Even I know more goes into it than that, Bruce. Thank you. And you under charged me. Don't think I didn't notice that, too."

He nudged her arm. "Consider it the godfather's gift to the twins."

Mae hugged one of his huge arms and bumped her head against his bicep. "TK is very lucky to have Uncle Bruce as their godfather."

The temptation to ask what Elise thought of it was strong, but she resisted. If he wanted to talk to her about their relationship, he would. Until then, she'd hold her tongue, even if it drove her crazy.

"So, that bump out over there? That's for the cribs and changing table and stuff. When they get bigger, you can put up one of those plastic, folding baby cage things."

"Baby cage things? You mean a playpen, right?"

"Cage, playpen, same difference."

She punched his arm. "Nice. Very nice, *Moose*."

He blanched. "It's so weird when *you* call me that."

"I know, right? Why *is* that?"

Bruce scratched his neck. "Different kind of relationship, I guess?"

He blushed a little and Mae pretended not to notice. Instead, she asked him about some other thoughtful details she'd noticed.

"A built-in bookcase? I hadn't even thought to ask for one. You're amazing."

"Aw, shucks," he drawled. Then, more seriously. "You're doing okay, right? I mean, you—"

"I'm fine, Bruce. Really. Doctor said so himself. No sign of repercussions, no lingering anything."

"And little Evvie?"

A worry line creased her forehead. "She's struggling to gain weight. They want to do a feeding tube. I'm scared I won't know what to do."

"Please. You're our Magnificent Mae. You'll be a pro in a flash." She blushed this time, and he pretended not to notice. He added, "You and William got this. No problem."

"If I can get the twins out of Gina and Feather Anne's hands, you mean? God, those two are baby hogs."

"Let them help, Mae. You're pale, skinny, and tired looking. You don't even look like you just had twins six weeks ago."

"I think there's a compliment in there somewhere?"

"You know what I mean. You've been taking care of everyone for a long time. Now let us take care of you a bit, okay?"

"Fine, fine." She sighed. "I guess I could get used to the pampering."

From the front counter, William called back, "Don't get too used to it, sweetheart. I'm an old man, remember."

She wagged a thumb in his direction. "This guy."

Bruce winked and yelled back, "Hey, old man, didn't you just run eight miles yesterday afternoon?"

William widened his eyes comically. "Tattletale."

"Sorry, man. My bad. Still bros?"

"Yeah, sure," said William with a shrug.

Mae rolled her eyes. It was so much easier for men to set aside their differences. Why couldn't women do the same? Sure, she and Elise had a friendly-ish relationship, but it was superficial. A current always flowed just below the surface. Wariness, reticence, distrust—it all rippled the normally calm waters. Frankly, Mae was tired of trying to win her over.

"All right, *bros*, time for me to get home and pry my babies away from their Gigi—that's Gina's chosen name for them to call her—and Feather Anne."

"You okay to drive?" Asked Bruce.

"Oh, my God, yes. I'm okay to drive. Do you need to see a doctor's note?"

"Well, somebody's testy," said Bruce with a smirk.

William chimed in again. "Don't poke the bear, my friend. I have scars."

Mae left out the back entrance, ignoring their childish banter. She had one more stop to make before home.

"Mae, my dear girl. What a wonderful surprise." Charles opened the door wide and called out, "Georgie, it's our Mae come for a visit."

"Mae," exclaimed Georgie, pulling off her gardening gloves. "did you bring—oh, answered my own question. No babies."

She looked disappointed but recovered quickly. "So glad to see you, of course. How are you feeling? Anything we can do for you?"

"Well, yes, actually. I do have a favor to ask. I was wondering if you'd be willing to be Evvie's godparents? Bruce and my aunt Tree are TK's, and we'd be so honored if you'd be—"

"Of course, of course," said Georgie. She clasped her hands to her heart. "But, dear, you realize we're in our seventies? Usually the role of godparent goes to someone able to care for the children if, God forbid, something should happen to you, the parents."

Mae waved a hand dismissively. "I know, but I don't care. You've both meant so much to me growing up. There's no one I'd rather have."

Charles and Georgie exchanged a look. He spoke what they both must've been thinking. "Won't Gina's feelings be hurt, Mae, dear?"

Mae grinned. "It was her idea."

Georgie seemed taken aback. "Her idea? Why, I'm stunned."

Mae cocked her head at them. "You have no idea how much your kindness affected her, do you?"

Again, the pair looked at each other, this time with bafflement. "Affected Gina Byrd? Us? How?"

"You were her third grade and eighth grade teacher, right, Mrs. B.? And you taught her how to play piano and the fundamentals of singing, Mr. B.?"

They nodded, recollection dawning on their faces. "I haven't thought about that in many years, but yes," said Georgie.

"She said you two—and my dad—were the only people in this town that ever showed her a moment of kindness." She looked at Georgie. "She said she knew her winning the writing contest was a crock because her paper was blank except for her name at the top."

Georgie grinned and looked away. Charles said, "You never mentioned that part."

"Didn't matter. I wanted the girl to have something positive. I never did feel like I did enough to help her. We didn't have those 'mandatory reporter' laws then. It was more, mind your business and just teach your class back then."

Mae turned to Charles. "And about you, Gina said you were the kindest, most patient man she ever met. She said she used to pretend that she was your daughter, and this was her home."

Georgie's eyes filled, and she dabbed at the corners with the handkerchief Charles handed her.

"You showed her what happy looked like, that it even existed, and that you gave her hope that maybe someday she'd find it herself."

"I-I'm flabbergasted, Mae. Truly, I am. When Feather Anne started coming around, Gina seemed so hostile toward us. Like we were trying to steal the girl away. I thought she hated us," said Georgie.

Mae shook her head emphatically. "No, she hated herself for not living up to your expectations. She was ashamed."

"My expectations? I don't—oh," said Georgie. She pressed her hand to her cheek. "Oh, yes. The book."

Charles looked confused, but Mae bobbed her head slowly.

"What book, dear?" Asked Charles.

Together, the two women said, "The Secret Garden."

"Do you remember what you wrote inside?"

Georgie did. "You will find your own secret garden, and you will thrive."

"And in mine, you wrote, *You are the secret garden.*"

Georgie leaned forward and took Mae's hands in her own. "You *are* the secret garden, dear girl."

"And you are very sly, Mrs. B."

"Indeed, you are, darling wife," agreed Charles.

"I was sworn to secrecy, you see." She cast a sad look to her husband. "And I had my own secret weighing heavy on my heart. I was torn. So, I did what I could and hoped for that someday when you two would connect."

"You did the best you could with a difficult situation. Thank you for caring about us and taking care *of* us all these years. Both of you."

"It's been our immense pleasure," said Charles.

"So, is that a yes, then? Will you be Evvie's godparents?"

Georgie clapped and spoke for Charles. "Yes, we would be thrilled."

On the way out, Georgie asked, "You and Gina, it's going well, I take it?"

Mae looked thoughtful, then said, "Yeah, it really is. There's still a big learning curve and we're still kind of navigating, but yeah. It's been good."

She slung her purse higher on her shoulder and laughed. "You should see her with the twins. I think Feather Anne might be a little jealous of *how* good she is with them, though. Stirs up feelings and memories of her childhood, and not such rosy ones, either."

"Time is a great healer. You'll see."

"Yeah, I hope so. Hey, speaking of healing. How is Mrs. Van Bergen? I haven't seen her since the memorial."

Georgie's eyes clouded. "Not well, I'm afraid. Married over fifty years to the same man, now she's alone. The house is too big, her kids want her to downsize, but... well, it's hard."

"I'm so sorry for her. But I'm glad she has you. I'm sure you're a great comfort," consoled Mae.

"I try. Charles, too. But nothing takes the place of a beloved."

They hugged and said their goodbyes. In the car, Mae allowed herself one of the rare moments when she considered her life without William. The van Bergen's and the Brightsider's had each more than fifty years of togetherness. In fifty years, she'd be seventy-eight and William would be...

She started car and Landslide blared from the radio. She'd been listening to her Fleetwood Mac playlist on the way over. Mae turned the radio off. Less than a minute later, she parked in her own driveway and hurried inside to hold her babies.

38 Charles

March 2015

Charles watched his wife make her way through the mourners to Mae's side. He hung back, wanting the women to have a moment. The girl looked like a breeze could carry her away any moment. Pale and drawn, and terribly thin, Mae Huxley wore her grief plainly.

"Sad business, this is," said Andrew van Bergen beside him.

"Indeed, it is," agreed Charles, glancing down at his wheelchair bound friend.

"Too young," said Andrew.

Charles wondered at which he meant—the girl grieving the loss of her father, or the father gone much to young.

"Both," said Andrew, reading his mind.

"We've watched her grow up before our eyes. Thinking of her alone in that big house, running that café on her own. Breaks my heart."

Andrew raised a shaky hand. "I'd already served in one war by then. You were traveling the country. She'll be fine."

Charles concurred on the fact, but also disagreed. "Different times. Now they're—"

"They're coddled. Do the girl a favor, Charles, and don't help her too much."

"I know, I know. Tell it to my wife, though." Both men chuckled.

It pained him to watch Mae walk to the casket, lay a white rose on top, then collapse over it with a silent sob. Her aunt and Georgie flanked her and walked her back to her seat. Several hankies rose to dab eyes. Gloria, sitting beside Andrew, made a small sound like an oh and a sigh. Andrew patted her hand.

An hour later they clustered in small groups at the Huxley house with plates of cold cuts and hors d'oeuvres as they spoke in soft voices and bolstered Mae with gentle assurances when she came around to thank them for coming, only to cast sad eyes at her back when she moved away.

"Charles, I'm going to stay on to clean up once everyone's left. You don't might, do you, dear?" Georgie clasped his elbow.

"Not at all, dear. I'll go home and take care of the puppies. Don't worry about a thing. How is the poor girl?" He glanced in the direction of the kitchen where Mae loaded another platter.

"Working manically, keeping busy. It's the time when there's nothing to be done when it hits the hardest. Katrina's trying her best, but she's grieving her brother, too."

"To be expected. They're lucky to have you, dear," said Charles.

Georgie cupped his cheek. "And I'm lucky to have you."

Charles kissed her palm and pulled her in for a hug. When he released her, she added, "Give Rufus and Mabel a treat from me and I'll be home as soon as possible."

Charles said his goodbyes and opened the door. Before he could say a word, Gina Byrd pushed past him with Feather Anne in tow. The child shrugged at him as she slinked past. No good could come of this. He closed the door and spun back around. Perhaps he could stop them.

His moment of surprise had been one moment too long; Gina made her announcement almost as he shut the door. He couldn't see Mae's shock, but he felt its wave as it shuddered across the room. Not everyone had heard, but enough had.

A grim Katrina Huxley escorted Gina out of the house and Charles, fearing she might hit the woman, followed them out.

"Don't come back here," said Katrina with barely controlled fury. She turned on her heel and almost smacked into Charles' chest. "You're welcome to deal with her if you want. I-I just can't even, right now."

The door slammed between her and them. Charles's head swiveled to the thin, scraggly haired, hostile looking woman at the foot of the steps. Her arms folded across her chest and her gaze shifted and swept over everything except Charles.

He said the first thing that came to mind. "Still playing the piano?"

Gina looked incredulous, then snorted. "Yeah, sure. My baby Grand in my trailer plays real nice."

"Touché, my dear." He tipped an imaginary hat. "If you don't mind my asking, what brought you here *today*, Gina. Today of all days." He admonished her as mildly as he could.

He expected an expletive-laced rebuke, but she raised and dropped her narrow shoulders. "I dunno. I guess I—I dunno."

Charles nodded. He couldn't guess with confidence why Gina Byrd had chosen the day of Keith Huxley's funeral to announce her role in Mae's life. If he had to guess, he'd say the woman simply wanted her turn in Mae's life. Then he supposed nothing was ever simple.

Instead of grilling her further, he said. "I've been working on a piece for months now. It's just finally dawned on me it needs a piano. If you're not busy, I could use the help. You play, I'll write?"

She kept her face impassive as one shoulder shrugged. "Sure, I guess."

When they were in the house and the dogs settled down, Charles led her to the music room. Over his shoulder, he said, "Not much has changed, I suppose. Except for the dogs."

"Oh, wow. Yeah, I remember the other ones. They were cool. How old are these two?" She sank down on the floor to receive gleeful wet kisses from the puppies.

"That there is Rufus, and that one is Mabel. They're six months. Sheet music is on the piano already. I'll grab my violin."

"Classical? Not jazz?" Gina's eyebrows scaled her forehead.

"I like to mix it up sometimes. What can I say?" He grinned at her. She didn't smile back, but he could tell she'd been close to it.

They played for an hour. Charles asked her nothing, and she offered no explanations. It wasn't his place. She stood from the bench and stretched.

"Been a real long time since I played. It was rusty."

"A little. But it came back to you quickly. As I told you then, you had the makings of a prodigy."

Gina bowed her head. "Yeah, well… life happens, you know? Well, I better scoot before Mrs. B. gets back."

"No need to hurry off. Are you hungry?"

"Nah. I'm good. Hey, listen. I, uh, wanna thank you for being good to Feather Anne. She's a handful, but a good kid. I-I'm not—"

"No thanks necessary. Any time. That goes for both of you."

Gina muttered her thanks and ducked out, making as little eye contact as possible. Later, when Georgie came home tired and heartsick, he felt no need to mention his visit with the woman who caused such a stir at the Huxley house. Especially after Georgie unleashed a torrent of ill feelings about the woman.

"Now, Georgie, I'm surprised at you. Being so hard on the poor thing. She's not had it easy. No reason to dislike her so."

"It's not her I dislike, it's her choices, Charles. Such a reckless, thoughtless, ill-timed and futile move. The day of her father's funeral, for heaven's sake."

Charles opened his mouth to speak, but his wife hadn't finished yet. "And now it's all for naught." She threw her hands in the air.

"W-what's all for naught, dear?" Charles was confounded.

"Why, everything. The opportunity for them to connect. A chance for Mae and Feather Anne to be sisters. All ruined by impulsivity."

He scrutinized his wife. Georgie's state of agitation on the matter surpassed what Charles deemed appropriate. "Georgie? Did you have something to do with—"

"I did nothing, thank you very much."

Charles waited, blinking at his wife. She'd changed into her nightgown and now brushed her hair vigorously in the mirror. She caught his eye in the reflection and wilted.

"I may have put the notion in Feather Anne's head that it was high time they got to know each other. I didn't think she'd tell Gina, or that Gina would pick now of all times to make a move toward our Mae."

When Charles exhaled, he let a low whistle escape. "I see," was all he said. He didn't admonish her for meddling. Or point out that some blame could be placed on her shoulders due to afore-*un*mentioned meddling. Nor did he say he'd told her so, weeks ago. But she heard the thoughts in his head as if they'd been shouted.

"Yes, yes. I know. I shouldn't have meddled. No need to rub it in." She smoothed lotion over her arms and climbed into bed.

"I wouldn't dream of it, dear," said Charles.

Georgie harrumphed and lifted her novel off the nightstand. He took it as his cue that the conversation had ended and lifted his book off his lap.

It had never been his habit to keep things from his wife, so Charles felt guilt at not mentioning Gina's visit. He glanced at Georgie. Her eyes were on the pages of her book, but they weren't moving.

Not for the first time in their marriage, Charles acknowledged to himself that his wife kept things from *him*. Secrets. Things she locked away deep down in the dark somewhere of her heart.

Flashes of memories skidded through his mind. Their wedding night; her mortification at his knowing it wasn't her first time. Her strange melancholy that came out of nowhere every spring. The incident with the boy in her class. Her intense opinions and involvement in the Huxley-Byrd drama.

All these things shared one commonality and Charles, for the life of him, could not put his finger on what it was.

"Charles, you're frowning. What is it?"

The fog cleared from his brain. His wonderful, loving, devoted wife gazed at him with concern.

Her agitations of just minutes ago receded like the tide at the sight of her husband's troubled brow.

Dear woman. I'd be a fool to doubt her honesty.

"Nothing at all, sweetheart. I—you know you can always talk to me, right? About anything, anytime, anywhere?"

She searched his eyes. He knew she would find only love there, because that was what he felt.

Georgie lifted a hand and caressed his cheek. "My sweet husband. Yes, I know it."

She looked as if she'd say more but instead leaned in to kiss him. What started as a tender peck became more. The Brightsiders set their books upon their respective nightstands, turned out their respective lamps, and made love like they were still in their thirties. All concerns drifted out the window, carried on the breeze.

39 Bombshells

"Rosie Posie!" Miles shouted upstairs. "Where you at, woman?"

From the backyard, Rosabelle answered. "I'm out here, geez. The whole neighborhood can hear you, big mouth."

"There's my girl. And screw them, let them hear." He shouted, "I am about to make sweet, passionate love to my lady, and if—"

Rosabelle's hand muffled the rest over his mouth. "Are you insane," she said, laughing despite herself.

He spoke, but her hand still covered his mouth.

"I'm going to take my hand away now. Behave. Now, what did you just say?"

He pulled her tight against him. "I said, do you want the good news or the great news?"

Her eyebrow darted up. "You did not just say all that. Whatever. Um, the great news. No, the good news, then the great news."

"The good news is," he kissed her, "we got the house."

Rosabelle squealed. "We got the house! Wait, that's only the good news? What's the great news?"

"The great news is," he dipped her backwards, "we can get married in your English garden before the closing."

She blinked at him. "You're serious? Are you serious? Oh, my God. You're serious?"

Miles tried responding each time, but she wouldn't let him. He blurted, "Yes, before you ask again: I'm totally, absolutely, incredibly… serious."

"B-but how? I thought the owner—"

"Turns out my dad and old St. Nick—don't ask me, that's what my dad calls him—are golfing buddies. Soon as he found out who was buying the house, he gave us the go ahead. All he wants is an invitation."

"Yes, of course. No problem, right? Hell, tell him to bring his whole family, too."

"Okay, okay, don't get carried away. That bar tab is on our dime."

"Right. Good point. So, August fourteenth it is?"

"August fourteenth it is, Rosie Posie."

She wrapped her arms around Miles neck, and he spun her. When he set her back down, she said, "We have a lot to do, Miles. Invitations. There's no time for formal invitations. Your mother will flip. Catering. We need a caterer. It's too much for Mae so soon after the babies. And—"

"Rosie. Relax. It'll all get done."

"I think we need to hire someone." She snapped her fingers in Miles's face. "I know just the person."

"You do? Who?"

"Brianna Baker, duh."

Miles released her so quickly she stumbled backward. "Oh, no. Not a good idea, babe. No way."

"Oh, come on, Miles. We're all grownups. So, you two had a little... flirtation way back when. You said her and Ricky were split up, so no big deal."

Miles became suddenly interested in his cuticles. Way too interested.

"Miles Hannaford. Is there more to this story? You better fess up right now."

He squinched one eye. "Promise not to get mad?"

She gave him an exasperated glare. "Do I promise not to get mad? What are you, twelve? And no, I do *not* promise to not get mad. What stupid thing did you do to ruin my chances of hiring the best party planner in the state of Connecticut?"

"Okay, okay. It was before you, obviously. I—"

"You slept with her. Of course, you did. How did I not read between the lines?" She mimicked his voice, "*Brianna, and I had a little flirtation.* Great. Just great."

"There's more."

"More? Miles, I swear to God, If you—while we—"

"No! No, Jesus. I told you, it happened B.R.—Before Rosie. There was a brief—very brief—period I thought maybe her kid… was mine."

Rosabelle dropped her head and massaged her temples. Without looking up, she asked, "Does Ricky Baker know you're the guy who almost destroyed their marriage?"

"No," said Miles emphatically. Less emphatically, he added, "Not that I know of."

She looked up at him with a stony face. "It's Ricky Baker. You'd know if he knew." Rosabelle shook her fists at him. "What am I going to do with you? Are we going to have random children knocking on our door in the future and calling you Daddy?"

"Come on, Rosie. Don't be like—"

"Uh-uh. Answer the question. How many other maybe-babies are out there, Miles? At least prepare me a little."

"You mean you're not dumping me?"

"No, dummy. I knew you were a cad before we started dating, remember?"

Miles smirked. "A cad?"

"Don't make me laugh, Miles." Her mouth twitched.

He approached her like she was a deer ready to spring away. "To the best of my knowledge, no maybe-babies will knock on our door in the present or future. I was careful… most of the time."

She crossed her arms over her chest. "Fine. Then you better find me a wedding planner. Fast."

"Say no more, Rosie. I'm on it." He kissed her nose and dashed back inside the house, dodging the swat she tried to land.

Rosabelle considered lobbing a tomato from her basket at him but didn't want to waste a good tomato. He deserved a spaghetti squash to the back of the head for being such an idiot. Miles actions and behaviors, in what she liked to call *his past life,* were nothing to be proud of but they were just that: his past.

Sure, she didn't like it. Yes, she wanted to chuck vegetables at his head. But the Miles she knew and loved was a much better man than the one he'd been before. People can change.

"They *can*," said Rosabelle.

She denied the voice of doubt whispering in her brain—the one that sounded suspiciously like her mother's voice—and went back to picking ripened tomatoes and imagining her perfect wedding day scenario.

In her idealized vision, everyone got along. Ruth and Jeannie passed tissues and beamed. Steven and Chet clinked bourbon glasses. Their friends and family surrounded them in the blooming English garden as she and Miles exchanged hand-written vows. Hummingbirds and butterflies flitted around them as they kissed for the first time as husband and wife. Rose petals—plucked from her rose garden, naturally—would rain down as they ran hand in hand through the parallel lines of well-wishers. She'd—

"Hello, there," called a voice from the deck.

"Mae! I wasn't expecting you today. And you brought the twins, yay!" Rosabelle dropped the tomato into the basket and clapped.

"Sorry for coming by unannounced. Miles let me in. He seems… spirited."

Rosabelle shook her fist in the general direction of the house. "That man will give me gray hairs before I'm thirty. Never mind him though. Hand over a baby and sit. I want to hear how *you* are."

Mae set down the baby carrier that cradled a sleeping TK and undid the contraption that held Evvie snug against her chest. She seemed unflustered, as if she'd been carting infant twins around forever. It amazed Rosabelle. Mae saw her expression and laughed.

"Incredible what becomes normal practically overnight, right? Here, take Evvie. And here's a bottle."

"I don't know if I could ever do what you're doing. Not with the same ease and calm," said Rosabelle, nestling the sweet bundle against her.

Mae chortled. "Ha, ease and calm? Try *controlled chaos*. Twenty-five minutes ago, I had sweat pouring down my face, my boobs leaked through my shields, and look—two different flip-flops."

Rosabelle looked down and laughed. "Okay, you're somehow making me feel better. You're looking more yourself. How are you feeling?"

Mae shrugged. "The good news is I have almost no time to dwell on how I'm feeling. These two take up the lion's share of attention. But I'm okay. Better every day. Thank God I have tons of help."

This came as no surprise. Mae's support system seemed to work like a well-oiled machine and William, Gina, and Feather Anne had been bursting with excitement when she'd seen them last.

Rosabelle tried to picture hers and Miles's parents in such a situation and shuddered.

Rosabelle tipped her head to Evvie's downy black hair and breathed in. "You are giving me baby fever." She sighed.

"Well, then let's hurry up and get you two married already," said Mae with a laugh.

"Oh, oh my God. I have so much to tell you!"

Rosabelle filled Mae in on everything. The house, the bombshell Miles just dropped, the wedding plans, all in that order. They'd switched babies, so by the time she'd finished, she held the blond-haired boy moniker'd TK by none other than Miles.

"Wow. That is a rollercoaster of good and... not so good news. Congrats on the house and the wedding. Do you want me to take a hit out on your fiancé for you? I might know a guy who knows a gal whose dad knows some guys. Allegedly, that is."

"Holy sh—sugar. Are you saying Elise Martino's father really *is*—" she whispered, "in the mob?"

"Don't say a word. Bruce swore me to secrecy. He doesn't know if Mr. Martino is one of the Goodfellas, he just suspects it."

"So, you and Bruce are good?" Rosabelle watched her friend.

Mae fussed with Evvie's onesie. "Yeah, you know. Hot and cold. There's a distance there still. Sometimes, not all the time. Actually, we're good most of the time. Until Elise starts up with him, or she's around. Then he gets all tense and professional."

"Yikes," grimaced Rosabelle.

"Obviously, I can't say a word," huffed Mae.

Rosabelle cocked her head. "Why not? You guys have been best friends for years. Just tell him what you think."

"That easy, huh? So, what *do* I think?"

"Well," Rosabelle bit the corner of her lip. "You tell him you think he's making a mistake if he marries Elise. And that you can see he's not as happy as he deserves to be. And that you don't want to see him get hurt."

Mae sighed and set Evvie back in the infant carrier. "That does about sum it up. Still, though. If it comes from me… I don't know."

"Because it's complicated between you two," finished Rosabelle.

A crease in Mae's forehead formed. "I-I feel like—underneath everything—I'm always causing him pain. Not, like, a knife stab but—"

"A dull ache," finished Rosabelle.

Mae exhaled. "Yes. Is that disgustingly vain of me to think?"

"No. It's accurate. I can relate to Bruce. Back when I pined away for Miles—years and years' worth of pining, by the way—I wore the same expression when he came into a room." Rosabelle blushed a little. "How do I know what my face looked like, right?"

Rosabelle set TK in the carrier next to his sister's and sat back. "I always faced the big windows in the cafeteria during lunch. Partly because I loved the view of the field and trees. The other reason was because I could watch Miles's reflection in the glass when he walked in with the team. They all sat at the table behind me, so I could—God, this is so embarrassing—watch him eat."

She waited for Mae to laugh at her, and when she didn't, she continued. "Anyhow, I'd been staring at him through the glass as per usual when I dropped my—I don't even know, a tater tot, I suppose—when I looked up again, I saw my own face. I-I didn't even recognize that sad, hopeless girl staring back at me."

"Oh, Rosabelle. That's—"

"Pathetic, I know. I'm not saying that's exactly how Bruce looks when he sees you. But it's there, in his eyes."

"Shit. Do you think Elise sees it? Is that why she's such a—she's so cold to me?"

Rosabelle made an apologetic face and nodded. Mae nodded back. Mae's emotions played plainly across her face. Sadness, embarrassment, frustration. Her position was a difficult one. Distancing herself from Bruce would be improbable if not impossible, even if it might help him truly move on. Their lives intertwined.

"What does William say?"

"Nothing, bless him. He's a smart man. Insightful. Observant. But he's so gracious about it all. If he's at all jealous, he never shows it."

Rosabelle smiled at her troubled friend. "It's because he loves and trusts you. He trusts Bruce, too."

Mae puzzled. "Sometimes I get this feeling like he's glad for Bruce's... attention to me. To *us*— Feather Anne, Gina, now the twins. It's like a relief to him, I think."

It was Rosabelle's turn to frown. "Yes. I can kind of see that now that you mention it. Why *is* that?"

Sadness filled her gray eyes. "Because he thinks someday, when he's... gone, I'll at least have Bruce to take care of us."

"Well, that's just sexist," said Rosabelle.

Laughter burst from both women at the unexpected statement. The twins startled, and they shushed each other, but still laughed as they did.

"I mean, seriously, though," continued Rosabelle, "you are a self-sufficient, successful business owner who can take care of her own self."

"I am woman, hear me roar," laughed Mae, shaking her fist in the air.

"Exactly. Tell that man to just chill and enjoy his wonderful life. As we've all learned, anything can happen to anyone, so just *live*."

Mae raised her glass of iced tea. "Cheers to that."

"So, speaking of Elise. Are you guys going to the grand opening of her boutique?"

"Wouldn't miss it," said Mae with a hint of tightness in her voice.

"It'll be fine. She'll be so busy bossing everyone around, she won't have time to glare at you."

They silent laughed again and moved on to cheerier topics. Before long, it was time for Mae to leave. Both women felt lighter in spirits by the time Rosabelle waved Mae out of the driveway. When she returned to the garden, it was with an easier mind and a happier heart. Miles might be a former cad, but he was her former cad. Whatever fall out there might be from the Brianna debacle, Rosabelle would stand by her fool of a man.

40. All Right IN TIME

"So, you're going to live here from now on, huh?" Feather Anne looked around the huge bedroom in admiration.

"Yeah. At least until things settle down at my parents' house," said Brandon. He tossed the bag of Doritos in her lap.

She shoved an orange coated triangle in her mouth and said, "Do you want to go back?"

"No. I mean, eventually, maybe. I never thought I'd say this about my sister, but she's really good at mom stuff."

"I get it. Same thing with Mae."

Brandon gave her a lopsided grin. "I knew you'd understand. You're my best friend, Feather Anne. I couldn't have gotten through it all if it wasn't for you."

Feather Anne didn't want him to see her blush, so she busied herself with searching for the most perfect, powdered cheese covered chip.

Brandon persisted. "I mean it, Feather Anne. A-and I meant what I said to you the other day."

Even though her face felt like flames were flying out of it, she looked at him then.

She said, "Same."

It was the best she could do, the closest she could come to saying, *I love you, too.* No one had ever said those words in the way Brandon had whispered them to her the day he left her house with Ricky.

"*I love you, Feather Anne.*" That's what he said and how he said it.

Gina had sometimes tossed an, *who loves ya, brat?* Mae pretty much always said, *love you,* at the end of phone calls and before bed. Bruce sometimes said, 'love ya, sport.' William was more of a 'shows his love' instead of 'says it' kind of guy. Katrina did a Kardashian kind of, *loves you, babe,* thing that always made Feather Anne chuckle. But no one had ever said, *I love you Feather Anne.*

It made her insides tumble and her heart go fast and slow at the same time. She half wanted to laugh, and half wanted to cry. Brandon Bourdreau loved her. *Her.* Feather Anne Byrd, garbage girl. The outcast, troublemaker, fatherless kid. Until as of late, that was.

Not-Fat Chris was her father. A boy loved her. Her mother was not a shitty human being anymore. She lived in a beautiful house with happy people.

The twins and Mae were okay now. Life was good. Better than good. So, why did that scare her more than waking up alone in a dark trailer?

Brandon grinned at her. "Good. Now stop hogging the Doritos."

Just like that, the universe shifted back onto its axis and Feather Anne slipped back into the safe space of her mind. She crumpled the top of the bag into a messy fold and chucked it back at him.

He shoveled a handful of chips into his mouth and spoke around them, crumbs flying. "Look at us, being all normal and shit, huh?"

Feather Anne pointed at him and swirled her finger around in circles. "You call any of *this* normal? Damn, we're fucked."

From the hallway came, "Language, you two."

They rolled their eyes at each other. "Come on," said Brandon, "lets blow this taco stand."

They raced down the stairs only to be halted by Brianna.

"And just where are you two little savages off to?" She arched one eyebrow and crossed her arms in front of her, but she smirked.

"Uh, to the beach?" Brandon blinked at her.

She narrowed her eyes at him, then at Feather Anne, then back to Brandon. "Fine. Check in when you get there. Stay out of trouble. Be back by five. Dinner is at six."

"You got it, sis." Brandon saluted and grabbed Feather Anne's hand to pull her along before Brianna could give any more commands.

Out on the porch, Feather Anne said, "She's a bossy one, isn't she?"

Brandon bobbed his head. "Yep. She is."

"It's pretty cool, huh?"

Brandon nodded again, smiling. "Yep. It is." He looked down.

Feather Anne looked down, too. They were still holding hands. When their eyes met again, a myriad of thoughts and unsaid words passed between them.

She cleared her throat and blurted, "Last one to Heron's Way is a rotten egg," and dove off the porch.

They raced at full speed to the street sign declaring Heron's Way and Not A Thru Street. Feather Anne won naturally. They curled over, hands on knees and panting until they'd caught their breath again.

"Okay," said Feather Anne, "Tell me everything. You know my whole story, so now it's your turn."

Brandon looked off in the distance, then nodded once. "Let's get to the jetty first. I think better there."

He took her hand again, this time with deliberate intent. Feather Anne let him. They didn't look at one another, but at the opposite sides of the street. She grinned and suspected he did as well.

The tide was rolling out when they reached the end of the long boulder jetty. An old man fished off the edge while his jolly black lab sniffed around. The man tipped his hat to them and the dog nosed their open palms.

At first, they sat without speaking. The waves crashed and ebbed, crashed and ebbed. The steady ocean breeze swept their hair across their faces then pushed it away again. Feather Anne breathed in until her lungs hurt. Inhaling the briny air always made her body relax in a way only the ocean mist could.

Most beach trips, she and Brandon brought their strings and chopped up hot dogs to catch crabs in between the boulders as the tide went out, but today was for talking about serious stuff. Today, Brandon would share his secrets with the only person who'd understand and not judge.

"You kids enjoy yourselves now," said the fisherman as he passed by. The lab snuffed at their ears and wriggled her fat body between them as if she wanted in on the conversation.

"Lola, you traitor. Leave them alone, girl."

"Ah, we don't mind," said Feather Anne, slinging an arm around the damp dog.

"Suit yourself. I'm right over at the end of Beach Access Road. For Sale sign in the yard and another that says puppies for sale right next to it. Walk her halfway then tell her *Go home, Lola*."

"Cool," said Brandon. "Thanks, Mister."

"Yeah, we'll keep a good eye on her," said Feather Anne.

"She's a smart girl. I'm not worried at all."

Lola looked after him once or twice, ears pricked and head cocked, but the attention she received from the two kids enticed her to stay. After a few minutes, she stretched out between them and as long as at least one of them hand a hand petting her, she stayed quiet and still.

"My father... he smacks my mother around. A lot. My sister, too, when she lived at home. Calls them all kinds of names."

Brandon said this matter-of-factly. His voice was flat, emotionless. But one glance at his balled fist in his lap told Feather Anne otherwise. She waited.

"Not me, though. Never me. I don't really know why. I fucking provoked him enough. Until he started punishing my mother for my behavior. He'd say—" Brandon gulped and reached around for one of the cracked mussel shells left cleaned and abandoned by hungry seagulls.

He side tossed one into the water. "He'd say, *It's not your fault you don't know how to behave, son. It's your mother's. But don't worry. I'm going to teach her a lesson.*"

"He smacked her if there was a crease in his shirt. Or if our dinner wasn't hot enough, or on the table fast enough. He punched her in the stomach once because she'd forgotten to send me to practice with my baseball mitt."

He scooped up more shells. One by one, with each clipped sentence, he hurled them.

"Where's my dinner, Martha?"

"This tastes like shit, Martha."

"You're stupid, Martha."

Brandon swiped the back of his wrist under each eye and kept his gaze locked on the horizon.

"If I tried to stop him, it made it worse for her. He tried to make it like we were, like, in it together.

Me and him against the stupid women. Nothing, nothing I did made it better. He just kept fucking—"

The rest caught in his throat, swallowed up by an involuntary sob. Lola cast her wet, doleful gaze at Brandon, then at Feather Anne. She blinked back her own tears and reached over the dog to take his hand.

Once he'd pulled himself together again, he went on. "I tried *everything*, Feather Anne. After I failed at taking some of his fucking rage off her, I figured maybe if I tried to be the best kid on the planet, he wouldn't hit her anymore."

"It didn't work, did it?"

"Nothing worked. That last night—when I left—I couldn't take it anymore. She did something—God knows what—wrong in the book of Gordon and he had her pinned against the refrigerator. He had his arm pulled back. I grabbed the first thing I saw—a metal spatula," he laughed mirthlessly. "I fucking swung that thing as hard as I could. At his hand, his back, his face. I got in three good shots—whack, whack, whack—before he yanked it out of my hand. You know what he said?"

He turned to Feather Anne and looked into her eyes with such bottomless despair that her breath caught.

"Thanks, son. This'll help teach her a lesson." He shook his head. "The fucker was bleeding. He had a welt the size of a, well, a metal spatula, and that was all he said."

"Then what happened, Brandon," asked Feather Anne. She watched his jaw clench.

His voice broke. "I ran. I ran like a fucking coward, Feather Anne."

"No, no. Hey. Brandon, *no*. You're *not* a coward. You're the bravest person I know. Don't think that, okay? He held all the power. He brainwashed all of you. At least he tried to. But you never gave in to his will. You never became like him."

His head bowed and Feather Anne couldn't be sure her words penetrated his tormented mind, or if they were even the right things to say at all. Lola picked her head up again and nudged their clasped hands. Brandon looked down at her and did the most surprising thing. He laughed.

Relief flowed from her in the gust of air. He wasn't all right, but he would be in time. Just like her. They'd both be all right in time.

41 The Brightsiders

Charles and Georgie sat on their small back deck and watched Rufus and Mabel frolic in the yard. The sun had risen over the house and now shone onto the garden. They drank mimosas for no other reason than *they could*.

"Cheers, my dear," said Charles before clinking his glass against hers and taking a sip.

"And to you," chuckled Georgie.

"Are you ready for the assault this afternoon?"

"Assault," laughed Georgie. "Come now, they're not that bad, are they?"

Charles winked. "Oh, now, I'm teasing. They're all a delight. All the ones we've met so far, at least."

"Yes, but… are you sure you don't mind any of this? It must be so—even for me it's—"

"Nonsense. Do you remember what I told you on our wedding night?"

She puzzled a moment, then her face softened. "Yes, of course. *The only things that matter to me are our present and our future.* You didn't care that I had a past."

"And I've never pushed you to tell me anything you didn't want to discuss, either. But that didn't—it doesn't—mean I was disinterested. I hope you know you've could've told me anything."

"Even if I murdered a man?" Georgie kept her face serious.

Charles blinked rapidly. "D-did you?"

Georgie scoffed then chuckled at him. "Of course not, you ninny."

"Well," muttered Charles into his glass, "I've seen your temper, Missy."

She cast him a reproving side eye, lifted her glass, and extended her pinky as she drank the mimosa. They sat in companionable silence observing the dogs and the slow creep of the sun along the deck. The silence went on so long that Charles startled a little when Georgie spoke.

"I would like to tell you what happened." She shifted her gaze from Rufus to her husband, then back again. "About... how I—how Craig came to be."

Fast approaching sixty years of marriage to Georgina Brightsider meant Charles knew that, when she had something difficult to say, she required absolute silence. He obliged. After several starts and stops, she told him of the night she,

Gloria, her brother Samuel and his friend James went to Shea Stadium to see the Beatles.

She spoke of the music, the people, the sights and smells. When Ed Sullivan announced the Beatles, the stadium erupted into a deafening roar. How she screamed, too, when Paul McCartney first took the microphone. Georgie smiled as she recalled these parts. When she moved onto the after-concert memories, the smile faded.

"I had too much to drink. We all had. But it was funny. It was *fun*. Then Gloria decided she wanted real New York-style pizza. So, two went downstairs, out to the street, and two stayed behind. *I* stayed behind."

Charles did not need her to go on. He guessed easily at what happened. It was good she didn't look at her husband then. Rage curled his hands into fists. That someone would force himself on—

"I didn't say no forcefully enough. I suppose he thought I was playing coy. I don't know. I just know I was embarrassed and ashamed, and I wanted to forget it ever happened."

Georgie detailed the aftermath—discovering she was with child, lying to her parents about a nanny position in Upstate New York—and concluded the sad, infuriating story with, "So, now you know all there is to know."

Charles had to use Herculean force to control his voice. "And this James, fellow. Whatever came of *him*?"

"James?" Georgie looked surprised and confused. "Oh, I suppose he went on to have—oh. Oh, I see. No, Charles. It wasn't James w-who forced himself on me. It was Samuel, Gloria's brother."

All the pieces slid into place. Fragments of memories floated to the surface of his mind and a new light shone on each. Most recent—Andrew van Bergen's funeral and the way Georgie had tensed when she and her brother slid into the pew in front of them. The picnics and parties they'd been invited to at the van Bergen's but declined with one excuse or another. Georgie missing two of Gloria's boys' baptisms.

Charles replayed the moment Samuel Olsen side-stepped into the pew. His gaze had lingered on Georgie and when she hadn't met his eyes, he'd turned slowly away. The smile never left his lips, though. If Charles could only have that moment back now, he'd have knocked that smug prick's dentures right out of his mouth.

"Charles? *Charles*. I know that look. You'll not be punching anyone's lights out, Do you hear?"

"Dentures," muttered Charles,

"What on earth—"

"His dentures. I'd like to punch the dentures out of him."

Georgie, despite the seriousness of the conversation, laughed. At first, it was a quick, *ha*, sound, followed by another. Next her shoulders began shaking, and she covered her mouth to hold it all in. It was a useless endeavor. Now she laughed in earnest and though he resisted it mightily, Charles began to laugh, too.

The dogs' ears pricked, and the charged up the steps to see what the ruckus was from their people. They found their loud guffaws and cackles more alarming than amusing and pounced in both laps to lick and whine in their faces until they stopped.

"All right, all right, you two. That's enough of that," said Georgie, sputtering away from the wet dog kisses.

"Yes, everything's fine now. We're all fine now." Charles's and Georgie's eyes met over the dog's heads. He said it again. "We're all fine now."

"Yes," agreed Georgie firmly. "We are."

Three hours later their house was full. Children—*Georgie's grandchildren*—ran amuck in the yard. Two boys and one girl. All blue-eyed, golden-haired, long-limbed, happy children who favored their father—Craig's oldest son—who favored his father… who favored Georgie.

The last to arrive was Craig and Marianne's middle son, Dylan and his fiancée, Lotus. When his open top, doorless Jeep rolled into the driveway, Marianne looped her arm through Georgie's, leaned her head in, and said, "What till you get a load of this one. She's… something."

Georgie patted the hand on her arm, and teased, "Spoken like a boy-mom, I'm sure."

Marianne implored Georgie to look into her eyes. "You're a boy-mom, too. We're so thrilled to have you and Charles in our lives now. Thank you. It couldn't have been easy."

Georgie was spared answering by a shout of, "So, this must be my new grandmother. Did those jerks already pick a name for you?"

"Hello, Dylan," said Georgie, welcoming the lanky man-boy into a hug. "Call me whatever you like… after you introduce me to your beautiful girlfriend and that precious bundle in her arms.

"Right, yeah. Georgie, this is Lotus, and that is Petal."

"It's lovely to meet you finally," said Lotus, kissing Georgie on both cheeks.

Lotus was indeed exceptionally beautiful. Long cornrows woven with ribbons and beads. Skin like café au lait, and soulful brown eyes with thick lashes. Glorious artwork wove up and around one arm. Perhaps around both. A scarf-like sack draped across her body, from which a matching café au lait infant arm peeked out.

"What beautiful tattoos you have, dear," said Georgie in awe.

"See, Mom. Told you Georgie would be cool," said Dylan.

Marianne laughed nervously and swatted her son's arm. Craig unwittingly saved her. "There they are." He beamed. "So glad you kids could make the trip."

"We wouldn't have missed it for the world, Pop," said Dylan.

He draped a proud arm around Lotus's narrow shoulders, and she leaned against him. They looked to be a sweet couple and Georgie took an immediate liking to them. She'd never say it aloud, but she suspected the tall, easy spirited young man would have been her favorite had she been able to watch him grow up.

Charles joined them, and perhaps sensing his wife's wistful thoughts, kissed her temple and gave her a wink. She introduced the new arrivals, and as she expected, he became enamored of the beautiful, doe-like Lotus who seemed mutually besotted. The two—three, including the sleeping, as yet unseen baby—strolled off together to view Georgie's gardens.

"Lo's usually pretty reserved around strangers," said Dylan. "Your Charles must be something special… Gram. Wait, no. That doesn't fit you."

Georgie took his arm and led him to the house. "You'll think of just the right thing, I'm certain of it." They left Craig and Marianne standing slightly agape.

***

Marianne looked up at Craig. "I-it's like they've all known each other forever, isn't it?"

Craig looked at them again—his mother and his middle son walking into the house, Then at Charles and their… quasi-daughter-in-law strolling in toward the garden and deep in conversation—and chuckled.

"I couldn't have dreamed of a better turnout, Marianne. Thank you."

"Me?" Marianne's hand pressed to her chest. "Why are you thanking *me*?"

"This was all your doing. I'd have chickened out if not for your—"

"Being a busy body?" She finished for him.

He tipped her chin and kissed her. "For your caring enough about me after all these years. For doing the things I couldn't bring myself to do. For raising our boys. For everything."

Marianne blinked the tears from her eyes. "Now, you stop that. You're going to make me cry. Craig Davidson, you are a good man. You deserve this."

She waved a hand at the scattering of family. It was what he'd always dreamed of; a large family, children laughing and playing, his wife beside him. Then there was the part he'd always believed impossible. His mother, a part of the image.

***

"Everyone," called Georgie from the front steps, "Come around back, if you would. Food's ready.

Thomas, Craig's oldest son, had volunteered to man the grill and his wife, Janie, had helped Georgie and Marianne in the kitchen with the rest of the food earlier. Nate and his latest girlfriend, Mia, had set up long tables in the shade and carried out the dishes and bowls.

Janie, Lotus, and Georgie piled food on plates for the children, then sent them off to sit under the willow tree to eat.

"And do not feed your food to the dogs," called Janie in her most stern mom voice.

Georgie spied their little one, Juliette, handing a bit of hamburger to Rufus. She looked up guiltily and met Georgie's eye. She nodded at the girl, put her finger to her lips, and winked. A little of hamburger wouldn't hurt old iron stomach Rufus.

Mabel was more delicate, and Georgie suspected there'd be a mess to clean up that night. But her *great-granddaughter* was bonding with her dogs, and Georgie's heart filled with joy at the sight. So, she let it slide.

"Let me put those in some water for you, dear," said Georgie to Lotus. She and Charles had picked a bouquet from the garden.

"Oh, thank you. Your gardens are amazing, Georgie. I'd love to have one someday."

"Well, until then, you can enjoy mine any time you like."

Lotus smiled. She had the most serene way about her, and Georgie told her so.

"Years and years of yoga, meditation, Reiki healing, crystals… you name it." She laughed a little, perhaps feeling that Georgie might find it all silly.

"How lovely. I imagine if more people did what you do, the world would be a happier place, now wouldn't it?"

Lotus practically glowed. "Thank you. Yes. That's actually my dream—to open a small studio where I can incorporate all the things I've learned during my travels. Eastern and western medicine really can work hand in hand, but most people don't understand their options."

"Oh, if only you lived here, in Chance," exclaimed Georgie. "The young woman who ran a yoga studio in town has been trying to sell it for months. Brittany Sheffield is her name. They own the apartment above the studio too. But I suppose it's silly of me to suggest it. You and Dylan live in New York, right?"

Lotus nodded. "Don't tell Dylan, but I hate it there. I mean, I love the culture and the diversity, but the—"

"Noise? Smells?" Georgie gave her a knowing smile.

"Exactly. It just, like, depletes my qi, you know?"

"I think I do," said Georgie.

Later, Lotus approached Georgie again. "Petal is awake now. Would you like to hold her?"

"I thought you'd never ask," said Georgie, her arms extended.

Petal was the clone of her mother, but with Dylan's bright blue eyes and Georgie's already full heart expanded more. After a few minutes, Lotus said, "Would you mind if I left her with you for a bit? I'd like to talk to Dylan about something."

"Of course, my sweet. Take him for a walk through the garden. There's a bench under the rose arch you may find enjoyable."

They held each other's gaze a moment, both with small grins pushing at their cheeks. Lotus bent and gave Petal a kiss on her soft, open palm and then winked at Georgie.

"What are you up to, wife of mine?" Charles came and sat beside her.

"Whatever do you mean? I'm sitting with my great-granddaughter, that's all."

Charles eyebrow went up, and he nodded toward Lotus, who'd taken Dylan's hand and led him through the arched gate that marked the garden's entrance.

"Fine," said Georgie, "I may have mentioned the yoga studio was for sale."

"The Sheffield girl's place? Next to Mae's?"

"Yes. That one. It's the only yoga studio in town, Charles."

"Mhm," was all he said.

"Oh, hush," said Georgie.

Later, as everyone packed up for the beach bonfire, Dylan called everyone's attention.

"Hey, before we head down. Lotus and I have an announcement."

"What, you eloped?" Thomas called out.

"You're having another baby," shouted Nate.

"You're getting married?" Marianne's voice rose hopefully.

It turned out she'd been more upset they'd had Petal without getting married first. When Marianne learned it was Lotus's idea to not marry, she'd been sorely disappointed and so the frosty air between them began. Georgie felt some guilt at suspecting the chill was because of Lotus's skin color and it relieved her to learn otherwise.

"Let the boy speak, will you," admonished Craig. He raised his beer and said, "Go on, son. The floor, er, grass is yours."

"Thanks, Pop. So, I just got off the phone with a realtor and... we're moving to Chance, effective immediately."

A flurry of congrats, holy shits from the brothers, and a smattering of questions—mostly from Marianne—followed a brief, stunned pause.

"I don't understand," she sputtered. "You're moving here? To Chance?"

"Yes, Mom. Georgie told Lotus about a yoga studio and an apartment for rent in town, and Lo's been dying to open her own place, but forget it in the city—too expensive—and I found the number for the realtor. He said it's ours for the taking."

"If we pass the background check and can come up with first last and security on both places," added Lotus with less enthusiasm.

"Ah, you're screwed, little bro. No way you're passing the background," teased Thomas.

"Very funny," said Dylan. He tossed a roll at him. "That's the easy part. The rest—well, we'll figure it out. We've got some savings, and well, never mind that. Let's go to the beach, people!"

More congratulations and hugs followed as they moved the party to the front of the house where some loaded Thomas's SUV with a cooler and blankets, and others took out a wagon and two strollers for walking.

Craig asked, "Who's driving and who's walking?"

"I'll ride," said Marianne. Janie, Craig, Charles, and Mia chose the car as well.

"Georgie, wanna walk with us?" Dylan's crooked smile welcomed her.

"I'd love to," said Georgie.

"Lo and I want to thank you for telling her about the studio. She's been dreaming about this for a long time."

"Yes, I really can't thank you enough. This is… it's everything," added Lotus.

"I'm glad for you, truly I am. But—forgive my intruding—is this a stretch for you financially? I don't ask to be nosy. I-I'd like to help if you need it."

Dylan put his hands up. "Oh, no, no. We couldn't ask you for help like that, Georgie."

"You didn't ask. I offered."

Dylan and Lotus exchanged weighted stares. It was obvious they needed the help, but pride battled necessity and rendered them mute. Georgie *tsked* at them both.

"Oh, now. Don't let pride stop you from pursuing your dreams. I'm your grandmother, and grandparents spoil their grandchildren. It's the law, you know. That means I've some lost time to make up for."

Lotus, with damp eyes, shook her head in amazement. "You're incredible, Georgie. We're so blessed to have you in our family."

"I'm the one who's blessed, my dear. Why don't you kids stay the night, and tomorrow we'll go over to—Miles Hannaford, I'm presuming?"

"Yes. Boy, everyone really does know each other here, huh?"

"Yes, we do. And I happen to know Miles rather well. So, he'll be in big trouble if he's not giving you the best deal he can."

As the sun set over the water, the men stacked wood and sticks into a pyramid and the women settled the children and themselves on blankets and chairs at a comfortable distance around it. The Villeneuve's, who'd been passing by with their children, stopped to say hello and ended up joining them. Georgie delighted when Marisol and Lotus gravitated toward one another and seemed to chat easily.

When Marianne sat beside Georgie, it didn't surprise her. She'd sensed the woman's trepidation at her son's announcement and felt what she thought might be a reproving glance in her direction when Dylan credited Georgie with their decision.

"Some news," Georgie said. She wanted to give Marianne an opening. No need for beating around the bush.

"Y-yes," agreed Marianne slowly. "I was… caught off-guard for a moment. Although, I shouldn't have been surprised. It's very Dylan-esque to make rash decisions."

"Is it?" Georgie turned to see Marianne's face. "Do you think it's a bad idea?"

She hesitated. "It's just—and I adore my son—but he's impulsive. Always has been. He gets an idea in his head, and the next thing you know, he's in Thailand. Or Prague. Or Spain."

Georgie chuckled. "Sounds adventurous."

"He bought a pig once. Not one of those cute pygmy ones, either. Full grown sow. Said he couldn't let her get slaughtered."

They laughed together. "All right, that might be on the impulsive side. Sweet, though. He's a good-hearted young man. You've done beautifully raising him—all three of your boys," said Georgie.

"Thank you, Georgie. I don't mean to be presumptuous, and I'm afraid this'll sound… wrong, but if he asks to borrow money, you should tell him no."

Georgie stayed silent.

"That sounds unkind. It's not that he's shifty or anything. He's just…"

"Impulsive," finished Georgie.

"Yes," breathed Marianne. "His intentions are always good, but his follow through, not so much. Please don't tell him I said anything."

"Of course not. Not a word will be said on the matter," promised Georgie.

On the opposite side of the growing fire, Charles watched the goings on of his newly adopted family. So many serious looking side conversations. His wife and Marianne. Craig and Dylan. Lotus and that lovely Marisol. Thomas and Pedro Villeneuve. A beach bonfire was no place for seriousness.

"Everyone, it's time for a sing-along," declared Charles.

A few groans mixed in with the general enthusiasm. From his back pocket, he pulled a harmonica. Thomas announced he just so happened to have his guitar in the SUV. Nate announced that Mia was a fantastic singer.

Often, Charles would look over at Georgie, at the way she glowed—not just from the firelight, but from joy—as she interacted with her son and family, and their eyes would meet. Hers said, *you're still my world*, and his said, *there's room for all, my dear*. They smiled and nodded and sang along together to *What a Wonderful World*. It was, indeed.

To Be Continued…

About THE AUTHOR

Elsa Kurt is a multi-genre author and speaker. She has written nine novels, several short stories and a book for aspiring and new authors called *You Wrote It, Now What?* When not writing or sharing her experiences in writing, publishing, and promoting, Elsa can be found gardening or spending quality time with her husband, daughters, and three dogs. To learn more about Elsa and her books, visit elsakurt.com or at @authorelsakurt across social media. Elsa loves to hear from her readers at authorelsakurt@gmail.com.

https://facebook.com/authorelsakurt/
https://instagram.com/authorelsakurt/
https://twitter.com/authorelsakurt
https://www.goodreads.com/author/show/15177316.Elsa_Kurt
https://allauthor.com/profile/elsakurt/
https://amazon.com/author/elsakurt
https://www.bookbub.com/authors/elsa-kurt
https://www.pinterest.com/authorelsakurt/pins/
and her website, https://www.elsakurt.com